Praise for Gayle Trent and her delectable Daphne Martin Cake Mysteries

"One day I found myself happily reading . . . mysteries by Gayle Trent. If she can win me over . . . she's got a great future."   —Dean Koontz, #1 *New York Times* bestselling author

"Gayle whips up a sweetly satisfying mystery that'll have you licking your lips for more!"
          —Christine Verstraete, author of *Searching for a Starry Night*

"A pleasant heroine."   —*Kirkus Reviews*

"For people who love a tasty cake and a cozy murder mystery, *Murder Takes the Cake* is a delicious read."
          —*Suite101*

"The breezy storyline is fun to follow. . . . Daphne is a solid lead character as she follows the murder recipe one step at a time."   —*The Mystery Gazette*

"The folksy names, dialogues, settings, and characters all promise a good cozy (culinary) mystery. This was an easy, entertaining read. It reminded me a bit of a comfortable, enjoyable game of Clue."
          —*A Bookworm's World*

"Trent has written an absolutely captivating cozy, complete with all the traditional elements of the genre. . . . I hadn't even read past page seven, and I had laughed out loud numerous times. The dialogue in this book is filled with snappy wit."
          —*Pudgy Penguin Perusals*

Also by Gayle Trent

Murder Takes the Cake
Killer Sweet Tooth

Battered to Death

A Daphne Martin Cake Mystery

GAYLE TRENT

POCKET BOOKS

NEW YORK   LONDON   TORONTO   SYDNEY   NEW DELHI

Pocket Books
A Division of Simon & Schuster, Inc.
1230 Avenue of the Americas
New York, NY 10020

This book is a work of fiction. Any references to historical events, real people, or real places are used fictitiously. Other names, characters, places, and events are products of the author's imagination, and any resemblance to actual events or places or persons, living or dead, is entirely coincidental.

First Pocket Books paperback edition October 2013

POCKET and colophon are registered trademarks of Simon & Schuster, Inc.

For information about special discounts for bulk purchases, please contact Simon & Schuster Special Sales at 1-866-506-1949 or business@simonandschuster.com.

The Simon & Schuster Speakers Bureau can bring authors to your live event. For more information or to book an event contact the Simon & Schuster Speakers Bureau at 1-866-248-3049 or visit our website at www.simonspeakers.com.

Manufactured in the United States of America

10 9 8 7 6 5 4 3 2 1

ISBN 978-1-5011-0042-0

For Tim, Lianna, and Nicholas

1

IT HAD been a long, bleak winter in southwest Virginia. Even though I was born and raised in the small town of Brea Ridge and should be used to the cold, often snowy winters, I was a warm-weather gal at heart. I sometimes wondered if I was adopted . . . if I'd been born to parents whose native climate was tropical . . . and if they ever wondered what had become of their dear Daphne and wished they'd have kept me there with them in their oceanfront mansion.

And so my thoughts were meandering now that

the weather was finally warming up. I was sitting at the island in my kitchen—as close to a tropical island as I was likely to get for a while—making flowers for the wedding cake I was entering in the first annual Brea Ridge Taste Bud Temptation Cake and Confectionary Arts Exhibit and Competition when Myra rapped on the door. The knock was a mere formality. She could see me and figured—rightly so—that the door was unlocked, so she came on in.

Myra is my closest—both in proximity and in relationship—neighbor. She's wonderful, she's exasperating, she's aggravating, she's endearing, and she's always entertaining.

"What are you doing?" she asked, cocking her head as she watched me using my cattleya orchid cutters to make petals out of fondant.

"I'm making orchids for the wedding cake I'm doing for the cake competition," I said.

"Oh, good. I thought you were making the weirdest-looking cookies I'd ever seen." She sat down on one of the stools across the island from me. "So . . . do you think anything crazy will happen at this cake thing?"

"Crazy?" I smiled. "There's always something crazy going on in the cake world. That much competitive spirit combined with all that sugar makes for some interesting shenanigans."

"No, no, no." She waved away my "interesting shenanigans" with a double flick of her left wrist.

"I'm talking about criminal activity. I'm hoping that with all these people coming to little old Brea Ridge, Mark and I will have at least one interesting case on our hands before the weekend is out."

Myra—an attractive widow in her early to mid-sixties—had been dating private investigator Mark Thompson for the past couple of months. Mark was good at his job and had plenty to keep him busy. He'd also had the good sense to keep Myra away from his investigations for the most part, but I suspected that was getting harder and harder for him to do.

"I didn't know Mark was looking for extra work," I said, gently picking up one of the orchid leaves and ruffling its edges with a ball modeling tool.

"He's not, but he's told me that if the right kind of case comes along, he'll be glad to have me help out."

The right kind of case . . . Well played, Mark. Well played, I thought.

I continued shaping the orchid. "Well, good luck, but I can't see anything too awfully crazy happening over the course of the next few days. I mean, any criminal activity would be handled by the police, so I don't know what could happen in that short amount of time that would require the services of a private investigator."

"That's the kind of stuff people say just before disaster strikes," Myra said, with a sage nod of her head that would've done any mountaintop guru proud.

"I guess you have a point there." I tried to change the subject. "I hope the confectionary arts exhibit and cake competition will go well. I know there are some people in Brea Ridge who aren't happy that so many people will be converging on the town, but I think it'll be good for the local economy. Don't you?"

"Well, honey, I hope it will. I know all the locals could use the money. Tanya's even put a sign in her window that walk-ins are welcome and that they specialize in updos."

I'd seen some of the updos that had been done at Tanya's Tremendous Tress Taming Salon. The words "beehive" and "shellacked" immediately came to mind.

"Hopefully, she'll get some business," I said, trying not to shudder as I imagined scores of out-of-towners with ten-gallon updos that would stand up to hurricane-force winds. I really did hope Tanya would get some business, though. Maybe new customers would be good. They could look at their new hairstyles as part of the whole Brea Ridge Taste Bud Temptation experience.

Myra looked down at the orchid I'd just finished. "Well, that's pretty after all. I didn't know what you were going to wind up with when you started."

"Thanks. I've not done many orchids before,

but I thought white orchids and peach roses would be a beautiful combination on the wedding cake I'm entering into the competition." I put the orchid on a foam square. "Hopefully, next year, I'll be able to incorporate the Australian string work I'll be learning in Jordan Richards's two-day class that starts tomorrow."

"Jordan Richards?" Myra leaned back and frowned at me. "He's that cake decorator from TV, right?"

I nodded. "He's a renowned sugar artist. A lot of people are coming to the cake and confectionary arts exhibit and competition just to see him. He only accepted ten students into his class. The ones who weren't able to get into the class will be attending his demonstrations at the show."

Myra scoffed. "Like he'll give two hoots of an owl's patoot."

"What?" I chuckled.

"He's the one who's so mean on television. He makes that Gordon Ramsay fellow look like Mary Poppins."

"I know he has the reputation of being hyper-critical and a . . ." I struggled to find the right word.

Myra didn't need to think about it as long and hard as I did. "Jerk . . . creep . . . rabid, inconsiderate, rude, hypocritical ball of snot?"

"Uh . . . yeah, I guess you could call him any or all of those things. But that might just be his TV persona. He might be nothing like that in real life.

At least, I hope he's not." I held up my crossed index and middle fingers. "Fingers crossed. Besides, I want to learn from the best."

"Oh, honey," Myra said. "Sometimes you learn just as many *bad* things as good from the best."

I put aside the orchid petal I was working on and asked Myra if she'd like something to drink. Experience had taught me that when Myra began an *Oh, honey* story, I might as well make myself comfortable and settle in for the long haul.

"No, thanks, I'm fine," she said.

I took a bottle of water from the fridge, uncapped it, took a long drink, and sat back down.

"Ruthie Mae Pruitt got to be purt near fifty years old before she learned to drive a car," Myra said. "She didn't really feel the need to learn to drive until after her husband died. The fact that he'd died as the result of a car accident didn't really faze her, since he'd been walking and was hit by the car that had the accident."

"So she figured she might as well learn to drive in case she wanted to hit somebody? Or was it because she was afraid to walk wherever she wanted to go after her husband's death?" I was being sarcastic, but Myra answered as if I weren't.

"Mainly, she didn't want to walk everywhere she wanted to go. And, of course, she got to thinking that driving herself could really broaden her horizons. She'd had to depend on someone else to take her wherever she'd wanted to go all her life.

With her own driver's license, she could go any-where she wanted. She'd even decided to visit her sister two states down and one state over, in the upper corner of Georgia. That was a big deal to Ruthie Mae. So she started asking around town be-cause she wanted to learn to drive *from the best*." Myra leveled her gaze at me. We were getting to the moral of the story.

"Now, everybody in Brea Ridge knew that Tony Barger was the best driver around. He could've probably gone pro on the NASCAR circuit or that Indy 500 deal or some other big-time racing racket had it not been for his drinking problem," she con-tinued.

"Please tell me Tony Barger wasn't drunk when he taught Ruthie how to drive," I said.

"Of course he wasn't. He had, however, tied one on and kept it on the entire weekend before he took Ruthie Mae for her first and only driving les-son on Monday afternoon."

"First and only?" I asked. "Did she decide she didn't like it after all?"

"More than likely, that was her final thought. Neither of them made it out of that driving lesson alive. You see, Tony was definitely not drunk when he was driving Ruthie Mae out to the parking lot of that closed-down grocery store where he was going to give her that first lesson in driving. He was very conscientious about that. He wanted to set a good example and that sort of thing. But the poor man did have the DTs something fierce," she said, slowly shaking her head. "Some say he might've even had a seizure."

"Wait a second. How do you know he had delirium tremens?" I asked. "Did someone see him having them?"

"Nah, honey. It just stood to reason. What would you think if a man who was normally a drunk who could drive circles around everybody else in Brea Ridge suddenly took a relatively young widow for her first driving lesson and drove her into the side of an abandoned grocery store at eighty-five miles an hour, instantly killing them both?"

"I'd think he was drunk at the time instead of suffering from withdrawal," I said.

"That's because you didn't know Tony. He could drive just as good drunk as he could sober," Myra said. "In fact, he drove better drunk than some people could drive sober. And had he been drunk, that accident never would've happened."

I took another drink of my water, figuring it was useless to argue the point with her. Even though I found it nearly impossible to believe that an intoxicated man could outdrive most of the sober citizens of Brea Ridge, why argue? After all, what difference did it make?

"Plus, there was no alcohol in his bloodstream at the time of the accident," Myra went on. "It was in the newspaper. That's how everybody knew it wasn't the alcohol that caused the wreck but the fact that he'd been off it since Sunday night that had been the problem. So you see? Sometimes learning from the best isn't all it's cracked up to be."

"I'll keep that in mind," I said. "Hopefully, Chef Richards won't be drunk . . . or sober . . . or in any kind of condition that would hinder him from instructing us all in the fine art of Australian string work. And even if he is, the worst he can do is frost us to death, right?"

She laughed. "I guess so. Just be careful he doesn't put you in a sugar coma."

"Or cause me to gain ten pounds overnight," I said.

"Oh, honey, that's my worst nightmare . . . well, one of them anyway."

At the time I didn't realize that taking a cake decorating class from Jordan Richards would not be too different from hitting a brick wall at eighty-five miles per hour. We live and we learn. And, to Myra's credit, it turned out that sometimes learning from the best was not everything you thought it would be.

AFTER MYRA LEFT, Sparrow, my gray-and-white, one-eyed Persian cat, came out of my home office-slash–guest room, where she had a bed in the corner in which she liked to hide. Her mewing reminded me that it was nearing dinnertime. Although she was a stray that I had inherited when I'd moved into my house last year, Sparrow had adapted very quickly to having her meals served on a regular basis.

As I opened a can of cat food and emptied it into her dish, I thought about how far I'd come these past few months. After my abusive husband had shot at me—fortunately, he'd missed—and had been arrested for attempted murder, I ended our fifteen-year marriage and moved from our home in Tennessee back to my hometown of Brea Ridge, Virginia. My sister, Violet, was a Realtor in Brea Ridge, and she'd found a house she knew I'd love. She was right. My cozy two-bedroom cottage suited me to a tee.

I also loved living closer to Violet's twelve-year-old boy/girl twins, Lucas and Leslie. My ex-husband, Todd, and I had never had any children—a good thing, looking back—and Lucas and Leslie were as close as I was likely going to get to having children for a while. Of course, I was forty, and nearing forty-one at breakneck speed. If I was going to be a mom, I needed to get started on the process fairly soon . . . whether naturally or by adoption. I had a vision of Marisa Tomei stomping her foot in one of her movies and telling her onscreen boyfriend that her biological clock was ticking. I was afraid that if I waited much longer, my biological alarm would start buzzing . . . and I wouldn't be able to hit the snooze button either.

Anyway, Leslie and Lucas had always held a

special place in my heart. I'd enjoyed spending plenty of time with them since I'd been back in Brea Ridge. It was just that sometimes watching them interact with Violet and Jason, their dad, I sensed the strength of the family's bond and longed to have that closeness with my own child. A husband would be nice too, of course. Yes, I wanted the whole package. I wanted everything I didn't have with Todd: a lover who cherished me, a man I could trust and respect, a provider and guardian who would shelter me and our child—or children—from life's storms. Suddenly, music from Franco Zeffirelli's *Romeo & Juliet* swelled in my head, and I nearly began singing "A Time for Us" at the top of my lungs. I restrained myself, though, because it would have really freaked out the cat . . . and any neighbors within earshot.

I'd worked for a government housing agency for over twenty years when I was living in Tennessee, so I was fortunate to get a severance package when I retired, which allowed me to realize my dream of operating a bakery out of my home when I moved back to Virginia. Pretty much ever since I'd been back in Brea Ridge, I'd been the sole proprietor of Daphne's Delectable Cakes. And now I was getting ready to put my cake-decorating skills to the test by entering not one but two cakes in the Brea Ridge Taste Bud Temptation Cake and Confectionary Arts Exhibit and Competition. In addition to the wedding cake I'd told Myra about, I'd sculpted a superhero cake to enter into the novelty cake division.

I washed my hands at the sink and then put away my orchid petals and the completed flowers while I wondered what to have for dinner. Ben, my significant other—the term "boyfriend" sounded too teenybopper to apply at our age, although I'd been envisioning him as the Romeo to my Juliet in my previously mentioned fantasy—was the editor in chief of the *Brea Ridge Chronicle,* and he was working tonight so I was on my own. I opened the cabinet and perused the shelves. Cold cereal it was.

I had several boxes on hand of various varieties. I'd learned cold cereal to be the most important staple of the single woman's diet. I took the box from the cabinet and put it on the table. Before I could get my bowl, milk, and spoon, the phone rang. Maybe it was Ben, and he was going to be able to have dinner with me after all. We could cook something together, or get takeout, or . . .

I answered the phone. It wasn't Ben. It was my sister, Violet.

"I finally talked her into it," Violet said as soon as I'd said hello. "Leslie is going to enter a cake in the kids' division of the cake competition."

"I'm so glad! Is she going with carved, traditional, or something a little more modern, like the topsy-turvy cake we discussed?"

"She's going to do a carved cheeseburger-and-fries cake."

"That's good," I said. "She'll be utilizing one of her strongest skills. She is great at eyeballing shapes and chiseling them out. How about Lucas? Is he going to enter a cake?"

"I'm afraid not," she said. "He still likes to bake sometimes, but he doesn't think it's cool to admit it anymore. He and Jason are attending a college baseball game Saturday, but they'll be stopping by the competition either before or after the game to see how everything is going."

"I'm glad. I can hardly wait to see him . . . them. I mean, it'll be nice to see their dad too, but I haven't seen Lucas and Leslie in over a week!"

"Hello? Don't I rate at all?"

"Of course you do," I said. "It goes without saying that I'll be happy to see you."

"Yeah, sure." She laughed. "Way to try and cover. Between you and me, how do you think Leslie will fare in the competition?"

"I think she'll do really well. She has a knack for decorating, and she learns quickly. The only problem I think she'll have at all is stressing out over it too much," I said. "Just remind her to do her best and then to let it go. Tell her to have fun with it."

"I'd like to take this opportunity to remind *you* of the same thing," said Vi. "You've been known to stress out too much over things like this yourself."

She was talking about the time that I went all the way to the Oklahoma State Sugar Art Show in Tulsa and then chickened out of entering my cake in the competition. I wound up giving it to the staff at my hotel, much to show-director Kerry Vincent's disapproval. Ms. Vincent had basically told me to come back when I was ready to put a little more faith in myself and my ability as a decorator. She was very kind and understanding. Maybe I would return to the Oklahoma State Sugar Art Show and compete . . . but I needed to see how I would fare in the Brea Ridge Taste Bud Temptation Cake and Confectionary Art Exhibit and Competition first. Then I'd think about frying bigger fish . . . in Oklahoma.

"In my defense, the hotel staff said my cake was gorgeous . . . and that it tasted delicious," I said.

"I'm sure it was. And I dare you to bail out of this competition at the last minute like you did that one," she said. "In fact, I'll be there to kick your butt if you try. If I'd been in Oklahoma with you, I wouldn't have let you squirm out of that one either."

"But, Vi, you didn't see all those incredible cakes!"

"I saw the pictures you took. Granted, they *were* magnificent—and there will be impressive cakes at this competition too—but you have to stop selling yourself short."

"I will," I said. "I promise."

"All right. And I'm not going to let Leslie back out either. Like her aunt Daphne, she merely needs to recognize her own worth and talents and feel confident enough to show them off."

"Preach, sister, preach!" I laughed.

She huffed. "Okay. I'll get out of my pulpit now and let you go back to whatever you were doing." She paused. "What *were* you doing?"

"Deciding which cereal to have for dinner," I said. "I'm thinking of going with a granola entrée and following up with either a chocolaty or fruity cereal for dessert."

"I take it Ben's working?" she asked.

"Yep," I said.

"How are things going between you two?"

"Great," I said. "He's wonderful. I should've never let him go all those years ago. I'm lucky he gave me another chance."

Ben and I had been childhood friends and later high school sweethearts. Although we had tried to make it work, our romance fell apart after we went to separate colleges and I met Todd.

"Then don't let him get away again," she said. She kept her tone light, but there was a word of warning there.

"Do you know something I don't?" I asked.

"No. I'm just saying that it's rare for a couple to get a second chance like the two of you have been given," she said. "Make the most of it."

"I am."

After talking with Violet, I took my bowl of granola into the living room and watched the episode of Chef Jordan Richards's program I had recorded on my DVR.

As the show came on, it showed Chef Richards addressing a petite brunette about her three-tiered wedding cake. "What's this *bleep*?" he demanded. "What color is this supposed to be?"

"Burnt orange," the brunette said, lowering her eyes away from his scalding glare. "It's what the client wanted."

"Well, it looks like *bleep* brown to me!" He used his right hand to forcefully push the center tier of the cake, effectively knocking the entire cake off the counter and onto the floor. "Clean that up! Then you can start over!"

The camera zoomed in on the brunette's face—particularly, her quavering lips—as she went to the corner of the kitchen to get a broom and dustpan. The cameraman followed, allowing the audience to see the woman's humiliating trip back behind the table to clean up the remains of her hard work. He then panned the camera over to Chef Richards, who was shaking his head in contempt as he wiped his icing-covered hand on a dishtowel.

I gulped, suddenly dreading tomorrow morning's class. I tried to reassure myself. I'd dealt with bullies before. Todd had bullied me for years before committing the act of abuse—trying to kill me—that was second only to the final act of abuse—succeeding in the murder attempt. At least Jordan Richards wouldn't try to *kill* me during the course of teaching his string work class . . . would he?

2

THE BREA Ridge Inn was one of the oldest and the fanciest resort hotels in the southwest Virginia, northeast Tennessee region. Its arched windows and four-sided hipped roof were typical of the Grand Georgian architecture in which it was styled.

I walked into the lobby, admiring as I always did when I had occasion to come here (which was usually only for a wedding reception or formal birthday party) the ornate oil paintings hanging over the massive fireplace. The paintings were said to depict the original innkeepers, and they had been restored at least once over the years.

A couple of older gentlemen were sitting by one of the large, floor-to-ceiling windows enjoying a game of chess. I smiled at them as I made my way to the reception desk. One waved a white bishop at me just before using it to take his opponent's queen.

"Hi," I said to the desk clerk. "I'm Daphne Martin. I'm here for Chef Jordan Richards's Australian string work class."

She politely directed me to Ballroom A.

I turned and made my way through lushly carpeted halls framed by walls that featured an intricately carved chair rail molding and was interspersed every few feet by a cherry crescent table holding a bold floral arrangement.

The double doors to Ballroom A were open. I nervously wiped my palms down the sides of my black slacks before walking in. I could see Chef Richards standing inside the room, but he was turned away from me talking with a man who was dressed in a white chef's uniform. Should I have worn a chef's uniform rather than the dress pants and geometric-print blouse I was wearing? Oh well, too late now.

Chef Richards was shorter than I had expected him to be. He'd always appeared taller on television. I wondered now if the people he worked with were also short, or if he instructed the camera crew to shoot him in a way that made him appear taller. Despite his height—or lack thereof—he carried himself with a confidence that bordered on arrogance. I supposed that when one was as successful as Chef Richards, one would be allowed a little arrogance . . . a little smugness. I just hoped the attitude didn't hop the fence and cross that border into full-blown overbearing, narcissistic superiority like it did on TV.

The chairs had been stacked and moved to the sides of the ballroom, while long tables had been evenly spaced throughout. There were tented cards bearing the students' names, two to a table. I spotted my table and was making a beeline for it when Chef Richards noticed me.

He had gunmetal-gray hair. His eyes were brown and, in person, his face appeared to be more weathered than was obvious on television. As he strode toward me, he had the bearing of a smug autocrat, and I felt myself cringing inside. Then, surprising me, he smiled and stuck out his right hand.

"Welcome! I'm Chef Richards, but I suppose you already know that."

"Of course," I said, shaking his hand. "It's a pleasure to meet you."

"And you are . . . ?" he asked.

"Daphne Martin. I'm a local baker, and I hope to learn a great deal from you in class today and tomorrow."

He nodded. "If you work hard, you will."

"I certainly intend to do that," I said. I'd started to say I planned to get my money's worth, but I felt that might sound too crass, especially given the fact that the class had been priced well out of my budget.

Chef Richards told me it was "nice to have me on board" and then went to greet another student who was just coming into class. I felt relieved. Maybe I'd been right in what I'd told Myra—the mean-guy persona cultivated by Chef Richards was for the benefit of the TV cameras. I was looking forward to going home at the end of the day and telling her how nice he'd turned out to be.

The student who'd just entered the ballroom turned out to be my table partner. His name was Lou, and he was wearing a black chef's uniform. At least we were wearing complementary clothing.

Lou was an affable guy with a dark-brown buzz cut and a goatee. He shook my hand and told me he'd come from South Carolina to take this class.

After everyone had filed in, been welcomed by Chef Richards, and filled all ten of the assigned spots, Chef Richards began the class.

"Good morning," he said. "As you can see, you each have before you a bowl of royal icing. I made the batch myself before you arrived, and it is of a perfect consistency. I trust each of you has a passable royal icing recipe, but I guarantee that your recipe won't surpass mine. I have, therefore, taken the liberty of having my assistant print out my recipe for you. It too is on your table. Don't bother to thank me—although you will every time you mix up a batch of this icing." He smiled. "Allow me to go ahead and say you are all welcome."

Chef Richards paused momentarily to give us all time to express our gratitude. Then he introduced us to his assistant, Fiona. Fiona was a petite woman with light-pink hair. The color was striking on its own but made even more so by the fact that every piece of her clothing was white.

Fiona said hello and started to say something else, but Chef Richards cut her off.

"There'll be time for you to socialize later, Fiona."

"Of course," she murmured as she moved back to the side of Chef Richards's table and resumed standing there as unobtrusively as possible.

"Students, go ahead and fill your piping bags with the royal icing," Chef Richards instructed.

I took the plastic wrap off my bowl of icing and used the silicone spatula provided to fill the pastry bag. We'd been provided eight-inch, fondant-covered round cake dummies on metal and porcelain turntables and a flexible plastic dividing wheel to determine where to pipe our string work.

"You'll notice there are some toothpicks beside your bowl of royal icing," said Chef Richards. "Please use one to score your cake for the first row of Australian string work, making your loops one and one-quarter inches apart." He nodded at Fiona, and she began scoring his cake as we scored ours. "Then stagger another loop—also one and one-quarter inches apart—above your original scoring."

"Everyone done with that?" he asked after a couple minutes. He looked around the room and noticed that there was still one student who was painstakingly marking her cake. He blew out a breath. "For cripes' sake, what's taking you so long? You *do* know how far apart an inch and a quarter is, don't you?"

With great difficulty, I resisted turning to see who was getting the dressing down. Maybe Chef Richards's crappy attitude wasn't entirely manufactured for television after all. On the other hand, he *could* simply want to keep things moving at a brisk pace. I mean, we only had him for two days, so we were on a tight schedule. I was trying to give him the benefit of a doubt and not write him off after one exasperated comment.

"Now, if Ms.—" He squinted to read the placard in front of her. "If Ms. Wilson has caught up with the rest of the class, we will continue. Ms. Wilson?"

She apparently nodded, because Chef Richards told her that a nod or a head shake was not a proper response to any of his questions.

"If I ask you a question, you will respond to me verbally and with respect. Do you understand?"

"Yes, sir," she said softly.

"Louder," he instructed.

"Yes, sir." Her voice was louder now but tremulous.

"Very well," Chef Richards said. "Now, have you finished scoring your cake, and are you ready to proceed with class?"

"Yes, sir," Ms. Wilson answered.

"All right, then." He went to the back of his table, picked up his piping bag, and instructed us on piping the first thin line of icing to follow the scoring on the cake. "Now, as you can see, this line is rather thick. Undo your coupler and replace the tip you're currently using with the tiny round tip before you." He gazed about the room to make sure everyone was complying. He blew out a breath. "Oh, come on! It's not rocket science, people. Get a move on!"

Chef Richards began to walk around the room impatiently. I'd already switched tips and reattached my coupler, so I was ready to go when he resumed teaching. I thought he had nothing to pick on me about.

"Good job, Ms. Martin." He nodded at my piping bag.

"Thank you," I said with a relieved smile.

"You're welcome." He rocked back on his heels. "Is your husband still in prison, Ms. Martin?"

My smiled faded. "Excuse me?" I couldn't have heard him correctly.

"I asked if your husband is still incarcerated in federal prison in Tennessee," he said.

I took a second to gather my thoughts. "I'm not currently married, and I don't see what my personal life has to do with this class."

His mouth turned down at the corners. "That was a satisfactory response, Ms. Martin." He turned his attention to the rest of the class. "You see, students, Ms. Martin's estranged or former husband was incarcerated for attempted murder—of *her*, no less. What I just demonstrated to her was the importance of holding up well under pressure. You never know what types of questions the public will ask you or what kinds of people you'll be required to work with." He looked back at me and nodded curtly. "Adequate job, Ms. Martin."

I didn't thank him.

He moved back to his table when he was satisfied that everyone had switched the cake decorating tips in their couplers and was ready to continue. "With this tiny tip, we are going to make a string from the bottom of the thicker string to the top of your next scored line. Like so." He demonstrated, making strings linking base icing to the scored section so close together that they were almost touching.

"Fiona, finish this up for me while I observe the students' progress." Then he went around the room to look over everyone's shoulders.

If he couldn't criticize, he said nothing. Where was the congenial, albeit arrogant, man who greeted me and the other students when we walked through the door?

He nodded at my string work, which I took as high praise. To Lou, my table partner, he said, "Little sloppy there, Mr. Gimmel. Steady hands . . . steady hands."

Once Chef Richards had passed on to the next table, Lou rolled his eyes at me. I rolled mine back. I felt like telling Lou that at least Chef Richards hadn't thrown Lou's personal life onto the ballroom floor for everyone to gawk at. I'm surprised my hands were steady enough to make my string work any neater than Lou's . . . which in truth wasn't bad at all.

"Your work is even sloppier than Mr. Gimmel's, Mr. Conroy," Chef Richard said. "I'd scrape that crap off with my spatula and try it again if I were you." He looked Mr. Conroy up and down. "Are you a professional baker, Mr. Conroy, or are you here simply because you had no other plans for these two days?"

"I'm a professional," Mr. Conroy said. "I currently work in a grocery store bakery in my hometown, but I hope to improve my skills enough to either open my own shop one day or to work in an upscale restaurant."

"Yes, well . . ." Chef Richards pursed his lips. "In addition to *greatly* improving your decorating skills, you need to cut that hair, lose about twenty pounds, and have that dreadful tattoo lasered off. Customers expect their bakers to look professional."

Mr. Conroy's eyes narrowed. "Have you ever seen Mario Batali?"

"I have," said Chef Richards. "His appearance is almost as bad as yours, Mr. Conroy, and I wouldn't eat anything he prepared for me."

"He'd never prepare anything for you," Mr. Conroy said. "He'd see right through your egotistical, odious attitude in a heartbeat and tell you to hit the road."

Lou Gimmel and I looked at each other wide-eyed. I was wishing I'd had the nerve and the quick wit to say something like that to Chef Richards. The class held its collective breath waiting to see how Chef Richards would respond. It was something of a letdown.

"You're probably right," he said, moving on to slam Mr. Conroy's table mate.

Still, I couldn't help but think that he was criticizing Mr. Conroy's appearance when his own assistant looked like a Japanese anime character with her light-pink hair. Granted, the rest of her appearance was tame in comparison. Maybe to Chef Richards, cotton-candy hair went along with the concept of a confectionary artist.

By the time Chef Richards had returned to the table, Fiona had expertly completed the string work all the way around his cake.

"When you've completed encircling the cake with the string work as I have done here, we will move on to the next step," he said.

My eyes flew to Fiona's face. It was expression-less. I supposed she was used to standing in the background and allowing the celebrity chef to take credit for her work. And although we'd all seen Fiona do the work, no one spoke up about what he'd said. Maybe I was feeling nitpicky since he'd been so hypercritical of everyone else.

WHEN I GOT home at about five o'clock that af-ternoon, I was both physically and emotionally ex-hausted. Myra wasted no time in rushing over to find out if Chef Richards was as big a jerk in real life as he was on television.

We went into the living room. I stretched out on my long white sofa, and Myra curled up in my pink-and-white gingham chair.

I sighed. "I think he's actually worse in person. When you're in the room with him, the humiliation he inflicts becomes tangible . . . almost like a poi-sonous gas or something."

"Did he say anything mean to you?"

"He said something mean to everybody in the class at least once," I said, trying to sidestep her question.

Myra straightened. "What did he say to you?"

"He asked if my husband was still incarcerated. Then he went on to tell the class the whole sordid story of how Todd had tried to kill me."

Her jaw dropped.

"He said it was to demonstrate the pressure that bakers can come under from the public or some such garbage," I said.

"That's a load of baloney," Myra said. "He just wanted to embarrass you!"

"That was how I looked at it." I shrugged. "At least, he didn't tell me to lose twenty pounds."

She gaped again. "He told somebody to lose weight? Was it a man or woman?"

"Man."

"That's probably a good thing," she said. "If he'd have said that to a woman, they'd probably be scraping him off the hood of her car about now."

I chuckled. "The guy handled it well . . . I've got to give him that. He quickly retorted that his appearance was no sloppier than that of Mario Batali."

"And what did Chef Richards say to that?"

"He said he wouldn't eat anything prepared by Mario Batali, and the student said that Chef Batali wouldn't offer him anything because of Chef Richards's odious attitude."

Myra laughed. "Good for him! It sounds like Chef Richards thinks he's better than everybody else . . . and that he needs to be taken down a notch or two. Carl Jr. had a baseball coach like that once. He was the biggest jerk I'd ever seen. He was nice to the kids until they'd agreed to play for him, and then he treated them like dirt. He'd even criticize them for things they did *right* . . . just, apparently, not right enough! Carl Jr. once made a run—earned the team the game-winning point, no less—and Coach Jerk Face yelled at him when he crossed home plate for not being in the proper position when the ball was hit."

"Did you take Coach Jerk Face down a notch or two?" I asked with a grin.

"I sure did. One evening after sitting at a game, seething and hating the man and feeling guilty because I was seething and hating the man, I told Carl Jr. that we were going to find him another team to play for. Well, the coach heard me say that to Carl Jr. and he wanted to know if Carl was being a baby and quitting the team." Myra's jaw tightened and her eyes became slits just remembering the encounter. "I said, 'No, he's not. He'd stick it out and keep playing for you, but I'm the one paying the bills. And I'm not giving you any more of my husband's hard-earned money. I'd rather give his money to a team where boys are encouraged, not torn down.'"

"Wow. You handled that very well," I said.

"Well . . . I left out the part where I told him that if he ever said another cross word to my son I'd kick his butt up between his shoulder blades," she said. "And I didn't tell you that when I left, I let the air out of his tires."

I laughed. "From the sound of things, even if you had given him the butt-kicking, it couldn't have happened to a nicer guy!"

"Except maybe for Chef Richards," she said. "Maybe Mark and I should check into that guy's past."

"You do that," I said. "It's hard to tell what'll turn up."

She nodded. "I bet you're right. Nobody that mean could be up to any good."

AFTER MYRA LEFT, I still needed some time to unwind. My best therapy for relieving stress was baking. I decided to make some cookies . . . maybe white chocolate chunk macadamia.

I thought about taking the cookies to share with the class tomorrow morning, but I quickly dismissed that idea. Chef Richards would either a) declare the cookies to be the most disgusting things he'd ever tasted, b) harangue me for making cookies when I should have been working on my lousy scrollwork technique, c) toss the cookies in the trash can immediately upon my arrival because he hadn't authorized my bringing them to class, or d) something even more nasty than any or all of the above.

Ben loved my white chocolate chunk macadamia cookies, and we were going out tonight. I'd make the cookies for him, put them in a bakers' box tied with a red ribbon, and present them as a "just because" gift.

With both my recipe and my purpose in mind, I

took out my favorite blue mixing bowl. There wasn't any special sentimental value to my mixing bowl . . . no particular reason it should be my favorite. It was simply a good bowl. Chefs, bakers, gourmands, and grandmothers—especially grandmothers—could always get a feel for the best kitchen tools. This bowl was uppermost in my arsenal of baking weaponry. I relied on it often and was never disappointed by it— it wasn't too deep or too shallow; it was just right.

I measured my flour into the bowl and wondered again about Chef Richards. *Was* he as harsh as he'd tried to come across today in class? He'd greeted us all nicely—I wouldn't go so far as to say warmly—when we got to class. He hadn't been impersonal or unfriendly. Then he'd begun the class and behaved like a complete ass. Was it part of his performance as the caustic celebrity chef? Could he turn the attitude on and off as if it were a light switch? Did he employ it only when he was onstage—with any venue in which he was performing as the celebrity chef serving as his stage?

He'd been critical of Gavin Conroy's appearance. Yet Chef Richards's own assistant had an unconventional hairstyle and fashion sense. Had Mr. Conroy been planted as a student in order to give Chef Richards someone with whom to argue? Given that Fiona had done almost all of the actual Australian string work, I had to wonder how much of Chef Richards's celebrity was due to his bluster and how much was to be credited to actual talent.

3

BY THE time Ben arrived to pick me up for dinner, I'd showered, put on a plum-colored wrap dress, reapplied my makeup, and felt like a brand-new woman. I'd even talked myself out of dreading tomorrow's class with Chef Jordan Richards. So what if the guy was a jerk? The rest of the class and I had survived the first day. We'd get through the second. Plus, I was learning some fantastic new techniques.

"You look beautiful," Ben said.

"You look pretty hot yourself," I told him. And he did.

Ben was gorgeous. He had wavy light-brown hair, sky-blue eyes, and a lopsided smile. He worked out at the gym every other day and had once won the Sexiest Male Editor of the Year award. Okay, I'm joking about that last part. To my knowledge, there was no such award. But had there been, my Ben would have won it. Tonight he wore navy dress pants, a light-blue shirt that brought out those eyes, and a tan sport coat.

"I have a surprise for you," I said.

"I have a surprise for *you*. I made reservations at that little Italian place outside of town," he said. "I hope that's okay."

I smiled. "You know I love that place."

"Yeah, I do." He kissed me. "Now what's your surprise?"

I stepped over to the island and retrieved the white box tied with a red velvet bow. I handed the box to Ben.

"Wow. What's the occasion?" he asked.

"It's nothing much. I guess the occasion is that I just wanted you to know I was thinking of you when I got home this afternoon."

He opened the box. "Oh, man . . . These are my favorites!"

"I know," I said.

He took out one of the cookies and bit into it.

"You'll spoil your appetite," I warned.

"No, I won't," he said. "Did you have fun in class today?"

" 'Fun' isn't exactly the word I'd use to describe it," I said. "But I don't want us to lose our reservation. Let me tell you about it on the way."

By the time we pulled into the parking lot at Geppetto's, Ben had heard the whole saga. He shook his head. "Chef Richards is lucky that the guy he called sloppy didn't punch him in the face . . . unless he *was* planted there, like you said. But *you* weren't planted there, and he wasn't kind to you. Someone will eventually put that man in his place. Bullies usually wind up meeting their match one way or another."

"Well, forgive me for saying so, but I hope I'm around to see it when Jordan Richards does meet his match."

Those words would eventually turn up on a plate served with sides of fear and regret, and I'd be forced to swallow them whole. But tonight, I was having pasta.

THE GEPPETTO'S HOSTESS showed us to an intimate table for two by a window that looked out upon the river. It was a lovely late winter's night. The sky was clear, and the moon was full. The hostess told us that our waitress, Kaitlyn, would be right with us, and then she returned to her post to seat the next arriving patrons.

While we awaited Kaitlyn's appearance, Ben reached across the table and took both my hands.

"You know how special you are to me, don't you?" he asked.

We hadn't yet got to the *L*-word stage of our relationship . . . not this time, anyway. When we were dating in high school, we threw the *L* word around like it was confetti. And we made promises we'd been unable to keep. This time we were much more mature . . . and cautious. We'd both been hurt in the past, and neither of us wanted to go through that again.

The seriousness of Ben's expression made my heart flutter. He was about to make a major revelation. Either he was going to dump me . . . or he was going to tell me he loved me. I leaned forward, desperately hoping for the latter.

"Hi there, I'm Kaitlyn, and I'll be taking care of you this evening. What can I get you to drink?"

I looked at the perky, ponytailed waitress and thought, *You can get me a big old glass of Give Us a Minute, Kaitlyn.* "I'd like a sweet tea," I said.

"And for you, sir?"

"I'll have the same," Ben said.

Kaitlyn said she'd be right back with our drinks. Since Ben had only let go of one of my hands when Kaitlyn had approached, I hoped the moment had not been lost.

"You were about to tell me something," I prompted.

"Let's order first." He let go of my other hand and picked up his menu. "That way, maybe we'll have a better chance of not being interrupted mid-way through our conversation."

It was definitely something big that he wanted to talk with me about . . . relationship-changing if not life-changing.

When Kaitlyn returned with our drinks and a basket of warm breadsticks and asked if we were ready to order, I jumped right in with my request for chicken Parmesan. Ben mulled over the menu for what seemed like two days and then said he too would like the chicken Parmesan.

This time, I took Ben's hands. "Alone at last. Now tell me what's on your mind."

He took a deep breath. "I got a call today from somebody I went to college with. Nickie Zane . . . she's, um . . . she's heading up a new, fairly large business magazine called *All Up in Your Business.*" He extracted one of his hands and took a drink of his tea. "She's offered me a lucrative position with the magazine."

"That's great . . . isn't it? Are you considering taking the job?"

"I am," he said. "It would be more money and less responsibility than what I have at the *Chronicle.* . . . The only drawback is that I'd have to move to Kentucky."

"Oh." I guessed it was the dump speech instead of the love speech. My heart sank into the pit of my stomach.

"That's it?" he asked, studying my face. "Oh?"

"What am I supposed to say?" In my mind, I followed up with *I don't want you to leave Brea Ridge and move to Kentucky. I thought we were building something wonderful here . . . together. . . .*

"I don't know," Ben said. "I thought you'd have something a bit more substantive to say than 'oh.'"

"Um . . . congratulations?" I pressed my lips together. "Ben, I honestly don't know what to say. I don't want you to leave Brea Ridge, but you have to do what's best for you. If this job is it, then I wish you all the best."

He released my other hand. "Okay. Thanks."

Wonderful. I'd said the wrong thing, and he was annoyed with me. I tried to make amends by further talking about the job. "Isn't that awfully far away from your parents?"

"Not really. Now that they're living in the condo in Tennessee, they don't need me as much as they once did." He leveled his gaze into my eyes. "I guess I don't really have anything holding me here in Brea Ridge. Do I?"

"That's not fair," I said. "What kind of person would I be if I tried to convince you to stay? You'd end up resenting me. Maybe not today . . . maybe not tomorrow . . . but soon, and for the rest of your life." It dawned on me that I was quoting *Casablanca*.

That realization hit Ben at the same time, and we both laughed.

"I do care about you, Daph, and my feelings for you will ultimately factor into my decision."

"And I care about you," I said. "A lot. That's why I have to let you make the decision on your own."

AFTER BEN DROPPED me off at home, I sat in the living room with my box of orchid petals and made orchids while feeling sorry for myself. Although the evening had ended on an upbeat note, there was still the possibility—a rather strong possibility—that Ben was leaving Brea Ridge. I tried to tell myself that he wouldn't go. After all, he'd spent his entire journalistic career at the *Brea Ridge Chronicle*. Why would he leave it to start over with a new venture in Kentucky? Magazine startups have a high fail rate, especially in this new age of digital publishing. Even if Ben would be earning more money and it would be a more prestigious position than that of editor in chief of the *Chronicle,* where would he be if the magazine faltered?

And the name: *All Up in Your Business.* . . . What kind of a name was that? Were today's professionals supposed to take a name like that seriously? It sounded more like the title of a television sitcom than that of a magazine intended to educate business leaders.

After making a few more orchids, I closed the plastic box and returned it to the kitchen. I went into my office-slash–guest room to check my mail. I looked at my mail—which was mostly junk—and then looked at my website statistics—visits were up a teensy bit, so that was good. And then I got to the real reason I'd logged onto the computer in the first place.

I opened up my favorite search engine and typed in *"All Up in Your Business* magazine." I scrolled through the links on the first page of search results and was beginning to think that maybe the company hadn't set up a website yet. But then there it was, near the bottom of the second page.

I clicked on the link. The *All Up in Your Business* home page featured "A List of Articles We're Working on for Our First Issue!" The list included such titles as "Small Business Networking," "Stop Stressing, Start Achieving," "Event Planning 101," and "Eco-preneurs You're Going to Love." There was a graphic of the first cover—farmland with skyscrapers off in the distance—to illustrate, I imagined, that the magazine's focus encompassed both the concerns of rural and urban business owners.

I thought that, given the cover and the proposed articles, the magazine would be off to a good start. The only drawback would be the magazine's inability to compete with the larger business magazines already in existence and the plethora of daily business blogs.

I clicked on the About Us tab at the top of the page. There was a photograph of an attractive dark-haired woman with a chin-length bob. Her name was Nickie Zane, and she was listed as the publisher. I clicked on the link embedded within the highlighted text of her name, and another tab opened with more photos and information about the adorable and ever-so-accomplished Nickie.

While I was skimming over the information, one of the photos caught my eye. It was a group shot from Nickie's college days. Smack dab in the middle of all those smiling faces—all but two of which were looking at the camera—stood Nickie and Ben. Nickie and Ben were the two people *not* looking at the camera. That's because they were looking tenderly at each other.

I felt a little sick to my stomach. Ben had described Nickie Zane as somebody he'd gone to college with, not someone he'd been involved with . . . someone he'd been in love with. . . . Why hadn't he told me more about his relationship with this woman? Obviously, there *had* been one . . . a serious one. And were Ben or Nickie—or both of them—eager to resurrect it?

I was a grown-up. I tried never to jump to conclusions. However, trying and succeeding were two different things. I also tended to rush to judgment every now and then. My current assessment of this situation was that this tramp Nickie was trying to steal my man.

I picked up my phone and dialed Ben's number.

"Hello." He sounded a little groggy.

I looked at the clock and saw that it was ten thirty. "I hope I didn't wake you."

"No . . . no . . . what's up?"

"Well, I was checking my e-mail and my website stats, and I just so happened to look up that magazine you were talking about . . . *All Up in Your Business,*" I said.

Silence. It was the guiltiest silence I'd ever heard.

"That *is* the name of the magazine where you were offered a job, isn't it?" I asked, keeping my voice ever so innocent.

"Yes," he said.

"I thought so. Nickie is as cute as she can be," I said.

"What are you getting at, Daphne?"

"What was your relationship with her?" I asked. "And what part does that relationship factor in to your decision to leave Brea Ridge and join her in Kentucky?"

He sighed. "Do we have to discuss this right now?"

"Over dinner, you seemed upset because I wouldn't help you make your decision," I said. "I feel like I didn't have all the information I needed then. Now I do, and yes, I'd like to discuss it."

Ben blew out another breath. "It's complicated."

This time, I was the one who was silent.

"Back when we were in college, Nickie was the coolest girl I knew," he said.

"Is this before or after we broke up?" I asked.

"After." His voice took on an edge. "It was after you dumped me for your perfect guy, Todd. Todd the football player. Todd the big man on campus. Todd, the abusive jerk you married. Todd, the man who tried to *kill* you."

At about the third "Todd," I was wishing I'd chosen to discuss the issue later. But, I'd insisted on talking about it, so I couldn't very well back out simply because the conversation was becoming uncomfortable for me.

"I get it," I said. "You and she dated after you and I broke up."

"We didn't exactly date, but she helped me get over you."

"Did you fall in love with her?" I asked.

"A little. I was closer to falling in love with her than she was to falling in love with me," he said. "Unlike you, she chose to stay with her high school sweetheart . . . to give their relationship a fighting chance."

"You don't have to continue to throw my past mistakes in my face," I said softly. "How many times do I have to apologize for them?"

"None. What good would it do anyway?" he asked. "I'm sorry. Our lives took the paths they took—yours, mine, and Nickie's. She married her high school sweetheart, and they were happily married for sixteen years. They have two beautiful daughters."

"You said *were*. Have they divorced?" I asked.

"He died. Eight months ago."

"I see." Here came that rush-to-judgment thing again. Had Ben been settling for me because he'd thought his beloved Nickie was happily married to someone else? Now that she was free, was he ready to run to her side? Tears pricked my eyes, but I fought them. No way could I let Ben think I was crying over him . . . especially if he was going to throw me over for Nickie the Wonderful.

"She needs me," Ben said. "She's trying to get this magazine off the ground. It was a dream she'd shared with her husband—they never suspected that he wouldn't be here to help her see it through."

"So you're just supposed to step into her husband's shoes, huh?"

"It's not—"

"Let me finish," I interrupted. "She might need you, but so do I." I took a deep breath and put my heart on the line. "I love you, Ben." I groaned on the inside. Being the first to say the *L* word was tough for a proud woman like me . . . especially without the reassurance that Ben felt the same way. But I was doing what I felt I had to do. "Your choices are your own, Ben, and I don't want to influence you . . . but I thought you should know how I feel before you make your decision."

"Daph, I—"

"Don't say anything right now, all right? It's late, and we both need to get some rest. We can talk tomorrow."

"Okay," he said. "Good night."

Okay? Good night? That was quick. No "wait, just let me say I love you too"? He was giving in awfully easily.

I firmly reined in my emotions and said, "Good night." Then I ended the call.

I slumped in my chair and finally let my tears fall. Had he been going to tell me he loved me before I'd interrupted him? Maybe. Or maybe not. But as much as I'd like to have heard those words right then, I needed actions more. I needed Ben to stay in Brea Ridge.

4

MY ALARM clock went off Friday morning, and I immediately hit the snooze button. When it went off the second time, I hit it again. I hadn't slept terribly well the night before, and I wasn't particularly looking forward to another episode of the Chef Jordan Richards's *This Is Your Pathetic Life* show.

When the alarm shrilled a third time, Sparrow stepped into the doorway and meowed. She wasn't comfortable enough with me yet to risk jumping onto the bed to see what was wrong with me, but she'd check things out from across the room. Being a former stray, she might never be willing to jump up onto the bed. But this morning, I was okay with that. I had enough problems without having tuna breath wafted in my face.

This time, I shut off the alarm, stretched, and got out of bed. Yawning, I stumbled into the bathroom and started filling the tub.

Sparrow followed, watching me intently.

"Yes, Sparrow, I'll take the time to feed you before I leave."

Seemingly satisfied, Her Majesty went to the kitchen to await the filling of her bowl.

I took a quick bath, slipped on my robe, and fed Sparrow. I then returned to my closet to stare in despair at my clothes. Nearly all the other students had worn chef's uniforms yesterday. I didn't have a chef's uniform. I didn't have *any* kind of uniform. Part of the joy of being self-employed was being able to wear whatever I wanted.

I didn't want to wear black pants again. I couldn't wear jeans—I didn't want Chef Richards to call me sloppy like he had Mr. Conroy. I certainly didn't have any snappy one-liners to come back at Chef Richards with. And even if I did, I was sure that he would somehow get the upper hand.

If I wore a pencil skirt, would it appear I was trying too hard? Maybe I could wear a houndstooth pencil skirt, a red blouse, and black flats. The flats, rather than heels, would make the look more suitable for a day of being on my feet and thus it wouldn't appear that I was trying too hard.

I growled under my breath at myself for being so concerned about Chef Richards's assessment of my appearance. I'd gone through years of being debased by Todd Martin, and I'd finally broken free of that. Was I really going to let this stranger . . . this bully . . . come into my life and tear down in two days what little self-worth I'd spent the past year trying to build up?

I huffed out a breath. It was so easy to lose ground . . . so easy to hear Todd's taunting voice in my head. In fact, it was harder to ignore Chef Richards's scathing voice in my mind than it was to make myself hear the voice of the self-confident, independent woman I was still struggling to become. At forty, you'd think I'd be better at self–pep talks. But I wasn't. I'd heard my negatives extolled all my life. Those negatives were difficult to replace with positives, no matter how hard I tried.

It was those numerous negatives that had made me feel so insecure when I'd looked at those photos of Nickie Zane . . . especially the one of her with Ben. All those venomous voices in my head kept telling me that of course Ben would choose her over me. Why wouldn't he? What did I possibly have to offer him that she could not?

I put aside those feelings. I didn't have time to ruminate on Ben, Nickie, and the fate of our futures. I had eight hours of Australian string work class with an insufferable teacher to get through.

ABOUT A HUNDRED yards from the Brea Ridge Inn, there was a roadblock. I saw a fire truck, an ambulance, and at least three police cars within the roadblock, all with their strobe lights on. I figured someone had been in a traffic accident. I was sorry for them, but I checked my watch. Chef Richards wasn't the type to forgive tardiness despite your having an excellent reason like being unable to make it to the inn.

I still had a little leeway before I became ensnared in the bumper-to-bumper traffic, so I went down a side street and parked at a convenience store. Hopefully, I could take a quick break sometime throughout the day—we got thirty minutes for lunch, although that was taken in the classroom— to come out and move my car before it got towed.

I grabbed my purse and hurried up the sidewalk to the inn, glad I'd decided to wear flat shoes. I went through the grass and around to the back parking lot in order to both avoid the scene of the traffic accident and to try to make it to class on time.

I was surprised to find that there were police officers in the back parking lot too. One of them stepped forward as I approached.

"Ma'am, what are you doing back here?" he asked.

"I'm trying to get to my Australian string work class," I said. "I'm one of Chef Jordan Richards's students. The class is part of the first annual—"

"The class has been canceled for today," the patrolman interrupted.

"What? You've got to be kidding! He's only here through Sunday," I said. "When is he going to make this up to us?"

Officer McAfee, with whom I was familiar and who happened to look like a younger version of Denzel Washington, joined us.

"Officer McAfee, what's going on?" I asked.

He took my elbow and began walking me away from the parking lot. "Chef Jordan Richards is dead, Ms. Martin."

I stopped walking and gaped up at him. "What?"

He nodded. "Somebody cracked him over the head with something hard and then drowned him in a big bowl of cake batter. That's how he was found . . . with his face submerged in cake batter."

I hadn't thought my eyes could get any wider, but apparently they could. And all I could seem to say was, "What?"

"Come on," he said. "Let's get you back to your car so you can go home. I'll probably be talking with you later. In fact, we'll be talking with all of Chef Richards's students as soon as the crime scene has been processed."

As he led me to the front of the building and

past the barricade, I tried to make sense of the whole Chef-Richards-was-murdered thing.

"Do you guys know who did it?" I asked.

"Not yet," he said. "Again, we'll be talking with you once our crime scene techs have gathered evidence."

"But do you have suspects?"

"From what I hear, Chef Richards wasn't Mr. Popular. Everybody who has ever been in contact with the guy could be a potential suspect," Officer McAfee said.

"Well, yeah . . . I imagine that's true."

He looked around. "Where did you park?"

"Oh. I parked at the convenience store. I can get back there on my own," I said. "Thanks for escorting me this far."

"No problem," he said, assessing my eyes.

I tried to keep my expression blank.

"You aren't too shaken up to drive, are you?" Officer McAfee asked.

"No. I'm all right. Thanks, though." I hurried toward my car and thought about Ben's words from the night before. *Bullies usually wind up meeting their match.* Chef Jordan Richards had obviously met his.

I WAS SHAKING when I got home. A man I'd learned from, been humiliated by, disparaged, and yet somehow admired for everything he'd accomplished in his baking career was dead. And not just dead—he'd been murdered. I shivered involuntarily. Had someone followed Chef Richards to Brea Ridge to murder him? Or had it been unplanned—someone acting out in a fit of rage? Had one of my classmates killed Chef Richards?

I put my keys and my purse on the island in the kitchen and then went to sit on the sofa in the living room. I didn't sit there long, though, before I got up, grabbed the phone, and called Ben. My call went straight to voice mail. Not really knowing what to say, I hung up.

I paced, phone in hand. I called Violet. Again, the call went straight to voice mail. I was beginning to get paranoid. Was everybody that busy or were they ditching my calls? I realized that Ben and Violet weren't "everybody," but in my little corner of the world, they *were* just about everybody . . . especially when I was in a panic and needed someone to talk with.

I continued pacing and decided to call Myra. Before I could dial the number, she knocked on the kitchen door. I knew it was her because she generally taps out "Shave and a haircut, two bits."

"Thank goodness you're here," I said, throwing open the door to let her in.

"What's wrong? Are you sick? I saw you come home early. You didn't deck the nasty little troll, did you?"

"I'm not sick," I said. "And I'm not the one who decked Chef Jordan Richards."

Her jaw dropped. "You mean somebody really did? Tell me all about it!"

"Somebody did more than deck him. Somebody hit him over the head and then shoved his face into a big bowl of cake batter."

"Well, good!" She laughed. "He had it coming. Did he have a big knot on his head? Did you sneak a picture with the camera on your phone?"

"Myra, he's dead!"

She staggered backward, clasping at her chest. "Oh, no! And I said he *deserved* it! I didn't mean it!" She looked skyward as if she were afraid of being struck by lightning.

I took her shoulders. "I know you didn't. You thought he just got knocked around a little bit."

"Exactly," she said. "I didn't *dream* he'd been killed."

"Let me make us some coffee, and we'll go into the living room and I'll tell you everything I know."

She nodded. "Sounds good. The sooner Mark and I can get to work on this, the better."

I busied myself with the coffeemaker to keep Myra from seeing me roll my eyes heavenward. It wasn't that I didn't appreciate her enthusiasm for detective work, but I figured that one, she was out of her league trying to investigate a murder, and two, Mark would wisely leave the investigation to the police. After all, he didn't have a dog in this fight. And without a client paying him for his time, wouldn't he rather focus on those clients who *were* paying him?

"I'll need a notebook and a pen," Myra said.

"There are several pens and a notebook in the caddy by the refrigerator," I told her.

"Thanks."

I heard her fishing the items she needed out of the caddy. I took two mugs out of the cabinet.

"Sugar and creamer?" I asked. That's how Myra usually took her coffee, but sometimes she only wanted sugar . . . or artificial sweetener . . . that depended on whether or not she was dieting that day.

"Please," she called. She'd already gone into the living room and, I imagined, set up her home-away-from-home detective office.

I poured the coffee into the mugs, added creamer and sugar to both, and put the mugs on a tray with a saucer of biscotti. I needed a little something to gnaw on, and I preferred it not be my fingernails. I carried the tray into the living room.

Sure enough, Myra was sitting on the floor in front of the coffee table with her back to the sofa. She was using the coffee table as an oversized lap desk. In my pencil skirt, I couldn't very well slink under the table with her, so I put the tray on the edge of the coffee table and sat on the pink-and-white gingham chair.

"The first thing we need to do is make a suspect list," she said.

I glanced at the paper in front of her and noticed that it had SUSPECT LIST written right at the very top. My brows rose when I saw that the first name on her suspect list was mine.

"Me?!" I made an indignant yelp. "Why is my name number one on your list?"

"Because yours is the only name I know," she said. "You'll have to tell me the other students' names."

"Myra, do you honestly think I'm a suspect?"

"Yes, honey, because you are. Trust me. The police will be looking at every student in that class as a suspect."

She was right. I ran a hand over my face. "Okay. So now what?"

"Tell me the names of the other students." She took a sip of her coffee before dipping a piece of the biscotti into it. She bit the cookie. "Mmm. This is good. Did you make these?"

I shook my head. "No. They're store-bought."

"Well, they're still good. You know, sometimes store-bought is just as good or better than what you can make yourself and even a better value once in a while."

"I guess," I said absently.

"Oh, honey, I *know*. Let me tell you, my grandmother Tilly couldn't cook worth a hill of beans, but not a one of us knew it until the day of her funeral."

I frowned. "How'd you know it then?"

"Because other than family and church members, the only mourners were chefs and bakers," Myra said. "They were gonna miss Nana Tilly. She'd kept them in business for years. See, she had all these 'special recipes' we thought she'd come up with on her own. At the funeral, my brother Alfred was moaning, 'Who'll make my favorite red velvet cake now that Nana's gone?' And Earl Watkins, who ran Watkins Bakery over in Damascus at the time, handed Alfred his business card. Alfred asked, 'What's this for?' And Earl patted Alfred on the shoulder and said, 'Whenever you want your Nana's red velvet cake, you call the shop, and I'll make you one.'"

"But didn't Alfred just think that Nana Tilly had given Earl her recipe? Or that Earl was offering to make him a cake *like* the one she'd made?" I asked.

"At first, he did. But then others started coming up and saying things like, 'And when y'all get a hankering for Nana Tilly's chicken and dumplings, let me know.' Or 'I'm the one who makes the lemon meringue pie Carl Jr. enjoys so much.' We figured out pretty quick that Nana Tilly was doing well to boil water on her own." She looked pensively up at the ceiling. "I reckon that's why she got so skinny after the Department of Motor Vehicles took her driver's license away. She'd told us she was too depressed to cook. Truth was, she couldn't very well have us drive her all over the country getting her famous dishes without giving her secret away, could she?"

"I guess not," I said. Part of me was dying to ask

why the DMV took Nana Tilly's driver's license away, but the other part of me was wise enough to keep my mouth shut and not ask a question that would lead her off on another twenty-minute tangent. After all, I was eager to have my name not be the only one on Myra's suspect list.

"So." She tapped the notepad. "Who are the other students?"

"I don't know all their names," I said. "But there were ten of us. There was Gavin Conroy—he was the one Chef Richards called a slob. There was a Ms. Wilson—I'm not sure of her first name, but Chef Richards almost made her cry. My table mate was Lou Gimmel from South Carolina."

"Slow down a little," Myra said. "I'm writing as fast as I can."

"Put down Fiona," I said. "I don't know her last name. And she wasn't one of the students. She was Chef Richards's assistant. Naturally, he treated her too like something offensive that he'd stepped in. Like I said, I don't know her last name, but unless there's a lot of turnover in his kitchen—"

"I imagine there is," Myra interjected.

"—we should be able to find her surname through an Internet search," I said.

"I'll let you take care of that. I'm not all that hot on computer stuff."

"Okay." I bit my lower lip in concentration. "Rival bakers should be added to your suspect list. I don't know who all is in town for this event, but there are bound to be some that Jordan Richards has angered at one time or another."

"Oh, I don't doubt it." Myra ran a finger down her list. "Our suspect list has grown to ten students, one assistant, and possibly hundreds of bakers." She shrugged. "Who knows that someone didn't sign up for this cake competition with the sole intention of coming to town, killing Chef Richards, and leaving with no one being the wiser?"

I blew out a breath. "What a nightmare."

Unfortunately, my nightmare had only just begun. There came a rap at my front door. Friends use my side door. Solicitors, census takers, and heavily armed police officers use the front door.

Myra and I shared a look of dread. She nearly upset the coffee tray as she scrambled out from under the table. She tucked the notepad into her bra.

I opened the door. "Can I help you?"

"Yes, ma'am," said the officer in front. He was the same patrolman who'd approached me in the parking lot. His nameplate said he was BAKER. How weirdly coincidental was that?

Officer McAfee stepped to the forefront. "Hello, Ms. Martin. Remember earlier when I told you we were going to have to question all the students?"

"Of course," I said, stepping back to allow them into the living room. "Please come in."

"Actually, we're going to need to take you down to the police station for questioning," he said.

"Oh." I looked at Myra, and my eyes filled with tears.

She hurried over and put an arm around my shoulders. "Now, look here, Officer McAfee, you've not even read Daphne her Mirandas. I know all about the Mirandas because I'm an avid watcher of both *Psych* and *Rizzoli & Isles*. Sometimes I watch *Law & Order,* and I usually watch *The Mentalist*—that little Simon Baker is a cutie—but I'm not as faithful watching those as I am the other two. They're my favorites. And, you know, I used to love—"

"Ms. Jenkins, we aren't arresting Ms. Martin," Officer McAfee gently interrupted. "We're only asking her to come to the police station for questioning."

"Why can't you question her here?" Myra demanded.

I rested my head against hers. *My surrogate mom*.

"We need to have her look at a piece of evidence that we can't take from the police station," said Officer McAfee.

She furrowed her brow and gave this some consideration. "Oh, all right, then. Just don't be rough with her." She jerked her thumb toward Officer Baker. "Him, I mean. I know *you* won't. You're sweet."

Myra had a little crush on Officer McAfee because he reminded her of the guy who played Agent

Morgan on *Criminal Minds*. I'm surprised she didn't quote that as one of the crime shows she avidly watched so she could tell him—again—of his resemblance to Shemar Moore.

She patted my shoulder before dropping her arm from around me. "Well, you go on with them, honey. I know Officer McAfee will take care of you. I'll come and give you a ride home if you need for me to."

So much for me and my *Mirandas*. I looked at Officer McAfee. "May I follow you in my own car? That way I won't have to impose on anyone for a ride home."

He nodded. "That'll be fine."

Myra squeezed his forearm. "Have you ever seen that show *Criminal Minds*?"

5

PULLED INTO the parking lot behind Officers McAfee and Baker. Officer Baker got out of the patrol car and directed me into the spot where he wanted me to park. Then both he and Officer McAfee waited to escort me into the building.

I left my purse in the car, taking only my keys inside with me. I didn't want the police searching my bag. I had a feeling this interrogation was going to be intrusive enough without the officers pawing through my tampons and breath mints.

With Officer McAfee on my right and Officer

Baker on my left, we strolled down the hallway of the Brea Ridge Police Department, which was conveniently attached to the Brea Ridge Correctional Facility. If they decided to arrest me, we'd have a short walk over to my new accommodations. Yay.

Officer McAfee, his left hand on my right elbow, led me to an interrogation room. It consisted of a table with an office chair pushed up against the side nearest the door, a metal folding chair across the table but pointed in the direction of the opposite wall, and another office chair—this one with casters—facing the metal chair. The setup was inclined to make me believe that the Brea Ridge Police Department was hurting for funding and that they'd just thrown a mishmash of furniture into the room, but Myra wasn't the only one who watched crime shows. I knew that the furniture was situated in such a way as to make me—the person being questioned—as uncomfortable as possible so I'd want to tell the police everything I knew and get out of the interrogation room. Well, little did Officers McAfee and Baker know, they could've put me in the most comfy rocker/recliner in town with my feet up and a masseur working out the knots in my shoulders, and I would be no less eager to leave the jail than I was at this precise moment.

As expected, Officer McAfee indicated I should sit on the hard, uncomfortable metal folding chair. He sat on the office chair in front of me and rolled closer, effectively hemming me in . . . as if I were planning on bolting out the door. I might've considered it were I not innocent . . . and if Officer Baker—who was much smaller than Officer McAfee—had taken that chair rather than the one across the table from me.

Officer McAfee nodded at Officer Baker and the other officer picked a cardboard box up off the floor and sat it onto the table. It was a rather large, square box, and I wondered . . . dreaded . . . what was inside. From my perspective, it couldn't be anything good. It was certainly not a bakery box—I doubted there were donuts or cookies or pretty cupcakes inside. This was just a plain brown box with a red EVIDENCE sticker on the side.

Officer Baker lifted a porcelain cake stand with a metal turntable out of the box. The metal turntable was dented.

"Ms. Martin, have you ever seen this cake stand before?" Officer McAfee asked.

"Of course," I said. "Or, at least, I've seen one like it. We were all issued cake stands just like that one to use for the duration of Chef Richards's Australian string work class. He supplied all the materials we'd be using himself. Of course, they weren't ours to keep . . . they were only ours to borrow." Great. Now I was babbling like Myra.

"*We* being . . . ?" Officer Baker prompted.

"The ten students in the class," I answered. "And Chef Richards . . . he had one of the cake stands too, naturally."

"Was there anything to distinguish the cake stands from each other?" Officer McAfee asked. "How would you know which one was yours?"

"The one sitting on the table next to my name card was the one I was assigned to use for that class period," I said. "Otherwise, they all looked the same." I tilted my head. "Until now, anyway. Someone has ruined that one." I turned my head in the other direction and kept talking despite my better intentions. "Well, maybe not *ruined*. Somebody might be able to get that dent out of it—it's not that big of a dent—and then it would be fine. I'd hate for that cake stand to simply be discarded. Those are fairly expensive, and—"

Officer McAfee interrupted me with, "Ms. Martin, your fingerprints are on this cake stand."

"Oh, then it must have been the one I was using," I said. "But it wasn't dented yesterday. Someone must've knocked it off the table after I left."

"No one knocked it off the table, Ms. Martin," he said calmly. "This cake stand was used to bash Jordan Richards over the head. He was hit hard enough to daze him—probably even knock him out—and then his face was submerged in the cake batter until he suffocated to death."

"That may be," I said, "but I'm not the one who did it. When I last saw Chef Richards, he was fine."

"And when was that, Ms. Martin?" Officer McAfee asked.

"Yesterday at about a quarter to five in the afternoon," I said.

Officer McAfee shared a look with the round-faced Officer Baker. Officer Baker took over questioning.

"Ms. Martin, do you know a Pauline Wilson?"

"If she's the Ms. Wilson who was a student in our class, then I met her yesterday," I answered.

"Did she also use this cake stand?" Officer Baker asked.

"No. She had her own. We all did."

"Did she use the same table as you?" he asked.

"No. My table mate was Lou Gimmel from South Carolina," I said.

"Ms. Wilson never came over and asked to borrow your cake stand or to look at your work?" asked Officer Baker.

I shook my head. "No. As far as I know, she had no contact—at least, during class time—with the cake stand that I was using. Why?"

"Because her fingerprints are also on this cake stand," he said.

I looked from Officer McAfee to Officer Baker and back again. "Well, there you go. I should be in the clear. If another person's fingerprints were found on the cake stand *I* was using, then that person obviously made use of it either before or after I was finished with it."

Officer McAfee rolled closer to me in his wheeled office chair. "Or that particular cake stand was being utilized by Pauline Wilson during class, and *you're* the one who picked it up either before or after the class was over."

"I'm telling you, I didn't see Chef Richards before or after the string work class," I said. "If you want me to take a polygraph test and tell you that again, I will do so."

"Some of the other students told us that Chef Richards antagonized some of you during the class," Officer Baker said. "Is that true?"

"I would have to say that he antagonized all of us at one point or another," I said. "And he antagonized his assistant, Fiona, too."

"Chef Richards brought up your past relationship with your ex-husband and the attempt Mr. Martin made on your life, did he not?" Officer Baker asked.

"Yes, he did."

Officer McAfee leaned forward. "He brought that up in front of the entire class? That must have been humiliating."

"It was," I said. "But it was nothing I can't handle . . . nothing I hadn't been through before. Besides, everyone in Brea Ridge knows about my past. So what if Chef Richards brought it up?"

"But it wasn't just people from Brea Ridge in that class, was it? It was fellow bakers from all over the country . . . or, at least, the eastern part of the United States. I mean, you said your table mate was from South Carolina, right?" asked Officer McAfee.

"That's right."

"These were your peers. And Chef Richards didn't just bring up your past history with your husband," Office McAfee said. "He made a joke of it—made a joke of *you*—in front of the entire class. He personally attacked you. Isn't that true?"

"He personally attacked *all* of us," I said. "Did you talk with Mr. Conroy, whom Chef Richards called a slob?"

"Not yet," Officer McAfee said. "But we will be interrogating all the students." He rolled even closer into my personal space. "However, since your fingerprints—and those of Pauline Wilson—are on the murder weapon, we will be taking a closer look at the two of you."

"Well, just don't look at me so hard that the real killer gets away," I said, praying that the two officers in the room didn't realize that my bones and every muscle in my body felt as if they'd turned to jelly.

"We're going to let you go now," said Officer Baker. "But don't leave town."

"I'll be right here in Brea Ridge." I hoped I'd be able to stand up and walk out of this room without my legs giving way.

I was weary when I got home. I started to finish my orchids for the cake I was entering in tomorrow's competition, but I figured what was the point? I might be in jail by tomorrow morning. I might just take a bath and then curl up in my bed underneath the covers and hide. So what if it wasn't even noon?

Myra's car had not been in her driveway when I'd pulled into mine. I was a tad relieved. I wasn't ready to talk things over with her yet. I didn't know whether or not I was ready to talk them over with *anyone*, which is why I ignored the frantic blinking of my answering machine light.

Sparrow brushed around my ankles.

"Thank you," I said softly. That's one of the good things about pets. They let you know they're there, but they don't needle you to talk about your feelings. They don't ask intrusive or scary questions. They don't speculate with you about what your fate might be if Chef Richards's killer isn't found and the Brea Ridge Police Department finds a way to pin the crime on you.

I adamantly did not want to talk about my feelings, answer any questions, or do any speculating. Any of the aforementioned activities would have me falling apart. I was a strong, independent woman. I was not going to fall apart.

As I was making this affirmation to myself, someone tapped lightly on the kitchen door. I turned to see China York standing there, looking like a cross between a wood nymph and Willie Nelson. She had gray braids that hung to her waist, and her tiny frame was swallowed up in a pair of jeans and a blue flannel work shirt.

When I saw her, my lips began to quiver. She opened the door and came on inside, enfolding me in her arms. I clung to her and wept.

"It's all right, sweetie," she said. "I heard about that chef on the scanner, and somehow I knew you'd be right in the middle of it. But everything's all right." China led me into the living room, and we sat down on the sofa.

I cried until I could barely breathe. "They . . . think . . . I . . . did . . . it."

"Hogwash," she said, rubbing my shoulder. "They know better."

"No, they don't." I shook my head vehemently. "They don't, China! My fingerprints are on the murder weapon. Well, they're on a cake stand that the police *think* is the murder weapon." I took a shuddering breath. "I'm going to go to jail, and Ben's going to take a job in Kentucky and marry his old girlfriend Nickie Zane."

"Thank the good Lord I brought this," China said, reaching into her shirt pocket for an airline-sized minibottle of bourbon. "Drink it."

"No, thanks. I'm fine." I let out another wail.

She uncapped the bottle and held it out to me. "Now, Daphne. You need this. Drink it and get a grip."

I put the little bottle to my lips and turned it up. It burned my throat, and had I not already been crying, I'd have said it made my eyes water. One more drink, and the bourbon was gone. I flung myself against the back of the sofa. "What am I going to do, China?"

"You're gonna quit this crying and pull yourself together, for one thing."

"I can't," I said.

"You can, and you will." She got up and went into the bathroom for a damp washcloth. When she came back, she handed it to me and ordered me to wash my face.

I buried my face in the cloth and began to cry all over again.

"Daphne Martin, you stop that! Get up from there and show me the cakes you're entering in the competition tomorrow."

I raised my head. "I'm withdrawing from the competition. If the Brea Ridge Police Department has its way, I'll be in jail tomorrow."

"Did you kill Jordan Richards?" she asked.

"You know I didn't."

"Then stop acting like you did. You hold your head up high at that competition tomorrow and keep an eye out for whoever *did* kill the old goat."

I lowered the washcloth. "You've got a point."

"Don't I always?" she asked.

"Yes," I said. "Yes, you do. The police think either I or one of the other students killed Jordan Richards. They're going to stay focused on me unless I can point them in some other direction."

"Right. Now you're sounding more like the Daphne I know," China said. "And although I imagine Myra would be much more of a hindrance than a help to him, I think you should get Mark Thompson to give you a hand."

"I can't afford Mark's rates," I said. "I blew my budget all to pieces on Chef Richards's class . . . which was cut short by a day . . . for obvious reasons, but I doubt that anyone will be refunding half my tuition."

She grinned. "You let Myra take care of Mark's fee. I imagine she'll take the case herself in order to gain some experience. He'll be forced to do all the real work to keep her from looking bad."

"Well, she did come over earlier and start making out a suspect list," I said. "Of course, I was at the top of that list. Wait until I tell her my fingerprints were on the murder weapon."

"What was the murder weapon?" China asked. "Did you say it was a cake plate?"

"It was a porcelain cake stand with a metal turntable . . . kind of like the one I use when I'm decorating cakes, except mine is plastic," I said.

"Is there a good reason why your fingerprints were on the cake stand?"

I nodded. "We were each given one to work with. Plus, another student's fingerprints were found on the cake stand too."

"So, there you go," she said. "You're not the only suspect. Turn Mark Thompson loose on this other student. What's his name?"

"*Her* name is Pauline Wilson," I said.

"Do you think she murdered the chef?" China asked.

"No. She just didn't seem to be the type. He humiliated her yesterday—like he did the rest of us—and it was all she could do not to cry," I said. "I felt sorry for her."

"Still, you don't know that her humiliation didn't turn to rage after class ended," she said. "Maybe the woman stayed behind to confront him. No one *ever* seems to be the type who would haul off and kill somebody, but just about all of us are capable of it under the right circumstances."

"I guess," I said.

"Other than this Pauline Wilson, was there anybody else that Chef Richards picked on . . . someone who wasn't afraid to give it right back to him?" China asked.

"There was a guy named Gavin Conroy who stood up to Chef Richards," I said. "And Chef Richards backed off of harassing him. At one point, I even thought Mr. Conroy might be a plant to show that not everyone was browbeaten by Chef Richards."

"Why would Chef Richards plant someone in his own class to stand up to him?" she asked.

"I don't know." I sighed. "I feel that I don't know anything anymore. Even Thursday's class is all a blur now. And I left in such a hurry, I didn't see what happened once Chef Richards told us he'd see us all tomorrow . . . or *those of you who are brave enough to come back*. That's how he put it. I all but sprinted to the door."

"Then go in there to your kitchen, work on your cakes, and let your mind relax enough to help you remember," she said. "You're bound to have noticed something. . . . You're just too upset to think about it right now."

6

AFTER CHINA left, I felt composed enough to check the messages on my answering machine. The first was from Violet.

"Hey, Daph. I heard about Chef Richards," she said. "I'm so sorry. Do you know what happened to him? I'm guessing with that temper he was famous for that he had a heart attack or a stroke. Call me when you get time. Love you."

The next message was from Ben.

"Hi, sweetheart. I'm calling to see if you're okay. One of my friends on the police force told me you're one of the suspects in Jordan Richards's murder. Call me when you get this . . . if you can. . . . Either way, I'll see you after work."

The last message was from Kimmie Compton, chairwoman of the first annual Brea Ridge Taste Bud Temptation Cake and Confectionary Arts Exhibit and Competition. Her message was professional and succinct.

"Good afternoon, Ms. Martin. The untimely death of Chef Richards has left us with some adjustments to make to the cake and confectionary arts exhibit and competition. Please call me back at your earliest convenience. Thank you."

I wondered about those adjustments. Was I being adjusted out of the competition because I was one of the suspects in Chef Richards's death?

Since Violet didn't seem to know—or, at least, hadn't when she'd called—that Chef Richards had been murdered, and since I wasn't quite ready to talk with Ms. Compton yet, the first call I returned was Ben's. That's what I told myself, anyway. The real reason was that he was the person I most wanted to talk with. Fortunately, he was at his desk and answered on the second ring.

"Hi," I said.

"How are you?" he asked. "I heard you were taken in for questioning by Baker and McAfee."

"You heard correctly. One other student and I are the two prime suspects in Chef Richards's death."

Ben drew in a breath. "Then the other student *has* to be the killer."

"That's what I told Brea Ridge's finest, but they're not so sure. And I'm not either. Both our fingerprints were found on the murder weapon, which is a cake stand, so there are a few scenarios I can imagine in which both our prints would wind up on it," I said. "What just dawned on me, though, is that neither Chef Richards's nor his assistant Fiona's prints were on the cake stand. One of them *had* to have distributed the supplies to the tables—and I'm not taking such a wild guess when I say Fiona—so why wasn't there another set of prints on the stand?"

"Did either Chef Richards or his assistant wear gloves during the demonstration?" he asked.

"Both did during, but I find it hard to believe that whoever set up our tables wore gloves while doing so," I said. "Why would they?"

"I don't know. It's worth looking into."

"Yeah," I said. "I'll see what I can find out tomorrow at the competition."

"The good thing is the police had nothing to hold you on," Ben said. "I'll bring a pizza by when I get off work, and maybe we can work on figuring this mess out."

"That'd be great. Thanks."

After talking with Ben, I called Violet. She was out again, and the call went to voice mail. She'd eventually hear—probably on the evening news—

that Chef Richards had been murdered, and then she'd call me all in a tizzy. Until then, I chose not to leave a message.

I wanted to work on the cakes I was entering into the competition, but I thought I should make sure I was still welcome in the competition, so I called Kimmie Compton.

"Kimberly Compton's office," a cultured female voice answered on the first ring.

"May I speak with Ms. Compton, please?" I asked.

"This is Kimmie."

"Hi, Ms. Compton. This is Daphne Martin. I'm returning your call."

"Good afternoon, Daphne," she said. "Isn't this business about Chef Richards simply dreadful?"

"It certainly is," I said.

"He was supposed to do three demonstrations during tomorrow's show alone," she said. "That's not even taking Sunday into consideration. I'm looking through my list of professional bakers and trying to get an idea of those I may call on to help throughout the day tomorrow. Are you taking part in the timed baking and decorating contest?"

"I am."

"Okay, then perhaps you'll be available to handle one of the demonstrations either before or after that one?" Ms. Compton asked.

"I'd be happy to help in any way I can," I said.

"Wonderful. Thank you so much, Daphne. I

look forward to seeing you tomorrow," she said. "I'll see where we're at with regard to the demonstrations tomorrow and speak with you after you arrive."

As I ended the call, I breathed a sigh of relief. Ms. Compton didn't want to cut me from the competition. She wanted me to help take up the slack Chef Richards's unexpected demise was causing with regard to the exhibitions. That had to mean that she, at the very least, did not suspect me in the man's death *and* that she thought I was capable of demonstrating cake decorating techniques to her spectators. I was ready to hit the kitchen with gusto.

My first order of business was putting the finishing touches on the cake that I was entering in tomorrow's wedding cake competition. As I arranged the completed orchids and roses on the second tier of the cake, I thought about Pauline Wilson.

Even though her fingerprints were also on the cake stand, I couldn't imagine her picking it up and smashing Chef Richards over the head with it. It was even less likely that, having dazed him or knocked him out completely, she would have held his head in a bowl of cake batter until he stopped breathing.

As I'd told Ben, there were a number of ways both our fingerprints could have come to be on the same cake stand. Perhaps Pauline Wilson had arrived before me, decided she didn't like the cake stand she'd been assigned for some reason, and switched hers with mine. She could have arrived early and helped Fiona—I couldn't for an instant see Chef Richards doing his own setup work—distribute the supplies to each table. However, I hoped that was not the case because then it would mean that Pauline Wilson's fingerprints were on *every* cake stand, and that would make me look even more suspect to the Brea Ridge Police Department.

I thought back to what I'd said to Ben about it being odd that neither Fiona's nor Chef Richards's fingerprints were on the cake stand. I could understand Fiona wearing gloves as she prepared the tables for class. After all, we each had a bowl of the perfect-consistency royal icing that Chef Richards had made—or that Fiona had made—so maybe she thought it was more sanitary to wear gloves.

The only thing I knew for sure was that I hadn't killed Chef Richards. Either Pauline Wilson was guilty, or the killer had worn gloves. I found the latter to be the most likely scenario. Of course, I'd been wrong in the past. Maybe Pauline *had* killed Chef Richards. But why?

BY THE TIME Ben arrived with the pizza, I'd completed both the wedding cake and the three-dimensional superhero cake I'd made for the adult division of the character cake competition. Both were boxed up, and I was wondering how to fit them into my Mini Cooper.

"You look deep in thought," Ben said, as he placed the box holding our ham-and-cheese pizza on the counter. "Having your fingerprints found on that cake stand is really weighing on you, isn't it?"

"Yes, but that's not what I'm puzzling over at the moment," I said. "Right now, I'm wondering how I'm going to get this 3-D cake and the three tiers of the wedding cake, plus all the accessories I need to decorate my allotted space, into my tiny car."

"I can help with that. You could almost fit your car into the back of my Jeep." He grinned. "I'll come by tomorrow morning and help you get everything to the inn."

I threw my arms around his neck. "Thank you! Have I told you today that you're the best?"

"Not today, you haven't," he said. "I was beginning to wonder."

"Don't wonder. You truly are the best." I gave him a kiss designed to show him how much I meant that sentiment and to drive all thoughts of Nickie Zane and her stupid magazine from his mind.

"Whoa," he said. "That was some kiss."

I smiled. Mission accomplished. "That pizza smells delicious. We should eat before it gets cold."

"I suppose."

I went to the cabinet and got us a couple plates while Ben took sodas from the fridge.

"Did you have a good day at work?" I asked.

"Well, it was an exciting news day," he said. "The fact that you were right in the midst of it did sort of put a damper on it for me, though." He poured our sodas into glasses and put them on the kitchen table. "You?"

"I got to meet some new people, such as Officer Baker." I put the pizza box and our plates in the center of the table. "And I got reacquainted with a couple folks I already knew." I got us some forks. "Officer McAfee comes across as nice as pie outside of the jail, but he can be pretty imposing in an interrogation room."

"I imagine he can." Ben put a slice of the pizza onto each of our plates and placed them in front of our chairs. Then he came around and put his hands on my shoulders. "I know you're not as all right with everything that has happened today as you're trying to pretend."

"I'm not," I admitted. "But I'm not the wreck I was when China York arrived just after I got home." I caressed his cheek. "I am starving, though. We can talk about it while we eat."

We sat down and for the first couple of minutes we both just stuffed our faces. The pizza was so good and hot and cheesy and comforting. Maybe it was the starches and carbohydrates releasing chemicals into my brain and body, but soon I was feeling as if I could weather this storm, even though it was the worst one I'd been in to date. Sure, I'd previously found two dead bodies and one of my cakes had been suspected of killing a third, but this was the first time my fingerprints had ever been on an actual murder weapon. And, yes, my former husband had shot at me, but he *had* missed.

I swallowed my bite of pizza and looked at Ben. "Don't you think that a cake stand is the most improbable murder weapon ever? I mean, did the medical examiner measure the dent in the cake stand and compare it to the wound on Jordan Richards's head to make sure it was a definite match?"

He nodded. "Of course. But what that means to police is that it wasn't a premeditated crime. The murderer used whatever weapon was at hand."

"And someone *planning* to kill Chef Richards would have not only taken along a more suitable weapon but would have worn gloves," I said. "That's why Pauline Wilson and I are the prime suspects."

Ben lowered his eyes but nodded.

"But what if the killer intended for it to look spontaneous?" I asked. "Then he or she might've worn gloves, used whatever could be found there in the kitchen—I mean, you know there's most likely going to be a rolling pin in a baker's kitchen, right? And . . . and . . ." I trailed off. "I'm not even buying that myself."

"We'll figure this out," he said. "I say the first thing we do is take a serious look at Pauline Wilson. I've done a little preliminary work and put out some feelers already. I'll let you know what I find out."

"Thanks."

He took my hands. "It's going to be all right. We'll get through this."

"What if we don't?" I asked. "What if the police zero in on me? What if they truly think that I killed Chef Richards?"

"One, I don't believe they do. Sure, they have to ask you the tough questions and they have to take a serious look at you because your fingerprints were found on the murder weapon," Ben said. "But if that's all the evidence they have—a cake stand with your fingerprints and one other woman's fingerprints on it—they can't arrest you."

"Somehow that doesn't give me much reassurance. Even if I'm not convicted, if Chef Richards's murderer is never brought to justice, people in Brea Ridge will still look at me suspiciously. My business will fail, and I'll be ruined here."

"Then we'll move to Kentucky."

I brought my head up sharply. "Does that mean you've made your decision about taking the job?" I asked.

"No," he said. "I was only trying to lighten the mood a little and to remind you that you have alternatives."

I studied his face, saying nothing.

"Seriously," he said. "I have until the end of next week to let Nickie know what I'm going to do, and I'm not going to rush my decision."

"Good," I said.

He ran a hand through his hair. "Why do I feel that you actually mean anything but 'good'?"

"I don't know," I said. "Because I do actually mean 'good.' It's an important decision, and it isn't something you should rush either into or away from."

"You don't want me to take the job, do you?" Ben asked.

"I want you to do what's best for you," I said. "If that means Kentucky and Nickie Zane, then so be it."

He grinned at my tone. "You're jealous!"

"Yes, I am," I admitted. "Now are you happy?"

"A little," he said, his grin widening. "Yeah."

"Did you love her very much?" I asked quietly.

"Not as much as I loved you," he said. "I never loved any woman like I loved you."

My heart leapt a little. And then I analyzed his statement. He'd said "loved." Past tense. I'd said the *L* word last night, but he had not. Maybe he didn't love me anymore. Maybe he'd thought he did when we started dating again, but maybe Nickie Zane had gotten him so entirely over me that she was the person who now maintained residency in his heart. After all, he and I had been apart for over fifteen years before I returned to Brea Ridge.

I got up, rinsed off my plate, and put it and my fork in the dishwasher. Ben came up behind me and put his arms around me.

"You really are jealous," he said with a little chuckle that infuriated me.

"Like I said, if she makes you happy, then go for it." My stiff posture and the hard edge in my voice probably screamed to him that I didn't mean a word of that.

Then he laughed. He actually laughed!

I slammed the dishwasher shut and squirmed out of his arms. "I'm glad you're amused by all this crap, because I'm sure not!" To my mortification, I began sobbing.

He pulled me back into his arms. "Shhh . . . I'm sorry. I didn't mean to make you cry."

I started to tell him not to flatter himself but figured that would be the proverbial cutting off the nose to spite the face. Instead I whimpered, "I just wanted to take an Australian string work class from an experienced celebrity chef . . . that's all."

"I know," he said soothingly. "I know." He led me into the living room where he sat down and pulled me onto his lap.

"I didn't kill Chef Richards." I nestled against his chest. "Please make this day go away."

"I wish I could, sweetheart." He kissed the top of my head and held me tighter.

"Don't let go," I whispered.

"Never."

I wondered if I could get that in writing, but I knew better. You get no guarantees in this life. You wake up in the morning expecting to finish up an Australian string work class and go to bed that night a murder suspect.

7

FIRST THING Saturday morning, Myra popped in. I was sitting at the kitchen table in my bathrobe.

"Hey, hon," she said. "I just wanted to check in with you and see if you're okay. I was going to come over last night, but I saw that Ben was here, and I didn't want to bother you."

"Thanks," I said. "I'm fine."

"You don't sound fine. Your face is longer than a rainy three-day weekend."

"Where do I begin?" I asked, as Myra pulled

out a chair and sat down opposite me. "I'm one of the prime suspects in a murder investigation, and Ben is probably getting ready to leave me and start a new life in Kentucky."

"Dang," she said. "That's a double whammy. The murder thing is bad enough on its own."

"Want some coffee?" I asked.

"Nah. I just had some before I left the house," she said. "Let's start with first things first. Mark and I have been looking into Jordan Richards's background. Did you know that last year he was arrested for assaulting his former spouse?"

"No, I didn't. Maybe that's why he mentioned Todd to me in class." I scoffed. "Maybe he was a fan . . . thought Todd was a hero."

"Maybe he did. Or maybe he thought Todd was stupid because he couldn't worm his way out of the attempted murder charge. The only reason Richards didn't do jail time was because his ex-wife dropped the charges before the case went to trial." Myra leaned back and folded her arms over her chest. "I think we need to see where the former Mrs. Richards was yesterday morning, don't you?"

"Sure," I said. "But that happened a year ago. It isn't likely she'd come after him now. Is it?"

"That might be what she *wants* us to think." Myra nodded, trying to appear sage. "That could be a major part of her plan."

"It could be." I was in an agreeable mood this morning. Or, at least, I wasn't in an argumentative mood. Sometimes the best thing I can do is simply go along with whatever Myra dreams up.

"Now, what's this about Ben moving to Kentucky?" she asked.

I sighed. "He's got a job offer from a new magazine, and the position would require him relocating."

She shook her head, her face showing her obvious skepticism. "He's not going anywhere, hon. Why in the world would he? He's the boss over at the *Chronicle,* he's got a beautiful woman here who loves him to pieces, and he's lived in Brea Ridge all his life. Don't get all up in the air over that one, Daphne. You're adding to your worries for no reason."

"I wouldn't be so concerned about it if his old girlfriend—who is gorgeous, by the way—weren't the one offering him the job," I said.

Myra's arms dropped to her sides. "What's her name?"

"Nickie Zane."

Myra's eyes dropped from mine to her lap.

"Myra, what do you know?"

She shook her head. "I don't know anything . . . except that you'd better get ready to go to the cake show. Don't you have to be there pretty soon?"

"Yes, but I want you to tell me what you know about Ben and Nickie Zane first," I said.

"Honestly, I don't know a thing," she said, pushing back her chair.

Myra *never* admitted to not knowing something. That meant she knew something, all right. She just didn't want to tell what she knew.

"I'll see you at the show," she continued. She gave me a quick hug and then hurried toward the door. "Oh, and Daphne, why don't you wear that emerald-green silk blouse you look so pretty in?"

I nodded. "I'll do that."

She knew something . . . something big. I got the distinct impression she was telling me to fight for my man . . . in green silk.

FORTY MINUTES LATER, I was dressed in the emerald silk blouse, a matching green-and-black-print skirt, and black boots. I was satisfied that my hair and makeup looked as good as I could get them, and I was resigned to the fact that my cakes were also as good as they were going to get. There was no time for any final tweaks.

I boxed up the superhero cake and was carrying it out to the car when Ben arrived.

"Good morning, beautiful," he said. "Need any help with that?"

"Good morning," I replied. "Actually, I've got this one. It's the wedding cake that's going to give me fits." I put the cake into the passenger seat of my car. When I straightened, Ben pulled me to him in a tight hug.

"Nothing is going to give you fits today," he said.

"I don't want you to worry about anything . . . not the cake competition, not Jordan Richards . . . not anything."

Not Kentucky wasn't said but was implied.

"You're right," I said. "Whatever happens will happen, right? I've done the best I can with the cakes. If I'm a winner, then great. If I'm a loser, then I'll deal with it." That comment also applied to more than just the cake competition.

"Whether or not your cakes place in this competition, you, Daphne Martin, are a winner."

I kissed him gently. "Thank you."

"You're welcome," he said. "Let's go get that wedding cake."

Ben was taking all three tiers of the wedding cake in separate boxes on nonskid foam to the Brea Ridge Inn. He was also taking all the accessories I needed for the wedding cake display table. Entries for the three-dimensional cakes didn't get their own tables, so I didn't have many accessories for that one.

When we were all packed up, I turned to Ben. "Please drive carefully."

"I won't go over eighty, and I'll try to keep my hairpin turns to a minimum."

"Don't joke about hairpin turns when you're transporting a wedding cake," I said.

He laughed and gave me a quick kiss. "I'll drive like an old lady. Happy?"

"Not particularly. Have you ever seen Myra drive?"

Ben's eyes widened. "You'd better *never* let Myra Jenkins know you referred to her as an old lady."

"It just slipped," I said. "It's an indication of how nervous I am."

"I thought you weren't going to worry about anything today," he reminded me.

"You told me not to worry. I didn't expressly agree to go along with that." I took a deep breath. "See you at the inn."

"All right."

When we arrived, the front entrance to the Brea Ridge Inn was a madhouse. Cars, trucks, and vans were crowding in, people were honking their horns, pedestrians were making obscene gestures . . .

I was contemplating the traffic and wondering what to do when Ben rang my cell phone. "Follow me," he said.

"Follow you where?" I asked.

"Trust me."

He pulled around the side of the inn to the guest parking area. He parked in front of one of the rooms. I impatiently maneuvered my Mini Cooper into the spot next to him. We were wasting valuable time.

I quickly got out of the car and opened the passenger-side door of his Jeep. "Ben, we can't park here. This area is for guests only."

He grinned as he took a key card out of his wallet. "We *are* guests. I reserved a room weeks ago, before it got filled up."

Tears pricked my eyes. "Ben . . ."

He winked. "You didn't think I'd let my girl down, did you? I knew this place would be crazy this morning. This entrance keeps us out of that mess out front."

The words "I love you" were the first to spring to mind. Instead, I said, "You really are the best."

"I know," he said, with a smile. "Are we starting with the wedding cake?"

I nodded.

"Then let's get everything inside and start setting up," he said.

Before we carried in the cakes, we took in the tablecloth and accessories. Ballrooms A and B had been combined to form one huge exhibition hall. Twenty-inch round metal tables had been set up in the wedding cake competition area. There had been one assigned to each contestant. I found my table located in what I thought was a pretty favorable spot. It was in the middle, not so close to the front or far from the end as to be forgotten by the time spectators had seen all the cakes.

I picked up the cards bearing my name and number. There were two number cards: one that also bore my name and was to be pocketed until after the cakes had been judged, and one bearing only my number. There was also a card on the table instructing passersby FRAGILE — PLEASE DO

NOT TOUCH. I put the cards on the floor and then spread my tablecloth—an ivory vintage lace—onto the table. Next came my round, half-inch-thick plywood cake board, which I'd covered with white fondant embossed with hearts and scrolls. I then returned the FRAGILE card and the number card to the table.

"Are we ready for the cake now?" Ben asked.

I nodded. "I've got a collapsible cart in my trunk that we can use to wheel it in."

"Great," he said. "The fewer trips we have to make, the better."

I trailed behind Ben as we walked to the car.

"Come on, slowpoke. What are you doing?" he asked.

"Looking for any bumpy or tight places where we might have trouble maneuvering the cart," I said.

He shook his head. "You're really paranoid about this cake competition, aren't you?"

"I have to be," I said. "One slip and all the hard work I've put into these cakes is lost."

"You've got a point."

I got the cart out of the car, set it up, and double-checked it to make sure all its parts were locked into place before we began placing the wedding cake tiers on it. I'd brought along a repair kit with extra icing, roses, orchids, and pastry bags and tips, just in case. I prayed I wouldn't have to do any touch-ups.

We returned with the boxed wedding cake tiers and noticed immediately that there was an argument under way a few tables over from mine.

"You *meant* to bump me!" a man shouted. He looked vaguely familiar, but I couldn't place him. I'd probably seen him at another cake competition somewhere.

"I did not," said a woman. "You're being ridiculous. Now leave me alone or I'll call security and have you thrown out of here."

I *could* place her. It was Pauline Wilson. She was certainly no shrinking violet today. Had her behavior in class simply been an act?

"Daph?" Ben asked. "Everything okay?"

I turned my attention back to Ben and my own cake. "Fine. It's just . . . that's Pauline Wilson."

"The woman whose fingerprints were found on your cake stand . . . or rather, *the* cake stand?" he asked.

"That's the one," I said.

"I thought you said she was timid," he said.

"It appears she got over it."

Ben helped me lift the bottom tier of the cake onto the table. I used a box cutter to remove the box, and then we slipped the cardboard from beneath the cake and discarded it. I centered the tier onto the cake board.

"That's gorgeous, sweetheart," Ben said.

I smiled. "Thank you, but wait until you see it finished."

We put the second and third tiers of the cake in place. I had a minor touch-up to make on one section of the scroll border. But overall I was pleased with how my cake and table looked. I placed one of the extra orchids onto the table as an additional decoration, and then I stood back and took a photograph.

"One for the scrapbook, huh?" Ben asked.

I smiled. "Yep." I moved around to take one from a different angle.

Actually, the photos were proof that the cake was in excellent condition when I left it. If sometime during the day the cake suffered any damage, I wanted to be able to show the judges how the peach-and-white confection had looked when I'd walked away from my table.

Assured that the wedding cake was as close to perfect as I could possibly get, Ben and I went to get the superhero cake and set it up on the long narrow tables dedicated to the novelty cakes. Similar tables were set up for competitors in various age groups—I thought of Leslie when I saw those—and for those who had made figures and flowers from gum paste. I didn't see Leslie and Violet yet, but then, I had arrived early.

"You're going to do great," Ben said, standing back with his hands on his hips, surveying my superhero in all his red-caped glory. "This is fantastic."

I smiled. "I think you like this cake even better than you do the wedding cake."

"Well, I do love my comic book characters," he said with a grin.

"And I like my heroes," I said. "Thank you again for coming through for me today. You've outdone yourself."

"The day isn't over, you know," said Ben. "But I do have to cut out on you for a little while. I need to run by the office. I'll be back by later on."

"Okay." I squeezed his hand. "I really do appreciate you, you know."

He kissed my cheek. "I know."

I watched him wind his way through the tables to the double doors at the back of the ballroom. I was thinking about how handsome he was . . . how thoughtful . . . how much I wanted him to stay in Brea Ridge . . . when I was jarred out of my reverie by a shrill, perky voice to my left.

"Daphne Martin, hello! I'm Clea Underwood, Channel Two lifestyle and entertainment reporter! How are you?"

I'd seen Clea Underwood on television before, but I hadn't realized she'd look like a bobblehead in person. Her head seemed huge in real life when you considered it in relation to her overly skinny body. The hand and arm Clea stretched out toward me seemed like some sort of raptor's talon. The talon clutched a microphone.

I pasted on a smile. "I'm doing well, Clea. How are you?"

"I'm terrific! I'm thrilled to be the celebrity host

of the first annual Brea Ridge Taste Bud Temptation Cake and Confectionary Arts Exhibit and Competition." She gave the cameraman a wide smile. "I'm here with Daphne Martin, owner of the local bakery Daphne's Delectable Cakes, which Daphne runs out of her home. Daphne, what cakes, if any, have you entered in the competition?"

"I have an entry in the wedding cake competition and one in the three-dimensional or novelty cakes competition," I said.

"Well, good luck to ya! It's great for all of us when one of our own comes out a winner!" She smiled at the camera and then made an almost comical tragic expression. "But already our first annual cake and confectionary arts exhibit and competition has been marred, hasn't it, Daphne? Celebrity chef Jordan Richards was found murdered yesterday morning, isn't that right?"

My smile faded. "Yes, Clea. That's true."

"And weren't you taken in for questioning about that, Daphne?" Clea asked.

"I was. In fact, all of the students in Chef Richards's Australian string work class were questioned."

"I see." She gave the camera a look that I couldn't quite read before turning back to me. "However, your fingerprints—and those of another student—were found on the murder weapon, if I understand correctly. *Do* I understand that correctly, Daphne?"

I glanced around the ballroom, wishing someone would come to my rescue or that the floor would open up and swallow me . . . or her. Although if the floor opened up and swallowed *me,* Clea Underwood would undoubtedly crawl into the hole with me to ask if the floor opening up beneath me was proof of my guilt.

"I'm not at liberty to discuss the investigation into Chef Richards's death," I said. "I feel confident, though, that the Brea Ridge Police Department will soon find the guilty party and bring that person to justice."

"Right . . . My sources tell me that—"

"Excuse me, please." Clea and her *sources* were cut off by Kimmie Compton. "I need to borrow Daphne. Could you please finish this later, Clea?"

"Of course." Clea gave her cameraman the slash-across-the-throat sign, indicating he should cut off the recorder. Then the two of them moved on away from Kimmie and me, but Clea kept watching me like a cat staking out a bird in a nearby tree.

"Thank you for rescuing me," I said. "I didn't realize that little woman was such a barracuda!"

Kimmie laughed. "I thought you were handling her quite well from what I could overhear. I need to let Ms. Underwood know in no uncertain terms, however, that she's here to cover the show, *not* the death of Jordan Richards. We are all saddened by that, but . . . well . . . the show must go on."

Kimmie was a beautiful woman, tall and thin, with a sense of humor but who nonetheless would not put up with any nonsense. Today she wore a red suit with a large jet brooch on the lapel.

"Speaking of the show going on," Kimmie continued, "would you mind taking Chef Richards's place in the cake carving demonstration today? He was scheduled to do several demos this weekend, and I was able to find replacements for all but that one."

"I'll be happy to do it," I said.

As Kimmie Compton walked away, I caught Clea Underwood gazing at me suspiciously. I was going to have to watch out for her. Before the reporter could pounce, I hurried in the opposite direction.

8

I WAS THRILLED to be leading the cake carving demonstration—it would be wonderful for business—but I was sorry that I was only doing it because Chef Richards was dead. And I hoped no one would attend the demonstration just to get a look at one of the *main suspects* in his murder.

Thanks, Clea Underwood.

Having not been prepared to do the demonstration beforehand, I walked over to the corner of the ballroom where a coffee and tea cart had been set up in a sort of snack area. There were baskets of pastries and fruit on a nearby table. I poured myself a cup of coffee, sat down at one of the small tables provided, and did a search for cake carvings using the Internet browser on my phone.

I noticed a young woman a few feet away with a boy who looked to be about ten or eleven years old. It seemed she was having a tough time getting him interested in anything that was going on around him. I decided to try to help her out.

"Hi," I called over to the mom. "I was wondering if you guys could give me a hand. I've just been asked to do the cake carving demonstration later today—the person scheduled to do it can't—and I have no idea what I should make. Do either of you have any ideas?"

With a little prodding from her, the boy accompanied his mother to my table.

"I'm Daphne Martin," I said to the mom. "Do you and your son live around here, or are you just in town for the cake show?"

"I'm Molly, and this is Alex." The woman looked down at her son. "Alex, can you say hello to Ms. Martin?"

Alex raised his right hand in a wave.

"Hey, Alex," I said. "Nice to meet you."

"We're glad to meet you too," said Molly. "We live about an hour away, and we drove in night before last to check out the town before coming to the show."

"Not much to see, huh?" I asked.

Molly laughed. "Not much. We'd be happy to help you pick out your design, though. Wouldn't we, Alex?"

Alex nodded.

They sat down beside me, and I began scrolling through cake designs. Ms. Compton had returned after I'd agreed to do the demonstration and informed me that she had checked the kitchen. Before Chef Richards had died, he'd made two large pound cakes for the carving demonstration. She had no idea what he'd intended to make with the batter he was found in, but I would have cakes to use in the cake carving exhibition.

"The design should be something relatively simple," I said. "I don't have a lot of time, but I want to be able to give a good demonstration of how to carve a cake as well as how to crumb-coat it, cover it in fondant, and decorate it."

"Van," Alex said.

"A van?" I asked. I'd recently done a Cadillac, so a van should be easy enough.

Alex nodded. "A cake delivery van."

A wide smile spread across my face. "What a wonderful idea! Thank you, Alex! You're a genius." It *was* a genius idea. I could put my logo on the van and get a little local publicity for the people in Brea Ridge who might not have heard of me yet. This kid was smart. I looked at Molly. "Do you decorate?"

She shook her head. "No, but Alex does. Or, at least, he used to."

"Used to?" I turned to Alex. "You don't anymore?"

He shook his head and looked down at the table.

"Oh, look," Molly said to Alex. "Here comes Uncle Chris."

A nice-looking man was approaching us. I could see the resemblance to Molly. Like her, he had dark-blond hair and brown eyes. Both were tall and lean. Alex had black hair and eyes, and he seemed a little short for his age. He obviously took more after his father's side of the family.

Molly introduced Chris and me, and then she asked Chris to take Alex to look at the cakes that had already been set up.

"Careful that he doesn't bump into any of the tables or touch anything, though!" she called after them. She smiled at me. "I appreciate your considering Alex's idea. That was sweet of you."

"Actually, he had a terrific idea. If I have time, I'm going to decorate the cake delivery van with my logo on it," I said. "It's an excellent marketing tool!" I took a sip of my coffee. "You said Alex used to decorate cakes. Why doesn't he do it anymore?"

"Alex has a mild form of autism called Asperger's syndrome," said Molly. "People with AS tend to have trouble communicating with others, socializing, and controlling their behavior. Unlike classic autism, children with AS tend to have an average or above-average IQ, and they often have a knack for mechanical things. That's what Alex did with cakes. He made these beautiful creations—especially for a child his age—and he added little touches like lights and movement."

"How wonderful," I said. "But why did he quit decorating?"

Her mouth tightened. "It was Jordan Richards. A few months ago Alex entered a cake decorating competition near our home. His design was a haunted house, complete with flashing lights, sounds, and ghosts that went back and forth across the windows. But rather than award Alex first place like he deserved, Chef Richards accused him of cheating. He said no eleven-year-old child could make something like that on his own." She took a steadying breath. "Alex went ballistic. He knocked the cake off the table and then turned the table over, destroying the other two cakes that were on it in addition to his own. He ran screaming from the room, and he hasn't been interested in cake decorating since."

"I'm so sorry," I said. "What a horrible thing for Chef Richards to do to him."

"Well, if you've spent any time with the man whatsoever, then you know that Jordan Richards was a horrible person." She blinked away tears. "I brought Alex to this competition hoping that Chef Richards would apologize to him. I'd made a video of Alex preparing his entry—the haunted house. After Alex's tantrum, I didn't have time to show anyone then, but I was going to show it to Chef Richards this weekend. . . . Of course, I get to the inn and find out that someone killed the sorry creature before we got here."

"If you think it would help, I'll watch the video and give Alex some encouragement," I said.

"Thank you, Daphne, but I doubt it would do much good. After Alex's meltdown last year, his doctor had to put him on antidepressants. He's just not the same child that he was. He had this brilliant creative outlet, and Jordan Richards took that away from him. It was up to Chef Richards to give it back."

"But you can't simply give up because Richards is dead," I said. "What about another kid who decorates? My niece, Leslie, is entering a cake in the competition. Do you think she could befriend Alex and possibly get him interested in the art of decorating again?"

"I don't know. It would be worth a try," Molly said.

I looked at my watch. "She and her mom are bound to be here by now. I'll go find them. You find Alex and Chris, and then come over to where the children's division cakes are located."

"I will," she said. "Thanks."

I spotted Violet first. She was hovering near Leslie and twisting her scarf in her hands.

"Why are you killing that poor scarf?" I asked quietly when I came up beside her.

She started. "Daphne! You scared the daylights out of me. I'm a nervous wreck." She looked around the ballroom before returning her gaze to me. "I don't know if Leslie was ready for this yet."

I looked over at Leslie, who grinned and waved as she touched up her cake, which had been—very expertly, I might add—made to look like a cheeseburger and fries.

"Leslie is fine," I told Violet. "I think it's you who wasn't ready."

"Oh, hardy-har," Violet said. "The cakes are judged twice, by the judges but also by popular vote. Votes are tabulated based on how many pennies are in the cups beside the cakes." She chewed her bottom lip. "I'm considering getting a five-dollar bill converted into pennies and—"

"Violet!" I interrupted.

"Oh, I'm not serious," she said.

Yes, she was.

"Unless I see someone else doing it," she continued. "If that happens, then you bet I will."

I strolled over to Leslie and gave her a hug. "This looks terrific, sweetheart. You've really outdone yourself."

She shrugged. "What can I say? I learned from the best."

"I do love you so." I dug in my purse for as many pennies as I could find and dropped them into the cup by her cake. I only had about seven, but I made a mental note to get some more later.

Leslie stood back and placed her hands on her tiny waist. "So what do you think, Aunt Daph? Size up my competition and give me your honest opinion about my chances."

For a twelve-year-old, she could be incredibly mature. That said, I needed to get a better look at the competition before I decided how honest to be in my answer. Maturity is one thing; telling a child you don't think her cake will win is another. I'm happy to say that after looking at the other cakes— and setting all bias aside while doing so—Leslie's was easily the best of the bunch.

There were other children's cakes that had been sculpted into items, like her burger and fries. One cake had a teddy bear, and another was a stack of pillows. But none of the other cakes matched Leslie's in the difficulty of the techniques she'd used or the overall neatness of the cake. Most of the other cakes in her age group were either single or double-tiered traditional cakes with roses and borders. They were pretty, and they were skillfully done. But I felt sure Leslie would win or at least place in the competition. I told her so.

She threw her arms around my waist and gave me a squeeze. "Thank you, Aunt Daphne!"

"You're welcome, but you did this all by yourself," I said. "You should be proud." I turned to see where Violet was and noticed that she was mentally counting the pennies in the cup next to the stack-of-pillows cake. "Violet, there's someone I want to introduce you and Leslie to."

"Who?" Violet asked. "It's not one of the judges, is it? That wouldn't be fair . . . would it? Would it be fair?"

"No, it wouldn't," I said. "Besides, their cakes are like ours. They're judged by their numbers—no names. The judges aren't supposed to know who submitted what cake." I saw Molly, Alex, and Chris approaching us. "Here are the people I wanted to introduce you to. They're coming this way now."

Alex held back. He seemed a little intimidated by Violet and Leslie. I wasn't sure if that was because there was now more than one of us and the three of us were too many for him to handle at once, or if perhaps he was more comfortable with adults than with children closer to his own age.

I quickly made the introductions. "Leslie, Alex can decorate cakes too. His mom said she had a video of a haunted house he made, complete with lights and movement. She said there were even little ghosts that went back and forth in front of the windows!"

"Way cool!" Leslie said. "Can I see it?"

"In a little while," Molly said. "First, tell us about your cake."

As Leslie was explaining to Molly, Alex, and Chris how she'd made her cake, Myra approached me.

"How are you holding up?" she asked. "I saw that nasty little Clea Underwood interviewing you on TV a few minutes ago. She's a piece of work." She scoffed. "*Clea Underwood*. Who ever heard of such a name? Whenever I hear it, I think 'clean underwear.' There's old Clean Underwear on television again."

I grinned but almost immediately turned serious. "Was the interview that bad?"

"It wasn't too awful bad. I thought you handled it gracefully. I was proud of you." She gave a dismissive sniff. "Nobody takes that little twit seriously anyhow. She's probably like Beulah Breckinridge."

"Beulah Breckinridge?" I asked. "Who's she?"

"Oh, honey. Beulah Breckinridge always went around Brea Ridge like she'd just stepped out of a bandbox. She acted like her . . . well, like her bodily functions . . . smelled like rose petals—if you know what I mean—and that she was above all the rest of us. Well, one day Beulah was in a car wreck and broke her leg. Her dress was so tight that the EMTs had to cut the thing off of her. And wouldn't you know it? Beulah Breckinridge's panties were full of holes, and her bra was dingy." Myra finished with a nod that indicated that this anecdote should make sense to me. It didn't.

"That makes Beulah like Clea because . . . ?"

"Because she's all flash and no substance," Myra said. "She looks nice on the outside, but on the inside, she's all holey panties and dingy bras." She patted my shoulder. "Don't you let her get to you."

"Okay," I said, still unable to make much sense of Myra's analogy. "I won't."

"And another thing—Mark and I are making some headway into this case." She took my arm, pulled me away from the group, and lowered her voice. "First of all, we looked into that assault case where Jordan Richards's wife dropped the charges. She also dropped him. She divorced him, and one website said she took a ton of money with her."

"Do you and Mark think she might've come here and confronted Chef Richards or something?" I asked.

"We're looking into it," she said. "We're also looking into the other woman whose fingerprints were on the cake stand."

"Pauline Wilson," I said.

"Yep," said Myra. "In college, little Miss Pauline was a shoplifter. So, she has a darker side than you'd initially thought."

I inclined my head. "Just because she shop-lifted a time or two when she was in college doesn't mean she killed Chef Richards."

"No, but it shows you very good and well that she's not all goody-goody either," she said.

China joined us. "I heard that last part about Pauline Wilson. Myra's right, Daphne. All you know for sure is that you didn't kill Jordan Richards. The only fingerprints on the murder weapon are yours and hers. You have to keep an open mind."

"I know," I said. "I'll keep an eye on her."

"So will I," said Myra.

I glanced at my watch. "It's almost time for me to get started in the timed cake competition. Four of us have an hour to decorate a cake with a beach theme using only the supplies we've been given. Wish me luck!"

"Good luck," Myra said. "I'll be mingling to see what else I can find out."

"Me too," China said.

Knowing that Cagney and Lacey were on the case, I returned to Violet, Leslie, Alex, Molly, and Chris to let them know where I was going.

"Ooh, I'm coming to watch," Leslie said.

"Alex, would you like to watch Daphne compete in the timed cake decorating competition?" Molly asked.

Alex nodded. Behind his back, Molly gave me a thumbs-up. I thought that must mean we were making progress.

As I walked toward the competition area, I overheard two celebrity chefs talking about Chef Richards.

"Did you hear that somebody drowned him in cake batter?" the man asked. "If that's not poetic justice, I don't know what is."

"Poetic justice would've been if they'd drowned him nude in a bathtub filled with batter," the woman said. "He was always quick to disgrace anyone he could. The tables would've really been turned on him then."

They both snickered.

"I just wonder who's going to get that plum TV spot he's giving up," the man said.

She grinned. "I hope it's me."

"And I hope it's me," he said.

"Hey, maybe they'll pick us both," she suggested.

His mouth turned down at the corners. "You know, that's not a bad idea. Let's do a demo tape and send it in."

They were excitedly making plans as I continued on to the competition area. There was certainly no love lost among Chef Richards and the two of them.

9

WHEN I got to the area where the timed decorating competition was to be held, there were
four long metal tables placed about two feet apart.
A place card indicated that I was at the table at the
far right. I was glad. I didn't want to feel I was the
center of attention. Plus, I would be less nervous if
I felt that not every other contestant in the competition was peeking to see how my cake was coming
along. This way, there would be only one other contestant who would have a clear view of me. I

glanced at the table to the left of mine. The place card said PAULINE WILSON.

Adjoining each metal table were smaller tables on each side that gave the decorator additional workspace. At the corner of the main tables, there were covered cake plates. Without looking, I knew the cake plates contained the two-tiered cakes we would be decorating in the competition. There were also items from our sponsors: molds for shell-shaped candies and chocolates, cookies, flavored fondant, icing, gel color, piping bags, and candies. There were chocolate and candy disks as well as a hot plate and two double boilers for melting them. Of course, we also had spatulas, cake tips, a fondant rolling pin, and some other decorating doo-dads.

Each contestant had also been given a sketch-pad and pencil to use to rough out his or her design prior to the commencement of the decorating. However, the design was part of the timed competition, so no decorator was able to sketch out his or her design until the official had read the rules and had said we could begin.

Kimmie Compton arrived just before the competition to ensure that everyone had the requisite items and that we were all ready to start. Assured that her competitors were ready to begin, Ms. Compton made a brief announcement to the audience who'd gathered in the metal folding chairs and risers approximately five feet in front of our tables. Ms. Compton announced that we—the competitors—would have one and a half hours to complete a beach-themed cake using only the items in our individual workspaces. Then she sounded a bell for us to begin.

I quickly uncovered my cake to see what I had to work with. I had a ten-inch round and an eight-inch round, two-tiered cake. I wanted to do something different from the traditional tiered cake. I didn't want to make a beach-themed wedding cake. I wanted to do something *different*. And I also had carving on the brain. This competition would be a good opportunity for me to practice my carving prior to the demonstration I'd be giving later in the day.

I stared at the cake for a moment, and then I flipped opened the sketchpad. I decided to cut the ten-inch layer to make a boat. I drew a circle and then dissected the sides to leave the long, rounded rectangular center. That would form my boat. I divided one of the sides in half to make a triangular front for the boat. I did the same thing with the eight-inch round layer, so that I could give the boat more dimension. This would make the top portion slightly shorter than the bottom, which would give me a space for the seats and windshield. The rest of the cake would form the waves and, possibly, a stretch of shoreline.

Once I'd sketched out my design, I separated

the cakes and began carving. It came together even better than I'd hoped. I was only about half an hour into the competition, and I had my cakes carved and my boat well under way.

I heard muttered curses behind me and figured Pauline Wilson wasn't enjoying the ease of seeing her design come together as quickly as mine had, but I didn't have time to worry about her. I knew I had precious little time to finish getting my boat together and finish my cake. One never knew what could go wrong at the last minute, so wasting time thinking about the competition was not an option.

Once I'd completed the carving of my boat, I crumb-coated it, and then I covered it in white fondant. I melted candy disks in the double boiler and poured the melted candy into the seashell molds. Hey, I was no fool, and I guessed that not using one of the biggest sponsor's gifts would result in a points deduction.

While I was waiting for the candy in the molds to harden, I made fondant figures—a boy and a girl—to go into the boat. I also took some of the remaining cake and carved it to look like water rising up on the sides of the boat. This, too, I crumb-coated and then covered in blue fondant.

I looked at the clock and saw that I had fifteen minutes remaining. My figures were blond—representing Leslie and Lucas. I had time to make one more . . . a brown-haired boy . . . for Alex. I then placed the figures into the boat, scattered the shells around the crushed-cookie "sand" covering the cake board, and then painted USS *Alex* as the name of the boat. I didn't want Alex to have any doubt that I was including him in my creation. I wondered if I should have named the boat the USS *Armstrong* and utilized Lucas's and Leslie's surname instead, but I would make it a point to explain the reason behind the USS *Alex* later on. I felt confident my niece and nephew would understand.

I was taking one final look at the cake trying to determine what—if anything—else it needed when the timer went off.

"Whoo-hoo, Aunt Daphne!" I heard Lucas yell from the audience. "Way to go!"

I smiled and winked at him. I was glad he and Jason had arrived in time to see the end of the competition.

"Contestants, your time is up," said Kimmie Compton. "No more work may be done on your cakes. Please step away from your tables."

Four chairs had been set up to the left of the audience members. Kimmie instructed us to go sit in the chairs while the judges perused the cakes. At last, I was able to look around and see what the other decorators had done.

Pauline Wilson's cake was an ivory wedding cake creation with a shell border and Cornelli lace. Like me, she used cookie crumbs to make a sandy covering for her cake board. Pauline also used the "sand" to decorate the top of her cake. The cake was sprinkled with shells she'd made using the candy mold supplied by one of the sponsors.

The competitor to Pauline's right was named Madge Koker. I'd never seen Madge before, but she was a short, heavyset woman with gray hair and kind blue eyes that were only slightly hidden by her glasses. Madge's cake had been iced turquoise to look like water and was decorated with fondant fish and candy shells.

The final competitor was Lou Gimmel. I smiled and gave Lou a little wave. He returned my smile and gave me a nod. His cake had been covered two-thirds of the way in blue frosting, with white waves cresting up over the cake to accommodate the fondant surfers who were riding the waves. The other third of the cake had been made to look like the beach, complete with fondant figures, a tiny sand castle, beach balls, chairs, and umbrellas. Lou's cake worried me. I felt I was probably looking at the winning cake on his table. It was beautiful.

As Kimmie Compton introduced the judges and then us, the competitors, Pauline Wilson glared at me. I had no idea what I'd done to deserve her ire, so I simply ignored her. As soon as Ms. Compton was finished with the introductions, however, I learned what Pauline's problem was.

She raised her hand in the air and shook it around like an elementary school student who needed to go to the bathroom. "Ms. Compton, I think Daphne Martin should be disqualified."

"And why do you feel that way, Ms. Wilson?" Ms. Compton asked.

"Because she cut up her cake. She didn't leave it in the traditional two tiers," Pauline said.

"There was nothing in the rules indicating that the cake had to remain in the shape in which you received it," said Ms. Compton. "I appreciate your concern, but the judges will decide what is and isn't appropriate and will be judging each cake based on its individual merits. Thank you."

I turned my attention to Violet, Leslie, Lucas, and Jason, who were sitting with Molly, Chris, and Alex. I was glad Leslie and Lucas had made friends with the boy. I was terribly sorry for what Alex had suffered at Chef Richards's hands. That man had been hard enough to contend with for an adult. How on earth were children supposed to deal with him and walk away unscathed?

Lucas got my attention and rolled his eyes before making a face in Pauline's direction. I nearly laughed aloud. I shook my head slightly to try to dissuade him from acting up, but I eventually had to turn my attention elsewhere.

Waiting for the judges to look at all the cakes, mark up their findings, and make their final decisions seemed to take forever. After one last consultation, they handed their final score sheets to Ms. Compton.

Smiling, Ms. Compton took the microphone. "Ladies and gentlemen, we award only two prizes in this competition, even though all four of these cakes are outstanding, as you can see for your-selves. That said, the second place prize goes to Lou Gimmel."

We all clapped heartily for Lou. He received a certificate, a red ribbon, and a basket of gifts sub-mitted by local merchants. I, for one, was shocked that he didn't win. I was even more shocked when Ms. Compton called my name as the winner.

I stood and accepted my prizes—a certificate, a blue ribbon, and a basket of local merchant gifts. "Thank you so much!" I exclaimed. "I can hardly believe it!"

"I certainly can't believe it," Pauline said. She'd said it low enough that I doubted anyone in the au-dience had heard her, but I had and I thought the odds were pretty good that the other contestants and Kimmie Compton had heard her as well.

"Let's give Ms. Martin a round of applause," Ms. Compton said coolly.

The audience duly applauded, and Lucas shouted more "whoo-hoos" for his favorite—albeit only—aunt.

Prior to leaving the competition area, we were allowed to pack up the items donated by the spon-sors. As I was gathering my items into a large plas-tic bag, Lou Gimmel came over to me.

"Great job," he said.

"Thank you," I told him. "But your cake should've won. I truly thought it was the best."

"It was good, but you showed more imagination and creativity when you carved your cake," said Lou.

I laughed. "The main reason I did that was because I'm doing the carving demonstration in about half an hour, and I needed the practice."

He laughed too. "Makes sense. I'm demonstrating characters made of modeling chocolate later this afternoon."

"I'll have to come and check it out," I said. "Your characters and the objects on your beach cake were spot-on . . . and that sand castle? Priceless."

"Thanks." He grinned. "I wondered if you'd like to have this." He handed me a coupon for ten dollars off a cut and style at Tanya's Tremendous Tress Taming Salon. "It was in my prize basket, and I seriously doubt I'll use it." He ran a hand over his buzz cut.

"I doubt I'll use it either, but I'll give the coupon to my neighbor," I said. "She's a braver soul than I am."

"You don't recommend the salon, then?" he asked.

"*You* might come out okay," I told him, "but my hair would be bigger than Texas."

Lou laughed and then excused himself as the thundering horde that is my family made their way to my table.

"Aunt Daphne, your cake rocked!" said Leslie.

"That guy who won second place had a cool cake too," Lucas added. "But yours was the best."

"I'm so proud of you," Violet said.

"Good job," said Molly. "Don't you think Ms. Martin did a good job on her cake, Alex?"

Alex nodded.

"Lucas, what are you and your dad doing here so early?" I asked. "I thought you guys were going to a ball game."

"We went to do a little batting practice before going to watch the game, and we decided we'd rather be here," Lucas said.

"Really?" I asked.

"Really," Jason said with a smile. "We didn't want to let our favorite bakers down."

"Thank you," I said.

Leslie gave Jason a bear hug. "Yeah. Thanks, Dad. And you too, Lucas."

"Can we eat that winning cake now?" Chris asked teasingly. "I'm starving."

"I'm afraid not," I said. "The judges will be taking the cakes to be photographed."

"I'm with you on the starving part," Jason said to Chris, looking around the ballroom. "There have to be some food vendors around here somewhere."

I told Jason where the snack area I'd found earlier was located. "It's where I met Molly, Alex, and Chris this morning."

"That's all we've got in the way of food? Oh well. I know where that is. I'll take you in that direction," Chris told Jason. "Maybe we can sit down and at least talk about something other than cakes. I'd like to get my mind off the stuff if I can't have a piece of any of them."

Lucas warmed to Chris's line of thinking. "Yeah. What's so great about a cake you can't eat?"

Molly shook her head. "All right, guys. Let's go get a snack."

"Will you show us the video of Alex making the haunted house while we eat?" Leslie asked.

"If it's okay with Alex, I will," Molly said.

Alex nodded to give his permission.

"Daph, you coming?" Violet asked.

"No. You guys go ahead. I have to get ready for the cake carving demonstration in about fifteen minutes, so I'll eat the protein bar I dropped into my purse this morning."

"Are you sure?" she asked. "I'll be happy to bring something over to you."

"That's fine," I said. "While I'm eating my bar, I want to walk around and see how my cakes are faring."

Her eyes widened. "Check on Leslie's too, would you?"

"I will," I said with a grin.

As it turned out, I went by the children's table first. Leslie's cheeseburger-and-fries cake had accumulated quite a few pennies, but I made a mental note to get some change after the cake carving demonstration so I could further contribute to the voting process. No one had said spectators could only vote once, and I saw plenty of relatives dumping pennies into cups. I didn't want Leslie to feel that her own family had let her down. Besides, I knew the pennies were going to a good cause. They were being collected for donation to the local food bank.

My cakes seemed to be doing well from a spectator-penny-vote point of view as well. I only hoped the judges would be as generous as the spectators. I was sizing up the other cakes in the three-dimensional novelty cake category when Myra rushed up to me and almost knocked me sideways.

"Congratulations on winning the beach cake contest," she said.

"Thanks!" I smiled.

"I knew you could do it. What did that nasty little Pauline Wilson say when you won?" she asked. "I know she said *something,* but I couldn't hear what it was."

"She said she couldn't believe I won." I shrugged. "Frankly, I thought Lou Gimmel deserved the grand prize, but I'm glad the judges disagreed."

"Lou Gimmel," Myra said. "His was the one with the surfboards and the sand castle, right?"

"That's the one," I said.

"It was pretty . . . not as pretty as yours, of course, but it was my second pick," she said.

I gave her a one-armed hug. "Thanks. Oh, by the way, Lou gave me the ten-dollar coupon to Tanya's salon that was in his prize basket. He has a buzz cut and lives in South Carolina, so he didn't feel he had a use for it."

"Probably not," she said.

"Do you want it?" I asked.

"Sure!"

I took it from my purse and handed it to her. "Would you mind considering it partial payment for all the detective work you're doing on my behalf?"

"I'll be happy to." She frowned slightly. "Of course, Mark is helping too. You think I should give him the coupon?"

"Nah. I'll bake him a cake," I said.

"Ooh, then I'll get a double win!" She giggled. "I can get my hair done and help him eat his cake!"

I laughed before glancing at my watch. "I'd better eat right quick." I took the protein bar from my purse, opened it, and took a bite.

"That's lunch, honey?" Myra asked.

I nodded.

"Make Ben buy you a nice dinner, then," she said.

"Have you heard any chatter about Chef Richards?" I asked.

"Not anything specific. Everybody seems to agree that he was a jerk. Mark is looking into the ex-wife's whereabouts." Myra gazed around the room. "He said he'd come by and let me know as soon as he finds out something."

I swallowed. "Thank you. I appreciate that. I

wish it would be something as simple as a murder of passion carried out by an angry ex-wife. Then I'd be off the hook, and everything would be hunky-dory. I'm just afraid I'm not that lucky."

"Well . . . we can hope." Myra took a tissue out of her purse. "Here. You've got chocolate on your face." She wiped my face with the tissue. "Let me see your teeth."

I glanced around self-consciously before baring my teeth to Myra.

"They're good," she said.

I gave her a quick hug before I hurried away. I might have a distant relationship with my own mom, but Myra more than makes up for it in times like these.

10

BY THE time spectators had begun filling up the metal folding chairs and risers in front of the demonstration table, I had a fairly firm grasp on how I was going to carry out the carving to make the cake look like a delivery van. When I'd done an antique pink Cadillac cake for the Elvis impersonators' convention a couple of months back, I'd used a stencil made from an enlarged photo of the exact type of car I was trying to replicate. With the van, it would be mostly guesswork. A van wouldn't be as complicated as a vintage car, though. I also wouldn't be doing the van as a three-dimensional cake—simply carving it into the shape of a van in order to illustrate the technique—so I was pretty confident I'd be able to pull it off.

About five minutes before my demonstration was to begin, an event volunteer hurried over to hook me up to a wireless microphone. I thanked him, and the audience tittered as my voice thundered throughout the ballroom. The volunteer adjusted the volume on my mike.

"Good afternoon," I said. "I'm Daphne Martin, and I'll be showing you how to carve rectangular layer cakes into the shape of a van. I'm a last-minute replacement for the person who was supposed to do this demonstration, so I have no idea what he'd planned to do. However, I'll do my best to teach you how to carve the cake and to answer any questions you might have." I looked around at the audience. "Does anyone have any questions prior to my starting the demonstration?"

A lady raised her hand and asked what the best types of cake for carving were.

"For carving flat cakes, just about any type of cake will do fine," I answered. "However, if you're carving a three-dimensional cake, you'll need a denser, sturdier cake, such as a Madeira or pound cake."

A muscular young man asked if the cake needed to be frozen prior to carving.

"That's entirely a matter of personal preference,"

I said. "It can also depend on how much time the baker has. Sometimes you get an order, and you need to carve something and have it ready quickly. At other times, you can make the cake at a more leisurely pace. I prefer the cakes to have been in the refrigerator, so they're firmer than they would be at room temperature, but not frozen when I carve."

Clea Underwood piped up from the back of the audience with, "I understand that Chef Richards was supposed to do this demo before he was . . . well, before he *died*. . . . Is that correct?"

"It is," I said. "And now, if you'll please hold the remainder of your questions until after the demonstration—or during, if you have a relevant question about the procedure—then I'll go ahead and begin carving our delivery van cake."

I spread a chocolate ganache filling on one of the long, rectangular pound cakes and then placed the other cake on top of it. "If I'd planned on doing this van as a three-dimensional cake, then I'd have cut the two cakes in half to make two additional cakes and then stacked them to facilitate sculpting all four sides of the cake. The van would have been smaller, but it would've stood upright. This cake will be larger and, in fact, easier to create."

I explained how cake carving is a lot like sculpting in that one starts with a larger design and then refines it to take the desired shape. I roughed out the outline of a van and then kept chiseling until the audience could see it too.

"You might want to make the design just a little bit larger than you intend it to be," I said. "The buttercream and fondant coatings will make the shape smaller once they're applied. Also, don't throw away the cake you've cut away. Save it and make cake pops!"

Someone immediately asked about cake pops. I was surprised by the question, since cake pops are so popular these days. Still, I explained that cake pops were cake mixed with frosting, formed into balls or some other shape, placed onto a lollipop stick, and then dipped into a candy coating.

I crumb-coated the cake and then covered it in white fondant. I cut around the windshield, windows, and wheels and used various cake tips to ice those details. Then I took a fine brush dipped in pink gel color and wrote *Daphne's Delectable Cakes* on the side of the van. I rinsed the brush, dipped it in black gel color, and outlined the letters in my logo before drawing the silhouette of a wedding cake beneath it.

I turned to the audience with a flourish. "And there you have it. Any other questions?"

"Why did you paint on the cake rather than use a writing tip?" asked a woman to my left.

"I wanted the writing on the van to look more like my logo and less like writing on a cake," I said. "I wanted it to appear more realistic. That's a wonderful plus to using fondant—you can paint some beautiful designs on it that you'd be hard-pressed to re-create in icing."

After everyone with questions had been satis-factorily answered—with the exception of Clea Un-derwood, of course—some audience members filed by the table for a closer look at the cake.

"Great job, Aunt Daphne," Leslie said.

"Yeah," Lucas said. He grinned. "The only way you could've made it any better would be to have the headlights and horn work."

I tilted my head toward Alex. "I wouldn't even know how to begin to do that. Would you, Alex?"

He nodded, and then looked up at his mother.

Molly encouraged him to tell me how to incor-porate lights into my design.

Alex spoke so softly that we all had to lean closer in order to hear him. "Before covering the cake with fondant, you could've carved a little hole where the headlight would be. Then you would have put a battery-powered LED light into the hole." He looked at Lucas. "The same principle would apply to the horn. Just put some battery-operated device into the cake where you could push a button and hear the horn blow. It's not hard."

"Cool!" Lucas shouted. "You're like Chef Duff and Buddy the Cake Boss and all those other guys rolled into one!"

Alex smiled slightly and then lowered his head. "It's not hard," he repeated. "You'd just have to be careful that no one got a piece of cake with a me-chanical device in it. That could be dangerous."

"That's good advice," I said.

"You've got to see the video of Alex making the haunted-house cake," Leslie said. "He did an awesome job!"

"Maybe I can see it later," I said.

Alex shrugged.

I wondered if we might be putting a bit too much stress on him with all our attention, so I asked Leslie if she'd like to go check on our cakes before Lou Gimmel's figure molding demonstration.

"I guess." She sighed. "I'm getting kinda nervous about the whole thing."

Alex shook his head. "Your cake is good. You'll be fine."

She smiled at him. "Thank you."

Molly gave me a grateful look over the top of their heads. I smiled and nodded. Hopefully, Leslie was just what the doctor had ordered to get Alex back to baking again.

As Leslie took me by the arm and propelled me toward the kids' division cakes, Myra headed us off.

"That nasty little Clea Underwood is going to keep on until I knock the ever-lovin' taste out of her mouth," she said.

I grinned. "She does wear a bit thin on the nerves, doesn't she?"

"She just wants to try to scoot poor Doug out of that head anchor chair, and she believes this is the story that'll do it for her," Myra said. "Well, I've got news for Ms. Clean Underwear, everybody in Brea Ridge prefers Doug to her—always has and always will. She's lucky Channel Two lets her do the spots she does get."

"I agree," I said.

"Leslie, can I borrow your aunt for just a second?" Myra asked.

"Sure." Leslie looked around at Violet.

"I'll take her on to the cakes," Violet said. "We'll either meet you over there or we'll see you at the figure molding demo."

"All right," I said. "Thanks." As soon as they were out of earshot, I turned to Myra. "What's up?"

Before she could answer, Chef Richards's assistant, Fiona, joined us. She had a small purse on her arm that matched her hair perfectly. Otherwise, she was once again dressed all in white. "Hi. You did a great job with the van cake. It looks fantastic."

"Thank you," I said.

"And you were excellent at explaining everything as you went along," Fiona said. "Have you done many demonstrations?"

"No, but I've attended my fair share." I smiled.

"You aren't looking for an assistant, are you?" she asked.

I shook my head. "If I were, though, you'd be at the top of my list." I introduced Fiona to Myra.

"What was it like working for Jordan Richards?" Myra asked Fiona. "Was he as big a jerk to you as he was to everyone else?"

"Bigger," said Fiona with a slight grin. Then she shrugged. "The pay was good, though."

"What will you do now?" I asked.

"I don't know," she said. "I might branch out on my own."

"You should," I told her. "From what I saw Thursday, you're every bit as skilled as Chef Richards was . . . probably more so. You did everything for him."

"I'm a good baker," Fiona admitted. "But I have trouble getting up and talking in front of people . . . or even in front of a camera crew. There's no way I could have handled that carving demonstration as well as you did. I'd have been so nervous, my hands wouldn't have held steady long enough to cut the cake."

"Oh, honey, you can overcome your fear of public speaking," said Myra. "I once knew a man who stuttered worse than Mel Gibson . . . No, wait, it was Mel Tillis who stuttered, wasn't it? Anyway, he got over his fear and started talking just as plain as anybody. He did that club where everybody toasts each other." She shrugged. I tried not to laugh at her description of the Friars Club. "Besides, if audiences could put up with Chef Richards being such a creep, they'd love you with your funky hair and cool persona."

Fiona smiled again. "I don't know about that. . . . Besides, not *everyone* could put up with Chef Richards, or else he'd still be here, wouldn't he?"

"You have a point," I said. "Still, I wish you the best of luck in whatever you decide to do." I reached into my purse and handed her a business card. "Please keep me posted."

"Thanks," said Fiona. "I will."

When Fiona walked away, I turned back to Myra. "Now, what were you getting ready to tell me earlier?"

"Well, first of all, Mark hasn't been able to find Jordan Richards's ex-wife," she said. "It's like the woman simply disappeared about six months ago."

I frowned. "That's weird. Do you think she left the country? Changed her name? Had some sort of . . . accident?"

"She hasn't had an accident that anyone knows about," Myra said. "If she had, there'd be a record of it. She isn't listed as a missing person either. Mark said he'd keep digging. With it being the weekend, his sources are limited."

"What does he think happened to her?" I asked.

"He doesn't know and would prefer not to speculate until he has more information." Myra's reply was so pat that I knew it had to have been copied from Mark verbatim.

"That's really strange," I said. "I hope she's okay."

"So do I," Myra said. "The other thing I wanted to tell you about was that I've been checking around about Nickie Zane. Not many people around here know her, but . . ." Myra sighed.

"But what?" I asked.

"Well, I'd heard that she and Ben were pretty hot and heavy back in the day, but I didn't want to say anything before until I got it straight from the horse's mouth," she said. "And Ben's parents reportedly told the woman who delivered their mail, who passed it along to a friend of Tanya's mom's, that they thought Ben was going to ask Nickie to marry him at one time. Of course, nothing ever came of that."

"Because Nickie wouldn't break up with her high school sweetheart," I said with a sigh. "Ben told me that much. He loved her, Myra. . . . He wanted to marry her."

"Only because he didn't have you anymore. Remember that."

"I'm trying, but it's hard," I said. "Now she needs his help, and he's ready to go running back to her."

"Not necessarily," said Myra. "You told me he said he had a week to think about it, didn't you?"

I nodded.

"If he was still head over heels for that woman, he wouldn't need a week to think about it," she said. "He wouldn't need a minute. He'd have accepted the job when she offered it."

"I guess," I said. "I don't want to think about Ben and Nickie Zane right now, though. It's too depressing. I keep going back to the worst-case scenario. Have you found out anything else about Chef Richards?"

Myra grinned. "That's my girl. Her love life is depressing, so let's talk about murder."

I giggled. "When you put it like that, it sounds really bad."

"It *is* bad," she said. "Wicked bad, as the kids would say."

I wondered if that was truly what the kids would say. Somehow I doubted it. "Hey, my life could be on the line in that capacity too if we don't find out who the real killer is," I reminded her. "My career could be ruined or, worse, I could wind up arrested for a crime I didn't commit. Don't forget, my fingerprints were on that cake stand."

"I know, honey. I'm only teasing you," said Myra. "It's good to see you smile. Mark is looking into the backgrounds of all the students who were in Chef Richards's class, based on the names and locations you provided him. He's also continuing the search for the former Mrs. Richards and scouring the Internet to see who had ongoing feuds with the chef."

"It might be easier to find out who *didn't* have an ongoing feud with him," I said. "I haven't heard anyone at this cake show utter a single kind word about the man. And he's *dead*. People are usually reluctant to speak ill of the dead. But not in Chef Richards's case."

"From what I've been hearing, it's hard for them to find anything nice to say," she said.

"That's true enough. Chef Richards even destroyed a child's dreams and fragile mental health, for goodness' sake. You saw the boy—Alex. He was with Lucas and Leslie." I groaned. "People were probably lined up to throw a punch at that man."

"Yeah, but it only took one of them to land a punch with a cake stand and then drown him in cake batter," she said. "I need to get back to loitering unobtrusively and listening in to people's conversations so I can see what I can dig up on this end of things. Call my cell phone if you need me."

"All right," I said. "I appreciate all your hard work." And I did. But I wondered how long it would take Myra to be forcibly removed from the premises by security. As I watched her sidle up to a group of people and try to blend in, I figured she had another hour at best.

11

Lou Gimmel was personable and funny while he did his figure molding demonstration. I hoped I came off both as knowledgeable and as friendly, but I'd been nervous and doubted I had related to the audience as well as Lou was doing.

"The first thing I'm going to make is a puppy dog," he said. His eyes sought out the children in the audience. "Does anybody here like puppy dogs?"

The children, as well as many adults, intoned, "Yes!"

"Yeah," Lou said. "I *thought* you people looked like dog lovers. And which kinds of puppies do you like best? Fluffy ones or mean ones with snarly teeth?"

"Fluffy!"

There were a couple of boys in the audience who yelled out "mean" and "snarly," but they were in the minority.

Lou laughed. "All right, then. You've come to the right place. I'm going to show you how to make a plump, fluffy, friendly puppy dog. First I'll need some fondant." He gestured toward the table where the fondant supplier who was sponsoring his demonstration was located. "I'd like to thank our good friends at Franklin Fondants for supplying this yummy buttercream-flavored fondant for me to use to make our puppy."

I heard a low male voice about two rows behind me and to my left say, "He's good. Not only is he likable with the audience, he plays to the sponsors."

Had I thanked the sponsors as I did my demonstration? I couldn't remember.

"We're going to start by rolling our fondant into two kinda large egg shapes, and then we're gonna make six smaller ovals. You'll see what they're all for in just a minute." As Lou talked, he quickly formed the eight ovals out of the white fondant. He put all but the largest oval into a plastic bag and zipped it shut. "I put the ones I'm not using into the plastic bag so they don't dry out before I'm ready to use them, all right? Now, this biggest fondant egg will be the doggie's body." He molded it a little more so that it would appear to be in a sitting position. "Okay. I told you this puppy was going to be fluffy, didn't I?"

The audience—especially the children—responded with an enthusiastic "yes."

"He *is* good." This time the voice—also male—came from my right. I guessed this man was talking with the other one because they both sounded close. "I like how he continuously keeps the audience engaged."

"So do I," the other man agreed. "And it's wonderful with a live audience, but will he be as charming when it's only him and the camera crew? I mean, it's one thing to entertain a live audience, but how will he come across to a television audience? Or maybe we should have a studio audience if we decide to go with him."

"I think we should test him both ways—with just a camera crew and with a studio audience—and see how he performs best."

"Do you think he'll be interested?" the first man asked. "I mean, he lives in South Carolina. That'll mean a lot of traveling for him."

"So? Paula Deen lives in Georgia," said the second man.

These were television producers. I knew they sometimes came to the bigger cake events to see if they could find any rising stars. I hadn't expected any to show up here in Brea Ridge, though. Had they seen my demonstration? If so, what had they said about me? Would they even consider me? Would I even *want* to be considered?

I turned my attention back to Lou who was now "fluffing up" the puppy with large dots of white icing.

"Well, now our little guy is fluffy, but he looks like his hair is sticking every which way, don't you think?" Lou asked. "He looks like he just rolled out of bed . . . and then maybe stuck his paw in an electrical outlet."

The audience members laughed.

"I'll fix that like this." Lou took a small paint-brush, dipped it into a ramekin of water, and patted down the peaks on the dots. "Ah, that's better. Now he's presentable to go out in public."

"Yeah, Richards would never have played to an audience the way this guy does," the man to my right whispered. "Gimmel is a natural with people. I think that would work well for him on the talk-show circuit. We should definitely test him."

"I agree," said the man to the left. "One reason Richards's show was in the crapper might've been because he wasn't nicer to the talk-show personalities. No one would have him back on after an initial visit. They went with Paula, Giada, Emeril, or some other person who was easier to work with."

"Can you blame them?" asked the one on the left.

"No." The man on the right sighed. "Richards was talented, though. He was really great at what he did."

"And this Gimmel guy isn't?" asked Mr. Left. "Look at how quickly he's taken what was essentially a mound of clay and half a cup of icing and turned it into an adorable puppy."

I was dying to turn around and get a look at these guys. Would I recognize them by their voices if they should talk with me later? I doubted it. They were whispering.

Well, good for Lou. He was a nice guy. And the producers were right—he'd do great on a baking show.

After making the puppy, Lou created a person for the audience. The person was a boy with a baseball cap, and he was created in proportion to the dog. Lou even linked them—both figuratively and literally—by having the boy hold a red leash that went to the dog's collar.

Ben came in as Lou was finishing up. He sat down and kissed my cheek. "How's everything going?"

"Lou Gimmel is doing a fantastic job," I said softly. "In fact, I think some people behind me believe he's destined for greater things."

"Really?" Ben asked.

I nodded.

Lou concluded the demo and asked if anyone had questions. Ben and I were quiet as the audience asked and Lou answered. When everyone began scattering, I tried to see if two men approached Lou; but so many people were headed toward the demo table, I couldn't tell. I assumed the men would wait until the fans that had gone up for a closer look at Lou's work had left before moving in to talk with him. But I wasn't able to watch long enough to see because Ben was pulling me aside.

He caught me looking toward Lou and gently turned my chin back toward him. "This is important."

"Okay . . . okay," I said.

"Wait. What is it?" he asked. "Do you think he might be the . . . you know, the *guy*?"

"No. I was just trying to see which ones the producers were." I shrugged. "You know . . . I wondered if they attended my demo . . . if I'd even recognize them. Not that it matters. It isn't like I could just walk up and say, 'Hey, what did you think of my demonstration?' Right?"

"Is that something you'd be interested in?" Ben asked. "Having your own TV show?"

"No . . . I mean, I doubt it. I just . . . it would be nice . . . you know . . . to be considered." I shook my head as if physically clearing away the crazy dreams of becoming the next celebrity chef. "What did you find out?"

Ben looked around to ensure that no one was paying any attention to us. Then he said quietly, "Fiona is the one who found Chef Richards's body and called nine-one-one. When the police arrived, she was pacing back and forth wringing her hands . . . and she was wearing white gloves."

"And if she was wearing gloves, then she could've hit him with the cake stand without leaving prints," I said. "So why are the police bearing down so hard on Pauline and me?"

"Because they haven't ruled out any of you as suspects. Sure, Fiona was wearing gloves, and she might've had more motive to kill Chef Richards than you or Pauline had, but that doesn't mean she did, in fact, crack the guy over the head with the cake stand."

"Have they looked into Fiona's past?" I asked. "Or how about *their* past—hers and Chef Richards's? Maybe the two of them were having an affair."

He shrugged. "I'm sure the Brea Ridge Police Department is exploring every possibility as quickly as they can. They know time is crucial in this case."

"Fiona has the next demonstration," I said. "She's doing the Australian string work demo."

"I think we should watch it," said Ben.

"Yeah . . . maybe she'll confess or something," I said. Of course, I was being sarcastic. I didn't really believe she would confess. In fact, I didn't believe she was the murderer. But then, like China had told me the day before yesterday, all I *really* knew was that *I* hadn't killed Chef Richards.

*   *   *

FIONA APPEARED SMALL, awkward, and too quiet to be heard as she introduced the subject of her demonstration.

"Australian string work is a lovely and prestigious cake decorating technique that makes it appear as if there is lace on your cake," she said.

"Could you speak up, please?" called someone from the back.

Fiona nodded, cleared her throat, and tried again. "I'll be demonstrating basic drop strings and lace points today."

It was better, but still not great. I could see why Chef Richards was the chef and Fiona was the assistant.

But then Fiona began decorating. And she became more confident. Her voice became stronger and louder as she explained what she was doing. Her work was magnificent—better even than Chef Richards's.

I looked at Ben, who was sitting beside me. He appeared unaffected by Fiona's talent.

"She's a master at this," I whispered. "I think she's even better than Chef Richards."

Violet, Jason, Lucas, and Leslie joined us. Violet sat beside me.

"Why is she wearing those white cotton gloves?" Violet asked.

I shrugged. "I don't know." I made a mental

note to ask her after the demo. Maybe they kept her hands from slipping or something.

The thought returned that Fiona could have bashed Chef Richards over the head with the cake stand and not left fingerprints on it if she'd been wearing the gloves at the time, but I dismissed it. If you're angry at a boss, you simply quit your job. A decorator as talented as Fiona would have no trouble whatsoever securing another position. Besides, statistics show that people are more likely to kill a lover than an employer.

That begged the question of whether or not there had been something other than a professional relationship between the two of them. Somehow I couldn't see that either. Fiona wasn't the femme fatale type. Plus, I couldn't imagine Chef Richards being attracted to anyone other than himself for long. A woman more ambitious than Fiona might've tried to seduce Chef Richards for whatever career boost he could offer her, but Fiona didn't appear to be comfortable in front of an audience. I doubted it was something she'd want to do for a living. I could see her happily working behind the scenes making gorgeous wedding cakes or working in a five-star restaurant as a pastry chef. I was guessing Fiona viewed her apprenticeship with Chef Richards as a necessary evil on the road to working in a more private, quietly prestigious position.

When Fiona completed her demonstration, I

excused myself from Ben, Violet, and her family, and I went to speak with Fiona privately.

Once the crowd had thinned, I stepped up to the table. "You did an excellent job. You're so much better than Chef Richards. I was thinking as I watched you that you should be head pastry chef in an extravagant hotel somewhere."

She shrugged. "That would be nice, wouldn't it? I guess I've never had much confidence in myself before." She lifted and dropped her shoulders again.

"I doubt Chef Richards ever helped you realize how talented you are," I said. "During our class, it appeared that if he couldn't belittle someone he didn't say anything at all."

"He could be all right once you got to know him. But, no, he wasn't terribly encouraging." She took off the cotton gloves.

"He was probably afraid he'd lose you . . . as an assistant . . . if you realized how good you were." I'd watched her face as I'd said he might be afraid of losing her, but I didn't detect any sign of her having more than a professional relationship with her boss. But then, I wasn't a facial expression or body language expert by any stretch of the imagination.

I nodded toward the gloves. "Do those help keep your hands steady?"

"They do. Plus, they're greener than latex gloves. I have several pairs of these, and I just toss them into the washer with my uniforms." She smiled.

"They can get a little warm in the summertime, but you get used to it."

I nodded. "I'll have to try those. Thanks."

Most of the time I didn't wear gloves when I was decorating . . . usually only when I was tinting fondant or using modeling chocolate. When I did wear gloves, I used thin, plastic ones that were very inexpensive. They might not have been as environmentally friendly as Fiona's cotton gloves, but I couldn't imagine tossing a pair of gloves with black gel coloring all over them into the wash with my other clothes . . . especially if my uniforms were white.

An announcement rang out in the ballroom: "Today's activities for the first annual Brea Ridge Taste Bud Temptation Cake and Confectionary Arts Exhibit and Competition have now concluded. Please make your way carefully toward the exits and plan to join us again tomorrow morning at ten o'clock for another day of delicious fun. Thank you!"

I smiled at Fiona. "I guess I'll see you tomorrow, then."

"Yeah. Have a good evening," she said.

"You too."

I turned and spotted Ben standing with Violet, Jason, Leslie, Lucas, Molly, Chris, and Alex. I made my way through the exodus to join them.

"We're talking about going to dinner," Jason said. "What do you think about us all descending on Dakota's like a pack of ravenous wolves?"

I laughed. "Sounds good to me. I'm not so sure Dakota's is ready for that, but . . ."

"Then they'd better get ready," Lucas said. "For a cake show, the food here wasn't much."

"I have to agree," Violet said. "Did they offer boxed lunches for the decorators or anything like that? Because all they had available for spectators were the fruit and pastries in those large baskets, and those went fairly quickly."

"That's all that was available for us too," I said. "If we're given an evaluation sheet tomorrow, I'll make a note that I heard *several people* saying they wished there had been a better selection and quantity of food available."

There was another announcement: "Thank you again for joining us today. The ballroom doors will be locked in ten minutes. Please gather your belongings and exit the ballroom at this time."

"They're definitely throwing us out," Ben said. "So, you guys will meet Daphne and me at Dakota's?"

Violet said she, Jason, Lucas, and Leslie would be there.

"Are you sure it isn't too much of an imposition for us to join you?" Molly asked.

"It's no imposition at all," Jason said.

"You *have* to come!" Leslie said.

Molly smiled. "All right, then. We'll see you there."

12

AFTER WE were seated at Dakota's and waiting for our food to arrive, we had plenty of time to chat since, being the only steakhouse in town, they were swamped. The staff had pushed two tables together to accommodate our group. Alex was seated between Lucas and Leslie, Violet was sitting beside Leslie, and Jason was on Violet's opposite side. Molly, Alex's mom, was directly across the table from him, Chris was beside her, Ben was beside Chris, and I was to Ben's right, facing Jason.

I peered around the men to catch Molly's eye. "What do you do for a living, Molly?"

"I write freelance articles for magazines—and websites, now that the print magazine market is dwindling," she said. "The writing allows me flexible hours and lets me homeschool Alex."

"That's great," I said.

"How about you, Chris?" Jason asked. "What do you do?"

"I'm a pitching coach," said Chris. "I used to play in the minor leagues, but I suffered a rotator cuff injury that pretty much put a halt to my playing professionally."

"Did you go to The Show?" Lucas asked.

"Afraid not, buddy," Chris said. "But I'm currently coaching a young man who I firmly believe will go all the way to the major league."

"That's wonderful," Violet said. "It must be rewarding to be able to help shape a career like that."

Chis took a sip of his soda before answering. "It is. It's terrific to be able to look at someone's face—especially the face of a child or a teen—and know he gets it. He understands what you're teaching him, he's applying it, and he's pitching better than you were at his age. It's a great feeling."

I smiled at Leslie and Lucas, thinking about how much fun we'd had baking together over the past year since I had moved back to Brea Ridge. And Leslie had come such a long way. I knew that

if she kept at it, she'd be an incredible decorator—
far better than me—one of these days.

"Did you get to meet any of the major leagu-
ers?" Lucas asked. "Like Big Papi, or Dustin Pe-
droia, or Jacoby Ellsbury?"

"Jacoby Ellsbury is cute," Leslie said, and then
blushed at her confession.

"You're not a Red Sox fan, are you?" Chris asked
with a grin.

"Yeah, I am. Me and Dad both are," Lucas said.
"Are you?"

Chris chuckled. "I like Atlanta myself, but the
Red Sox is a super team. I'm sorry to say I haven't
ever had the pleasure of meeting any of those guys."

"Not yet," Molly said. "Chris is very talented. I
expect the majors to snatch him up and give him a
plum pitching coach offer any day now."

"If only my sister were the general manager for
some team with deep pockets," Chris said.

"Well, if I were, I'd hire you in a heartbeat," she
said.

We all laughed. Even Alex grinned, and it didn't
appear he was predisposed to many displays of
emotion.

Then the food arrived, and the small talk
turned to the cake show. Everyone thought all the
cakes were beautiful, but they nicely told me they
thought my wedding cake would win. After seeing
the competition, I did not. I did say—sincerely—
that I believed Leslie would win her competition.

"I think so too," Molly said. "Your cake is gorgeous, Leslie . . . and, at first glance, it does look exactly like a burger and fries!"

"Just be glad Jordan Richards wasn't around to try to disqualify you," Chris said to Leslie. "He'd have thought no child was capable of making a cake like that without considerable help."

Molly's eyes flicked from Chris to Alex to Violet and Jason. "That's what he told Alex at his competition . . . Alex's last competition, I mean," she explained. "We—Chris and I—had hoped to confront Chef Richards . . . to try to make him apologize to Alex."

"That doesn't matter now," Leslie said. "Who cares what that guy thought? We know Alex is an awesome cake decorator, and he's going to be in the contest next year. Aren't you, Alex?"

Alex nodded.

"Really?" Molly asked. "Darling, that's wonderful!"

Alex shrugged.

Chris squeezed his sister's hand. "I told you this trip would be good for him."

Molly nodded, blinking back tears.

I was curious about Alex's dad. Neither Molly nor Chris had mentioned him, and it was obvious that Chris was the major father figure in Alex's life. Maybe Molly had confided to Violet about Alex's dad. I'd ask Vi once we were alone.

"I heard some producers talking during Lou

Gimmel's demonstration," I said. "I think he might be television's next big celebrity chef."

"Cool," Lucas said. "I'll be sure and get his autograph tomorrow."

"Good idea," Leslie said. "I'll get it too."

"He seemed really nice during the class we were taking from Chef Richards," I said. "He was my table mate."

"How did Chef Richards behave during the class?" Molly asked.

"About as domineering and condescending as you'd expect him to be," I said. "But he knew his stuff." I frowned. "But then, so does Fiona, his assistant. She did the string work demo today, and she did a better job than he did in class."

"I don't know how anybody who was that much of a jerk could get to be where that man was," Chris said. "Some people work so hard . . . treat everyone with respect . . . and never rise to the level of success he achieved." He shook his head. "It makes me sick."

"But professional success isn't everything," Molly said. "Chef Richards had to have been a miserable man deep down to have had so much anger and hatred in his heart. It makes me think he didn't enjoy much *real* success at all."

I couldn't help but glance at Ben. Molly was right. Professional success wasn't everything. But then, Ben wasn't only considering his career in his decision to take—or to decline—the job in Kentucky. His personal feelings factored into the decision as well . . . maybe even more.

He winked at me, and I gave him a small smile.

AFTER DINNER, WE all said our good-byes and went our separate ways. Ben and I walked to the parking lot and got into his white Jeep.

"I have to run home and feed Sandy, and I know you probably need to feed Sparrow," he said. "I can run you by your house, go home and feed the dog, and then come back to get you."

I wasn't sure what he was getting at, so I simply didn't answer.

"It *would* be easier for you to already be at the hotel in the morning when the ballroom opens and the judging gets under way, wouldn't it?" he asked. "You wouldn't have to worry about making yourself any breakfast . . . tidying up . . . What do you say?"

"I think it sounds like a good idea," I said slowly. "Are . . . are you staying too?"

"No. Something has come up at work, and I need to go back in," he said. "I don't know how long I'll be, and I know you're tired."

"Oh." I nodded. "Then I'd rather go back to the hotel and get my car . . . if you don't mind. If Sparrow gets out and I have to wait for her to come back, or if something else has happened, I don't want to delay your getting back to work."

"Are you mad that I can't stay with you?" he asked.

"Not at all," I said. "I just don't know what might happen or what might be waiting for me when I get home."

"Okay." He started the car. "I did reserve the room for the whole weekend, you know." He shot me a glance from the corner of his eye.

"Good."

"And, hopefully, we'll have lots to celebrate tomorrow," he said.

I smiled. "I hope you're right." I also hoped we *wouldn't* be celebrating his upcoming move to Kentucky.

"I hope so too."

After we pulled into the parking lot at the Brea Ridge Inn, I gave him a kiss that assured him I would miss him this evening and that—I hoped—was better than any kiss he'd ever received from Nickie Zane. I didn't know I could feel such resentment against someone I'd never met, but I bitterly resented that woman.

We reluctantly separated, and I drove home. I'd no more than pulled into my driveway than my cell phone rang. I was hoping Ben was missing me already, but it wasn't him. It was Myra.

"Thank goodness you're home," she said.

"Myra, what's wrong?"

"There's the meanest-looking dog I've ever seen on my porch. I'm afraid to get out of the car," she said. "I tried to call Mark, but his phone is going straight to voice mail. He might be on a stakeout or something. Anyway, would you come over and shoo the dog away?"

"Maybe we should call animal control," I said. "How big is the dog?"

"It looks kinda like the one that used to sell tacos in those commercials," said Myra.

"A taco-selling dog?" My mind raced until I could remember the commercials Myra was referencing. "The scary dog on your porch is a *Chihuahua?*"

"Well, I don't know!" She huffed. "I started to get out of the car, and it ran up barking and growling at me. I didn't try to make conversation by asking its name and nationality."

I sighed and rolled my eyes . . . albeit the eye roll didn't have the desired effect of letting Myra know that I thought she was being ridiculous. "I'll be right there."

I got out of the car and stepped into the kitchen to get a slice of ham. Then I walked across both our yards until I was at Myra's porch. I'd always gotten along with animals, and I didn't see any reason—at least, nothing obvious—why I should be afraid of this one. As Myra said it did her, the little dog stood up and began barking at me as I neared.

"What's the matter? You hungry?" I tore off a piece of the ham and tossed it to the dog.

The dog wolfed down the ham and hurried to me with its tail wagging. I gave it another bite of ham.

"Now, that's a good boy," I cooed. "Or girl . . ." I looked over my shoulder at Myra, who was still barricaded in her car. "I think it's okay to get out now."

"Are you sure?" she called.

"I'm almost positive," I called back.

"I'll wait until you're a hundred percent sure!"

I groaned. "I'll toss the rest of this ham, and when the dog goes after it, you come running, all right?"

"Okay!" she called. "Just don't throw it between me and the porch!"

Didn't she give me credit for having any common sense at all? "Fine! Ready, set . . ." I tossed the ham. "Come on, Myra!"

Myra got out of the car and sprinted to the front door. She quickly unlocked it and got inside. "Ha! You didn't get me, you little demon! Hurry, Daphne, and get in here!"

Shaking my head, I stepped through the door.

"Quick! Shut and lock the door!" she demanded. She frowned. "I think I have some leftover pot roast we can use to help you get back home."

"Myra, if you'd have stomped your foot at that dog, I bet it would've run off."

"You never can tell. It looked awfully mean to me. And just because it was small, that doesn't mean a thing," she said.

"I guess that's true," I said, and then I threw out that old chestnut about looks being deceiving.

"Oh, honey, you don't have to tell me a thing

about deceitful looks," Myra said. "I could rant on about women I've known for the rest of the night, but instead I'll tell you how I know not to ever underestimate someone—or some*thing*—based on its size."

I went ahead and stepped out of my shoes, padded into the living room, and sank onto Myra's sofa. *This ought to be good.*

Myra followed me into the living room and sat on the other end of the sofa. "There was this boy in Carl Jr.'s tenth-grade class. He was cute as he could be, but he wasn't big as a sixth grader. A lot of the other boys gave him a fit . . . well, at least, the ones who didn't know him well did. He was little, but he could be as mean as an old cross-eyed barn owl."

"I've heard they're pretty mean," I said. I actually hadn't heard that—I mean, how many cross-eyed barn owls were flying around in the world anyhow—but I was getting into the story.

"Oh, honey, they are," Myra said. "Well, one day this long, tall, skinny boy started making fun of the little one—they called the little one Buck. I can't remember the skinny boy's name. Anyway, Slim—I'll call him Slim—kept putting his elbow on Buck's head and leaning on him and taunting him that Buck wasn't as big as Slim's sister who was in the third grade. Well, Buck didn't take kindly to that, but he tolerated it as long as he could. Finally, he got so mad that he balled up his fist, stuck it up as high as he could, and started jumping up and down right there in the hall punching Slim in the nose!"

I giggled. "The little guy put his fist over his head and *still* had to jump up to hit the other one?"

"Oh, yeah, honey, Slim was the tallest boy in the class," she said. "Buck managed to hit Slim twice, and then Slim's nose started bleeding. Either Slim walked away after that or a teacher broke up the so-called fight—I can't remember which—but people pretty much left Buck alone after that."

"I guess so," I said. "How did you hear about the fight?"

"Carl Jr. told me. He was proud of Buck. They'd always been good friends, and Carl Jr. was tickled that Buck had stood up for himself." She nodded. "Still, that story proves my point. Just because something is little doesn't mean it won't bust your nose and make you bleed. That little demon dog out there might not have big fangs, but they'll break the skin just the same."

"But, Myra, I think the poor thing was just hungry and lost. Maybe it belongs to somebody around here."

"Maybe it does," she said. "And if you want to babysit the thing, have at it. I don't want any part of it."

"All right," I said. "It might find its way home now that it's had something to eat."

"Let's hope so." She stretched. "Can I get you something to drink?"

"No, but before I go, you can give me some of that leftover roast beef you mentioned earlier," I said.

We both laughed.

"Did you overhear anything about the murder today?" I asked.

"Not a lot. The people who were there at the cake show mainly to look at the cakes or to participate in the competitions didn't have much to say about Chef Richards," she said. "The others—like Clean Underwear—were there trying to sensationalize his death and see if they could find a juicy story—make that a *juicier* story than the one they already knew."

"I know," I said. "It's sad how little we've been able to uncover."

"I agree. I still think the best bet is one of the students—maybe that Pauline."

"Maybe." I frowned. "You didn't hear any gossip about anyone Chef Richards might have been having an affair with, did you?"

"An affair? Who'd want to have an affair with that creep?" she asked.

"I don't know. I thought maybe his assistant, Fiona, might. It seems farfetched, I know, but I'm grasping at straws."

Myra tilted her head back and looked up at the

ceiling. "I didn't hear of any torrid affairs. But it'll give me something to work with tomorrow."

"Oh, by the way, did you see the figure molding demonstration?" I asked.

She looked back at me. "No. What happened?"

"I heard some producers talking. Lou Gimmel—the guy who did the demo—might be the country's next celebrity chef."

Myra's mouth turned down at the corners. "Then I definitely need to check him out tomorrow. And I'll have Mark look into his background too."

13

I HAD NO need of Myra's roast beef to get back to my house. When we opened the door, the little dog was gone. I hoped it had found its way back home. But if it had no home, it would make a terrific companion for Myra. Seriously. The two of them just needed to come to an understanding . . . get to know each other . . .

I fed Sparrow, and then I called Violet.

"What's up?" she asked when she answered.

"I just wondered if Molly said anything to you about Alex's dad today," I said. "I think it's great that her brother has taken such a strong role in the boy's life, but no one mentioned his dad at all."

"She didn't say much," Vi said. "When Jason met Chris, he thought Chris *was* Alex's dad. Molly corrected the misassumption and then said, 'Alex's dad isn't with us anymore.' I don't know if that means he's dead or that he's just not part of their lives."

"Either way, it has to be tough," I said. "I'm glad Molly has Chris in her life."

"So am I. It's a shame, though, that they live so far away from each other."

"They do?" I asked. "I thought they were from the same town . . . maybe even lived together."

"No," Violet said. "While we were talking over lunch, we learned that Chris lives in a suburb of Atlanta, and Molly and Alex live in North Carolina. Chris had this weekend off and decided to come to the cake show with Molly and Alex."

"I'm glad Alex got along so well with Leslie and Lucas," I said. "I think they did him a lot of good, especially Leslie."

"Yeah. She even managed to convince him to start baking again. Of course, he might've just been telling her that, but I hope not."

"I hope not too. Molly said his personality really changed after he quit," I said. "Well, I'd better hang up. I promised Steve Franklin I'd make some brownies and cupcakes for the Save-A-Buck and get them to him by the first of the week. Since Ben had to go back in to work, I thought I'd go ahead and get that job taken care of early."

"I'll let you get to it. If you have any that turn out ugly or get smooshed or anything . . ."

"I'll bring any rejects to you guys in the morning," I finished for her. We both laughed.

After talking with Violet, I went into the kitchen, got out my favorite blue mixing bowl, and made a double batch of chocolate fudge brownies. While the brownies were in the oven, I went into my home office and booted up the computer. I checked my e-mail and website stats—visits were up considerably since I'd won the timed decorating competition!—and then I did a search for Chef Richards. I hoped to see for myself if there was any gossip about his having an affair with Fiona or anyone else. If not, maybe there was something about rivalries he might've had with other chefs.

There was nothing on any of the more credible sites that listed anything other than well-known facts about Chef Richards—where he was born (Massachusetts), how old he was (sixty), and where he studied (Le Cordon Bleu in Boston). However, the more reader-generated blog forums had plenty to say about the notorious baker.

"Rudest man I've ever met!"

". . . not even as good as I'd heard he was. His assistant did all the hard work."

I wondered if the assistant this person was referring to was Fiona. I scrolled down.

"All of his assistants have been better than he is," another poster said. "I hear he changes them like other people change their undershirts, but they're all more skillful than he is. And yet *he* takes all the credit for their work."

Another commenter said that she saw a woman at a cake show in Maine throw water in Chef Richards's face. "The woman said it was an accident, but no one believed her, and she got ejected from the venue! LOL! Who could blame her, though? He was so insulting!"

The timer went off on the oven, and I went to the kitchen to take out the brownies. I put them on a wire rack to cool. I realized I could very easily waste the entire night reading "I hate Chef Richards" posts on the Internet, but that wouldn't get me any closer to learning who had killed him. The only post that had possibly helped at all was the one that indicated that Chef Richards had changed assistants often. I should ask Fiona how long she'd been working for him.

I took out my recipe for pistachio cupcakes. I thought they might be a novel purchase for some residents who were up for trying something other than the typical vanilla and chocolate varieties.

As I scooped out a cup of cake flour and leveled it with the back of a knife, I realized that I hadn't seen Gavin Conroy—the baker Chef Richards had called sloppy—at the competition today. I dumped the flour into the mixing bowl and wondered if Chef Conroy had left after learning that class wouldn't take place on Friday. Didn't he have a cake entered in the competition? I tried to remember how he'd done in class. I thought he'd seemed to get the hang of string work pretty quickly and had done a decent job. Maybe he had been at the show today, and I simply hadn't noticed.

I added the rest of the ingredients to the bowl and looked up at the clock. It was after nine o'clock. I wouldn't be making it back to the Brea Ridge Inn tonight. And that was okay. I decided I'd rather stay at home anyway.

I wondered what had been so pressing that it had necessitated Ben's working late into the night. Had it been a new development in Chef Richards's murder case, he'd have told me. Wouldn't he? What else could possibly be going on in Brea Ridge right now that was more important than that? Unless whatever it was *wasn't* going on in Brea Ridge but in Kentucky.

Once the cupcakes were baking, I returned to the computer and looked up the name "Gavin Conroy." I found a football player, a CEO, and a martial arts expert. I didn't find a pastry chef. Had he been a plant hired by Chef Richards to be in the class after all?

I did a search for "Lou Gimmel" and found, not surprisingly, that he was the darling of his hometown. He ran a small but successful bakery there, served on the city council, and mentored children from area schools. He deserved his shot at stardom, and I was genuinely happy for him.

Before I logged off of the computer, I went to the *All Up in Your Business* website and looked once again at the photo of the collegiate Ben with Nickie Zane. Fortunately, the oven timer dinged, and I had no more time to torture myself with the photo. I shut down the computer and went to get the cupcakes.

THE NEXT MORNING, I delivered five packages of four iced brownies and six packages of four pistachio cupcakes to the Save-A-Buck. (I had saved one of the boxes of brownies for Lucas and Leslie.) Since the small, family-owned grocery store didn't have an in-house bakery, I supplied the store with baked goods on commission. They were displayed on a table at the front of the store.

I got out of the car, retrieved a shopping cart, and loaded the packages of brownies and cupcakes into it. When I wheeled the cart into the Save-A-Buck, I saw that a poster board sign had been stenciled with BAKED GOODS PROVIDED BY DAPHNE MARTIN, AWARD-WINNING CAKE DECORATOR and taped over the table.

I caught the eye of my favorite cashier, Juanita, jerked my thumb toward the sign, and said, "What's up with that?"

Juanita smiled. "Do you like it? We heard about

your winning the beach cake competition yesterday, and we thought we should brag about you. Congratulations!"

"Thank you," I said with a laugh. "I'm not so sure I'd go as far as to call myself an award-winning decorator because of that, but I guess it'll work."

"Of course you should call yourself an award winner," she said. "You *did* win, did you not?"

I nodded. "I did."

"Then embrace it," said Juanita. "Feel special."

"Thank you." I had a hard time embracing my successes and feeling special. The years I'd been married to Todd had made me feel anything but. Even though I was now out from under his control, I could still hear his taunting, malicious voice in my mind. It was hard to ignore. In fact, it was almost easier for me to accept failures than it was to bask in the glory of wins.

"I heard about Chef Richards," Juanita said. "I know his death must have cast a shadow over the cake show. I'm sorry for that."

"Me too," I said. I was also sorry that I was a suspect in his murder, but I didn't say that. If Juanita—and the rest of the Save-A-Buck staff—didn't know I'd been questioned about Chef Richards's death, I didn't want to be the one to spread the news.

"I get off work early today, so I'm hoping to get to the inn in time to see all the cakes," she said.

"They're gorgeous . . . especially the wedding

cakes. The sculpted cakes are great too. And wait until you see the kids' cakes! You'll find it hard to believe that kids in their particular age groups made those cakes." I smiled. "My niece Leslie made a cake that looks like a cheeseburger and fries. It's fantastic."

Juanita clasped her hands together and pressed them to her chest. "I can hardly wait to see them all."

I glanced at my watch. "I'd better get going. The ballroom doors open in fifteen minutes."

"I will look you up when I get there," she said.

As I left the Save-A-Buck, my cell phone rang. It was Ben. "Good morning," I answered.

"Where are you?" he asked. "Is everything okay?"

"Everything is fine. I just dropped off some pastries at the Save-A-Buck, and I'm on my way to the inn," I said. "Is everything okay with you?"

"Yeah . . . I just got here and wanted to surprise you, but you weren't in our room," Ben said. "And unless they did a superspeedy job of cleaning it this morning, you didn't sleep here last night."

"No, I decided to stay at home and get some baking done." I unlocked the door to the Mini Cooper with my key fob. "It wouldn't have been the same without you there anyway."

He blew out a breath. "I just thought it would be nice for you to be here. You've been under a lot of stress, and I hoped that staying here last night would help."

"Are you upset with me?" I asked.

"No," he said, although I wasn't entirely convinced. "You had work you needed to do."

"As did you," I reminded him.

"Right. Yeah. No, that's fine," Ben said. "I'll see you when you get here."

"Okay." As I drove to the Brea Ridge Inn, I wondered about Ben's attitude. He'd sounded disappointed that I hadn't spent the night in the room he'd reserved. I supposed he'd felt that he'd given me a gift and that I'd rejected it. I'd be sure and express my gratitude when I saw him this morning and tell him again that it simply didn't feel right to stay there alone.

When I stepped into the lobby, I was stopped by Molly. She looked as if she was about to burst with excitement.

"What's going on?" I asked.

She took hold of my upper arms. "Alex is doing the demonstration for the children's group today."

My eyes widened. "That's wonderful. Are . . . are you sure he's ready?"

"I hope so," Molly said, dropping her hands from my arms. "Chris ran into Kimmie Compton at the bar last night. The poor woman was stressing out over the fact that the person who'd been scheduled to do a decorating demo for the children today got sick and had to cancel."

"So Chris volunteered Alex for the job?" I felt like that might not have been the best idea in the world, but then, what did I know? Alex's mother and uncle knew the child. I'd only met him yesterday. Still, it seemed to me that a child who'd suffered a traumatic experience at his last decorating event—so traumatic that he'd had to go on antidepressants—shouldn't be in front of a crowd the next time he picked up a pastry bag.

"Well, Chris didn't exactly just sign Alex up." She frowned. "But he did tell Ms. Compton that Alex might be willing to do it. So then Chris came upstairs and told Alex that Ms. Compton needed his help, and Alex said he'd do it."

"He isn't nervous about it?" I asked.

"I think he was at first, but I went out last night and got him some of the things he'd need to practice with—fondant, icing, tips—and he picked it up right where he'd left off," she said. "It was as if he'd never quit. Chris told him that the bad man who'd said mean things to him last year wouldn't be here today and that we'd all be at the demonstration to support him."

"Of course we will."

"Do you think Lucas and Leslie would stand at the table with Alex?" Molly asked. "They wouldn't have to do anything . . . just be there."

"I think they'd be happy to help," I said. "I'll call Violet and make sure Lucas was planning on being here today."

"Thanks." She smiled. "I'd better get back upstairs and see if he needs anything."

As Molly got into the elevator and waved good-bye, I called Vi. I told her about Chris volunteering Alex for the children's demonstration.

"Molly said that Alex readily agreed, but she said she'd like Lucas and Leslie there for moral support," I said.

"Of course," Vi said. "I only hope that Alex is ready to do it. To get up in front of a crowd of people and give a demonstration is tough even if you're totally prepared, much less if you're an eleven-year-old child. To do it when you haven't practiced cake decorating in months is something else entirely."

"Tell me about it," I said. "I was a nervous wreck myself yesterday, and I've been decorating every day. And then to see how seamless Lou Gimmel made it all look . . . well, that made me feel even worse about my performance."

"You did great," she said.

"Spoken like a good sister."

"I am, aren't I?" She chuckled. "We'll be there in about half an hour. I wish there was a way we could let Alex know that it's okay to back out if he isn't comfortable doing the demo."

"I think Leslie will tell him if she senses any hesitation at all on his part," I said. "Like her mom, she's pretty intuitive and has a good head on her shoulders. Oh, and by the way, tell the kids that I have a box of brownies for them."

"Just for them?" Violet asked.

"There's one for each of you in the box," I said.

"All right, then. I thought I was going to have to storm the Save-A-Buck and take what was rightfully mine," she said with a laugh.

For some reason, her comment made me imagine myself dressed as a Roman soldier taking my sword and shield and heading for Kentucky.

14

I PUT MY phone away and went into the ballroom. I checked on my superhero cake, Leslie's sculpted cake, and my wedding cake. All of the above were fine—no spectator damage, no damage caused by settling or changes in room temperature or anything weird. That was a huge relief. I'd have been mortified if any of our cakes had been marred.

I spotted Fiona near the wedding cakes and went over to say hello.

"Did you enter a cake in the contest?" I asked.

She shook her head. "I'd have liked to, but with

Chef Richards's demanding schedule, I didn't have time to make one."

"I'm sorry about that," I said. "I think you'd have done a wonderful job. How long had you worked with Chef Richards?"

"About three and a half months," Fiona said.

"You said he had a demanding schedule." I inclined my head. "So he had you working some pretty long hours?"

"Yes, we did work long hours, and he traveled extensively," she said. "And, of course, wherever he goes—or rather, went—his assistant went too."

"I imagine a career like that would make having a personal life almost impossible," I said.

She shrugged. "I didn't have much of one anyway. My parents and siblings are scattered throughout the country, and I haven't had a partner since before I began working with Chef Richards." She lowered her eyes. "I'd hoped the sacrifices I was making would advance my career. I'd like to open my own restaurant someday . . . manage a staff . . . do all the pastries myself."

"That's terrific, Fiona." I placed my hand gently on her arm so she'd raise her eyes back to mine. "You can still realize that dream, you know."

"I'm not so sure," she said. "Jordan had so many connections . . . connections that I don't have without him."

"But you're great at what you do," I said. "Your talent and hard work will open doors for you."

"I used to think so," she said. "But I saw how Jordan could make or break careers with a single phone call. He could be brutal. Still, without him, I wouldn't know where to begin to find investors for my restaurant."

I didn't have a clue where to tell her to look, so I merely reiterated my confidence that she could realize her dream even without Jordan Richards. Then I changed the subject. "Did you ever meet Chef Richards's ex-wife?"

"Lily?" Fiona asked. "I'd met her once or twice. I didn't actually know her, though. Why?"

"I heard talk that he'd been abusive to her," I said, glancing around to make sure no one would overhear us. "I wondered if she might be the one who bashed him over the head with that cake stand."

"I highly doubt it," she said. "From everything I heard about her, she moved on and never looked back."

"I wish his murder *were* something as simple as a domestic dispute," I said. "Doesn't it make you nervous to think that there's a killer at large . . . probably right here at this cake show with us?"

Fiona laughed. "No. I don't think we have a thing to worry about, Daphne. It's not like there's a serial killer out there destroying all the cake decorators of the world. He merely—for whatever reason, and I'd imagine it's a personal reason— did in one horrible guy. I'm sorry it happened, but

I'm not afraid the murderer might kill one of us next."

I smiled. "Yeah, you're probably right. I'm letting my imagination get the best of me." I noticed Kimmie Compton posting the schedule of events and excused myself from Fiona.

"Good morning," I said as I approached Ms. Compton. "I thought I should come over and get a peek at the lineup today."

She turned and smiled. "It's another jampacked day. I think it'll be fun and exciting. Plus, there's the awards ceremony. That will begin at four this afternoon."

"Yeah . . . I'm not sure I'm ready for that."

"I doubt you have anything to be concerned about," Ms. Compton said. "I haven't seen the judges' notes—and, of course, the entries are anonymous—but I know you do fantastic work, Daphne."

"Thank you," I said. As Ms. Compton walked away, I scanned the list of events.

"Hmph."

I turned in the direction of the derisive grunt. It was Gavin Conroy. "Hi," I said to him. "It's Daphne Martin. . . . We were in Chef Richards's Australian string work class together."

"Of course. I remember who you are."

"I didn't see you yesterday and thought you might have left Brea Ridge," I continued.

He shook his head and then emitted a long,

drawn-out breath. "No, I stayed here in town. As a matter of fact, I'm rooming here at the inn, but I avoided the competition yesterday out of respect for Chef Richards." He jerked his head toward the events schedule. "And, just as I expected, there's no tribute to be paid to him today or anything. It's business as usual . . . and I think that's tacky."

"I suppose it would've been nice had there been time to coordinate a tribute on such short notice, but I don't think anyone could've possibly had time," I said. "I didn't realize the two of you were friends."

"We weren't friends," Gavin said. "But we *were* colleagues. All of us were his colleagues. And I think it's a shame that his work isn't being honored here."

"I believe his work *is* being honored," I said. "Fiona did an Australian string work demonstration yesterday using the techniques we learned in Chef Richards's class."

"Did she mention him at all during the demo?" he asked.

"No," I said. "But it was obvious she was very nervous. I don't think she enjoys being in front of an audience. Still, everyone knew it was to have been his demonstration. I took over one of his demos yesterday as well. And, no, I didn't mention Chef Richards as I worked either. I merely told the audience what I was doing. Like Fiona, I was nervous."

Gavin expelled another breath and shook his head.

"If you're so concerned about honoring Chef Richards's memory, Gavin, why don't you do a memorial yourself?" I asked. "I doubt Ms. Compton would mind."

"I might just do that." He stalked away.

"Who was that?" Ben asked as he approached from the direction in which Gavin left.

"He's Gavin Conroy, the guy that Chef Richards criticized for being a slob in class the other day," I said. "Now he's acting all sanctimonious because no one at the cake show is honoring Jordan Richards's memory."

"Chef Richards just died Thursday evening," Ben said. "What did that Conroy guy want—for the event to be canceled?"

"Either that or a tribute given," I said. "I told him that if he was so concerned about it, he should host a memorial himself."

"Good for you. But, given what you've told me—and what I've heard here—about Chef Richards, the sloppy guy will probably be the only one to show up if he does host a memorial." Ben stepped closer to the schedule of events. "It looks like you have a fairly relaxing day today. I don't see your name on here anywhere."

"Nope. No demonstrations or anything from me," I said. "All I have to do is hang around, watch other people's demos, and wait for the awards ceremony."

"That's great. . . . Right?"

I shrugged. "I'm actually nervous about the awards."

"But you've already won the timed cake competition," Ben pointed out. "Even if you don't win in your other divisions, you still leave here a winner."

I smiled. "I guess. How'd your work go last night? Did you finish everything you had to do?"

"Pretty much." He turned back to the schedule. "Wait, this isn't the Alex we met yesterday doing the kids' demonstration, is it?"

"It sure is. His mom told me about it when I first got here."

"Does she think it's wise to put him in the spotlight at the first cake show he's attended since he was bashed by Chef Richards for being *too good* at his last competition?" Ben asked.

"Molly thinks he'll be fine," I said. "Frankly, I'm concerned about him too. But his mom says that as long as we're there to support him—and that as long as Lucas and Leslie are willing to help him—Alex will be all right."

"I hope he will be. That's a lot of pressure for any kid," he said. "But a kid with Asperger's Syndrome who hasn't decorated a cake in months . . . ?" He spread his hands and widened his eyes in exaggeration.

"I know. But we have to trust that Molly knows him well enough to be aware of what he can and cannot do," I said.

I spotted the three judges—two women and one man—gathered around my wedding cake. I clutched Ben's arms. "Oh my gosh, there they are."

"Who?" He looked around the ballroom, oblivious to the cause of my alarm.

"The judges," I hissed. "They're grading my cake right this very moment! See them?"

Ben smiled at someone behind me. "Hi, guys."

I whirled to see Myra and Mark.

Myra took my shoulders. "Honey, what's wrong? You look like you've just seen a ghost or something."

"They're grading my cake, Myra. See their scorecards?"

She nodded her frosted blond head. "I'm on it."

"No, wait . . ." It was too late. She was on her way. I put my hand to my forehead and groaned.

Mark, a broad man in his early to midsixties with a gray buzz cut and bushy eyebrows, chuckled. "Once the gun has gone off, you can't take the bullet back, Daphne."

"I know. I just . . ." I sighed. "I know."

Mark patted me on the back, and I nearly stumbled. The man didn't know his own strength. "It might be better just to turn away," he said.

I knew he was right. And yet I stood there watching in horror as Myra approached the judges and began talking with them. It was apparent that they were trying to nicely shoo her away, but she was insistent.

Mark's gravelly voice drew my attention back to

him. "I've been looking into the backgrounds of the various students who signed up for Chef Richards's class. I took a look at Fiona too. Other than the shoplifting charge Pauline Wilson received when she was in college, all their records appear to be clean." His eyes suddenly widened, and I spun around to see what Myra was doing.

She was facing the judges with her hands on her hips. It appeared they were arguing.

"Oh, no," I groaned. "Oh, no. My cake is going to be disqualified."

"I'll go run interference," Ben said.

"Here's something interesting I learned," Mark told me as Ben walked away. "One of the students—Gavin Conroy—once applied to become Chef Richards's assistant. He didn't get the position."

"He must've really idolized Chef Richards, even though the chef treated him like crap," I said. "Conroy was pretty upset this morning because there was no memorial planned for Chef Richards. He was disgusted that it was, as he said, business as usual."

"Did Mr. Conroy give you any indication during the class that he thought so highly of Chef Richards?" Mark asked.

I shook my head. "In fact, it was the opposite. I got the impression that he didn't like Chef Richards any more than the rest of us did—maybe even less. But he *was* the one person who wasn't afraid to snap back at Chef Richards. At one point, that made me think that Richards had planted Conroy in the class to prove to us that he could take insolence as well as he could dish it out."

"You don't think that anymore?" Mark asked.

"No," I said. "I'd already decided that Chef Richards was too cocky to plant someone in one of his classes who would stand up to him. But, then, with your news about his applying for the job of Chef Richards's assistant, I think that theory is completely bogus. Don't you?"

"Probably. Maybe Conroy is one of those people who feel that once a person is dead, they couldn't have been as bad as they seemed," he said. "He could have been raised not to speak ill of the dead. Or it could be that he's feeling guilty over his treatment of Chef Richards in class on Thursday. How insolent *was* he with Richards?"

"Gavin Conroy only gave back as good as he— and the rest of us—got. If anyone should've felt guilty over the way he treated people, it was Chef Richards," I said. "That man was unbearable."

Ben returned with Myra.

"What did you do?" I asked her.

"I simply strolled by to see what was happening," she said.

"You didn't tell them that was my cake, did you? That could disqualify me."

"Of course, I didn't tell them it was your cake.

This is not my first investigation, nor my first time going undercover." She winked at Mark.

Mark closed his eyes and shook his head. Ben patted him on the shoulder.

"I simply commented on what a lovely cake it was," said Myra.

"It didn't look like that was all you were saying from our vantage point," I said. "It looked like you guys were arguing."

She shrugged. "Well, they asked me if I could look at the other cakes while they were judging yours, and I said that I'd wait. They didn't want me to do that, but I pointed out that the workmanship on your cake was so much better than that on the other wedding cakes that I wanted to study yours. I told them that I wanted to take photographs of your work so I could learn to duplicate it. I said I was a beginning cake decorator—which is just a tiny white lie because I made Mark a cake just last week and swirled the icing around on the top real fancy, and it looked nice. Didn't it, Mark?"

"It was gorgeous, dear," said Mark.

"That's when I went and got Myra and told her it was time for her medication," Ben said.

Ben and Mark had a hearty laugh over that, but Myra just glared at them.

"I might've been able to find out some good stuff from those people had I been allowed to linger," she said.

"Thanks, Myra," I told her. "You're doing well in your investigation. I only hope you can find Chef Richards's killer before the day is out." I turned my attention back to the schedule of events. "I see that Pauline Wilson is doing a gum paste flower demonstration in just a few minutes. I'd like to see that."

"I'll go with you," Myra said.

"I think I'll wander around and look at the cakes a little bit," said Ben. "Mark, care to join me?"

"Sure," Mark said.

"They're up to something," Myra noted as they walked away.

"More than likely," I said. "Maybe they have a good lead on a suspect, and they're going to take the guy down."

"Without me?"

I should've been commended for not laughing out loud. "That's probably just wishful thinking on my part, Myra."

"Yeah . . . you're probably right."

15

WHEN WE arrived at the demonstration area, Pauline was placing RESERVED signs, black-and-white head shots of herself, and small bags of chocolates on each front-row chair.

"What're you doing?" Myra asked her. "Trying to catch yourself a man?"

Pauline gave her an icy stare. "No."

"Because I'd never thought about it, but it makes sense . . . other than the fact that most of the men here are only at this cake shindig because their wives or girlfriends dragged them here," Myra said. "But, in theory, the way to a man's heart is through his stomach, so if he sees that you can bake a decent cake . . ."

"This row is reserved for *invited guests*," Pauline said.

"Oh, well, now, that makes more sense. Who are they? Local National Reservists? Marines?" Myra was still fully fixated on the premise that Pauline had reserved the front row for eligible bachelors.

I didn't think so. I was right.

"They're television executives, producers, and directors," said Pauline. "They sometimes come to these kinds of events looking for new talent. And now that Jordan Richards is dead, they'll all be looking for somebody new . . . somebody to be the next darling of the baking world."

"Well, I've seen Jordan Richards on TV plenty of times," said Myra. "I doubt he was anybody's darling."

I introduced Myra and Pauline before saying, "Good luck with the producers."

Her face softened slightly. "Thank you. I don't know whether or not I'm what they're looking for, but I won't know if I don't try, will I?"

"That's absolutely right." I smiled. "You're braver than I am. I wouldn't dream of inviting producers to my demo. If I'd had the slightest inkling they were in the audience, I'd have been a nervous wreck. Or rather, I would've been even more nervous than I was already."

"So you have no interest in becoming a celebrity chef?" Pauline asked.

"None. I had more than my fair share of fame—or, I should say, notoriety—in Tennessee once." I was talking about my experience with Todd and the news coverage of that entire mess. "That was plenty."

"You're talking about . . ." Pauline glanced at Myra, not wanting to reveal too much if Myra wasn't already aware of the situation. "About what Chef Richards mentioned in class?"

I nodded. "During that time, I had cameras in my face everywhere I went. I hated it."

"But this would be different," Pauline said. "It would be something good."

"I don't think it would be for me," I said with a smile. "But for you, I think it could be wonderful. Again, I wish you the best. I'm looking forward to watching your demonstration."

"So am I," Myra said. "And you never know. One of those producers might be an eligible bachelor. I'm not seeing a ring on your finger."

As Pauline laughed, a woman in a tailored navy suit approached us. She had short, dark-blond hair, and blue eyes that were accentuated by the suit.

"Excuse me," the blonde said in a soft, cultured voice. "Are either of you Pauline Wilson? I was told she'd be doing a gum paste demonstration here shortly."

"I'm Pauline. Are you one of the television executives?"

"No, I'm Lily Richards. Jordan was my husband."

Pauline's eyes cut to me and back to Lily. "And you're looking for me?"

"Yes," said Ms. Richards. "I'd like to speak with both you and Daphne Martin."

"I'm Daphne Martin." I was guessing the police had mentioned to Ms. Richards that the fingerprints found on the murder weapon belonged to Pauline and me, but if that's what she wanted to talk with us about, I wasn't going to hurry the conversation along.

"Oh." Ms. Richards's face softened into an expression that wasn't quite a smile. "This is a bit of luck, then. Do either or both of you have just a minute to talk?"

Pauline nodded. "Let's step over here behind the demonstration table, where we can have a little privacy."

I started to excuse myself from Myra, but the expression on her face told me that there was no way I was keeping her from being privy to this conversation. The four of us walked over to the demo area. I was well aware—as I assumed Pauline must be—that people were starting to take their seats in the audience, and I prayed that Lily Richards wouldn't make a nasty scene. My mind raced as I began mounting a defense before the woman even began speaking.

"Thank you for taking this time," Ms. Richards

said. "I know you're both very busy. I remember very well all the events I attended with Jordan, and I realize that things can get hectic in the blink of an eye."

I struggled for something to say. "Chef Richards was a talented man."

Ms. Richards nodded slowly. "He was. I realize everyone is in a rush, so I'll get right to the point. The police told me that your fingerprints—both your fingerprints—were found on the cake stand used to hit Jordan over the head." She held up her left hand. "I'm not here to accuse anyone of anything. I merely want to know what happened to my . . . to Jordan." She took a steadying breath. "I viewed the body last night . . . and, frankly, I find it hard to believe that even after smashing Jordan over the head with a cake stand, a woman could . . . could do that to him. Jordan was strong. He'd been in the military. He kept in good shape."

My eyes flew to Pauline. She looked as helpless as I felt. She and I hadn't discussed the fact that our fingerprints were found on the murder weapon, and now it was not only the elephant in the room, but there was an entire circus going on around us. Myra was leaning in as wide-eyed as a barn owl, Ms. Richards was fighting back tears, and I heard someone I presumed to be a television producer exclaim, "Yum, chocolate!"

"I . . . I . . ." After those two failed attempts, Pauline said nothing.

I managed to say, "I'm so sorry for your loss, Ms. Richards."

"Yes. So am I," said Pauline, appearing grateful that I'd given her the words she might've been groping for. "I really should get ready for my demonstration, though."

"Of course. I simply wondered how Jordan was acting on Thursday during the class," Ms. Richards said. "Did it appear anything was wrong?"

"How could you tell?" Myra blurted.

To my surprise, Ms. Richards laughed softly. "You've got a point. Jordan was always a bit abrasive. But did it strike any of you that there was anything out of the ordinary going on with him?"

"I didn't think so," I said. "I'd only just met him, but I didn't get the impression that he was concerned or upset about anything."

"Thank you. I'll let you go now," she said.

"Wait. Could we talk later?" I reached into my purse and handed her a business card. "This has my cell phone number on it. Like you, I'd love to figure out what happened to Chef Richards. Maybe if we could talk it over together, we could come up with an answer."

"I'd like to try," Ms. Richards said. "Could we perhaps meet for lunch?"

"That would be great," I said.

"I'd like to join you too," Pauline said.

"As would I," said Myra.

Pauline frowned. "But I didn't think you were in our class, Ms. Jenkins."

"I wasn't." Myra lifted her chin. "But I am a private investigator, and I would be happy to offer my expertise in this matter."

I looked at Myra and felt like Ethel Mertz, wondering what Lucy Ricardo was going to do next.

"I appreciate your help, Ms. Jenkins," Ms. Richards said. "I'll look forward to seeing all of you at lunch, then."

"I'll let you get ready for your demonstration," I said to Pauline. "Good luck."

"Thank you," she said.

Myra and I went and found seats on the risers well behind the reserved front row.

"What do you think of Ms. Richards coming to town?" Myra whispered.

I shrugged. "I suppose she's still listed as Chef Richards's personal contact or something. She seemed genuinely upset about his death."

"Wonder if she's the primary beneficiary to his estate?" Myra asked.

"I don't know. I imagine she probably is. She seemed like a class act, though, don't you think? I wonder what she ever saw in him."

"Well, don't you forget, we were just talking last night about looks being deceiving," she said.

"What I can't figure out is, if she's still going by

the name Lily Richards, why couldn't Mark track her down?" I asked.

"That's a good question," said Myra. "I'll send him a text and see what he says."

I nodded and tried to act like I was paying attention to Pauline as she set up her materials for the gum paste demo. I was actually thinking about Lily Richards and Pauline and Fiona and Gavin Conroy and the other students in the class and wondering which one of them—if *any* of them—had killed Jordan Richards. Ms. Richards had said she didn't think the killer was a woman, and I was inclined to agree . . . unless she was telling us that because she was the killer and was trying to throw us off her trail.

Still, my fingerprints and Pauline's were the only ones found on the cake stand. Had someone used that particular cake stand in order to set one of us up? Or was it merely the most convenient object with which to hit Chef Richards?

I sighed, and Myra patted my hand.

"Everything will be all right," she said, giving me her infamous wink-nod combo. "Now that Lily Richards is in town, the killer is bound to turn up."

"What makes you say that? Do you think he'll want to hurt her too?" I asked.

"I don't know. But in a bunch of those detective movies—especially the old ones—the police inspectors are always saying to 'searchay the female.' That means find the woman."

Cherchez la femme. Once again, I felt I should have been commended on my ability to stifle a giggle.

"So now that the woman is here," Myra continued, "another piece of the puzzle will fall into place. Just you wait and see."

Fortunately, the front row began filling up, and Myra focused her attention on seeing if she recognized anyone famous.

"What do you want to bet that's some of Pauline Wilson's family or somebody she's paid to come here and pretend to be TV producers so we'll all think she's a big shot?" Myra asked.

"I doubt it," lowering my voice in the hope that Myra would take the hint and lower hers. "I heard some producers talking during Lou Gimmel's demonstration yesterday, so I know there are some here."

"Yeah, but they showed up on their own," she said. "They didn't have to be wooed to his demonstration with chocolate."

"I don't want to break it to Pauline, but I think they'll probably end up going with Lou. . . . That is, if they're truly interested in anyone from our little corner of the world. I'm sure they sent out feelers to the Oklahoma State Sugar Art Show as well as to events hosted by the International Cake Exploration Societé," I said. "I doubt there's a shortage of chefs who want to be in the spotlight."

"Speaking of which, were you just blowing smoke when you told Pauline you wouldn't want a gig like that?" Myra asked.

I shook my head. "After Todd tried to kill me, the media was all over me. I was much easier to get to since Todd was in jail without bond, so they bugged me to death. Then there was the trial and the endless questions. I never want to go through anything like that again."

"But Pauline's right—a TV show would be different," she said.

"Not for long," I said. "Some gossip columnist would find out about Todd, and I'd have to relive the entire thing all over again."

"I see your point," she said. "I'm sorry."

I gave her a one-armed hug. "I'm not. I'm happy with my life here in Brea Ridge."

She grinned. "I'm happy you're here too . . . although, if you ever *do* get on TV and need an assistant, I'd be glad to help out."

"I know you would," I said. "Oh, look. Clea Underwood is taking one of the reserved seats. I wonder if Pauline invited her, or if she invited herself?"

"The little snot probably just stole somebody else's chair," said Myra. "She likes to act like she's a big shot, but she's far from it."

"Well, Pauline only put RESERVED signs in the chairs," I said. "Clea probably thinks that means VIPs and that she's certainly one of those."

She scoffed. "VIP, my butt."

Pauline gave herself a detailed introduction, and I really had to wonder about her timidity during Thursday's Australian string work class. Had that been an act? Had she thought that if she appeared to be über vulnerable, Chef Richards would be nicer to her? If she had thought that, she'd been wrong.

"Today I'm demonstrating how to make a gum paste calla lily," she said. "They're one of the loveliest . . ." She put her hand up to her mouth and said in a stage whisper, "Albeit *easiest* gum paste flowers to make."

She kneaded the pre-made white gum paste prior to applying gel color.

"As you can see, I'm using this toothpick to apply yellow gel to my gum paste. This will be used to create the center of my calla lily." She put on plastic gloves and kneaded the gel into the gum paste until the color was uniform. "Now I'm taking what I'll need to make a cone-shaped center to my flower, and I'm putting the rest in this plastic wrap to keep it from drying out so it'll be pliable when I need it later." She raised an index finger. "Always keep gum paste either in plastic wrap, in use, or drying." She winked.

"I hope they don't put her on TV," Myra whispered. "She'll make people puke with that fake, peppy, yippee attitude."

"Before you guys got here, I prepared a slurry using warm water and a little dollop of gum paste," Pauline said. "The slurry is a sort of glue that will help us make the gum paste adhere to itself and to other substances. I also pre-made my wire hooks."

As Pauline was talking, she was shaping her

ball of yellow gum paste into a rounded, tapered cone. She then inserted a wire hook into the center of the cone.

"Since I want the center of my calla lily to seem pollinated, I'm going to brush a little slurry onto the cone and then roll the cone in this finely milled cornmeal." She held up a little dish to show us that it was, indeed, filled with cornmeal. As she'd stated, she rolled the cone around in the cornmeal until it looked . . . well . . . furry.

"Who'd want to eat that mess?" Myra asked.

"I doubt anyone would," I answered. "Most people don't eat gum paste flowers."

"They don't? Why have them, then?"

"For decoration," I said.

Myra shrugged.

"Of course, we have to allow the center of the flower to dry for three or four days before we can make the rest of the flower," Pauline said. "You don't want to sit here with me for *that* long, do you?" She laughed. No one else did. She continued. "That's why I made some of these centers before-hand and brought them with me today. Now let's make our petal."

Pauline unwrapped a ball of lavender-colored gum paste. She took the plastic rolling pin and flattened the dough into a thin sheet. She then used a sharp knife to cut the gum paste into a teardrop shape.

"If you're uncomfortable using guesswork when making your gum paste flowers, there are all kinds of gum paste and fondant cutters on the market to help guide you along," she said.

Her words made me feel guilty and ashamed that I had to use the cutters rather than the knife to make my orchid petals. I knew it was merely because I wasn't that experienced a decorator yet, but I felt that if Pauline could whip out a knife and cut a calla lily petal just by eyeballing it, then I should be able to do it too.

She placed the petal on a foam board and began ruffling the edges with a ball tool. "See how pretty this makes your flower?"

"Ain't this the one you told me was a shrinking violet in class?" Myra asked.

I nodded.

"The shoplifter . . . ?"

Again, I nodded.

"Interesting," she mused.

"With a little bit of slurry all the way around the bottom edge of the petal, I'll attach it to the center piece," Pauline said. "And to make our flower fan out prettily, we'll wrap a bamboo skewer around the edge like so."

Myra made a *pfft* sound. "Prettily. La dee dah."

"At this point, we would have to let the flower dry and harden for a couple of days. But, once again, I made one beforehand so we could do this last step." Pauline smiled as she produced another lavender calla lily with a flourish. "We're going to take a little luster dust—you can see here that I have yellow, orange, purple, and red—and with a dry brush, I'm going to just paint a little of the luster dust into the center of the flower. You can mix up your colors however you'd like. And, *voilà*! You have yourself a calla lily."

"No, you don't," Myra muttered to me. "You have a cake decoration that you can't even eat. With a real calla lily, you could at least put it on your table until it wilted and died."

I started to protest that the gum paste flower would last a lot longer and wouldn't wilt or die, but I decided not to waste my breath.

Pauline was taking questions from the audience, and Clea Underwood predictably asked her about being in Chef Richards's Australian string work class and how his death had affected her. Pauline ignored Clea and took a question from someone who asked her to demonstrate again how to insert the wire into the flower.

"Of course," Pauline said. She took another hooked length of wire and was in the process of inserting it into the flower when something distracted her and she jabbed the wire into her finger. Alarmed, she grabbed a paper towel and wrapped it around the wound. "Well, obviously, you don't do it like *that*." She tried to laugh off the incident, but she kept looking at whatever it was that had distracted her. I followed her gaze to see Gavin Conroy standing to the left of the front row.

16

Myra, Mark, Ben, and I were sitting in the Brea Ridge Inn's restaurant awaiting Lily Richards and Pauline Wilson.

"Be very careful what you say to either of these women," Mark warned me. "They aren't your friends. And if it comes right down to it, they might be your enemies."

"Mark's right," Ben said. "Even if Pauline is innocent of Chef Richards's murder, she's in the same boat you're in. She needs someone else to pin it on."

"That sounds awful," I said. "I don't just want to pin his murder on someone else to get myself off the hook. I want to find the real killer . . . *and* get myself off the hook."

"But you don't know Pauline," Myra said. "She might not care *who* takes the blame as long as it isn't her . . . and she might be the one who smashed him over the noggin. You just never know."

"Myra's right," said Mark. "And as for Lily Richards . . . she wouldn't have shown up at this event if she wasn't looking for justice . . . or trying to cover her tracks. She'd have simply identified the body and left the rest of it up to the police. She'd been able to hide for a long time without anyone finding her."

"How?" I asked. "And why?"

"As far as I can tell, she used an alias to go underground after her separation from Jordan Richards," Mark said. "As for why she did that, I have no clue. She might have been afraid for her safety since she was claiming that Richards had been abusive toward her, or she might have wanted to avoid the publicity of the estrangement. They weren't Brad and Angelina by any stretch of the imagination, but there were still a few paparazzi who wanted to hang out and get gossip for the tabloids."

"Here she comes," said Myra. Raising her voice slightly, she asked, "Wasn't that cake that looked like it had been embroidered pretty? Not as pretty as yours, Daphne, but it was still nice. Oh, here's Ms. Richards. How nice to see you again."

Did I mention that Subtlety was Myra Jenkins's middle name? Okay, actually, it was Sue . . . but it should've been Subtlety.

"Hello," said Ms. Richards as she hung her purse on the back of the chair and sat down. "Thank you for agreeing to have lunch with me."

"It's our pleasure," I said. "You've already met Myra, Ms. Richards. This is Myra's friend Mark Thompson, and this is Ben Jacobs."

"It's nice to meet you," Ms. Richards told the men. She turned to me. "Will Pauline be joining us?"

"Yes," I said. "She should be here any time."

"I hope she's all right," Ms. Richards said. "It looked like she stabbed that piece of floral wire all the way through her finger."

"I believe she was distracted by that Conroy fellow," Myra said. "Do you know him, Ms. Richards?"

"We've met," she said. "He once applied for a position as Jordan's assistant."

"Really?" I asked, as if that were news to me. "The two of them didn't act as if they knew each other during class."

Ms. Richards shrugged. "Well, Mr. Conroy didn't get the job, so maybe they were more comfortable maintaining their distance."

"That's probably it," I said. "Chef Richards *did* criticize Mr. Conroy's appearance. Is that why the chef thought the two of them wouldn't be able to work well together?"

"It's hard to tell why Jordan chose and rejected

the assistants he's worked with over the years," Ms. Richards said. "Some of them he'd like one day and despise the next."

"Was he crazy or something?" Myra asked.

Ms. Richards laughed. "He had some mood swings, that was for sure."

I wondered how extreme Chef Richards's mood swings might've been and whether he could've initially lashed out at his attacker. Maybe the murder had been done in self-defense. I immediately rejected that theory on the basis that the blow to the head could have incapacitated Chef Richards long enough to let the other person get away. Drowning him in cake batter would have been unnecessary for someone who was simply hoping to escape with his or her life.

Pauline hurriedly approached our table. "I hope I haven't been keeping you waiting long. The official cake and confectionary art exhibit and competition medic insisted on giving me a tetanus shot, and that darn thing hurt worse than the wire I stuck in my finger." She pulled out a chair and sat down beside Ms. Richards. "I probably blew my chances with the producers." Her eyes widened as she turned to Ms. Richards. "I'm sorry. That was insensitive of me."

"Not at all," said Ms. Richards. "I understand that up-and-comers are seeking every opportunity to better themselves. In fact, Jordan was discovered at a cake competition in Colorado."

"Really?" Pauline asked.

"Oh, sure. There are typically producers on hand at these types of events, and one—the one who eventually produced Jordan's show—watched him do a demonstration and thought he was particularly dynamic." She smiled. "And when Jordan got a little caustic with an audience member, the producer was sold."

"So see? They might like it that you stabbed yourself," Myra told Pauline. "It might prove that you're quirky or something."

I took that opportunity to interrupt and introduce Pauline to Mark and Ben.

Noticing that the last expected member of our party had arrived, our waitress hurried over to take our orders.

After the waitress left, Ms. Richards decided to get down to business. She took a sip of her water, then folded her hands and asked softly, "Daphne . . . Pauline . . . why were both of your fingerprints found on the cake stand used to hit Jordan?"

Pauline bit her lip. "I think I can answer that one. We—the students in Chef Richards's Australian string work class—were all given cake stands to use for the duration of class."

"Yes, Jordan was particular about his classes and the supplies that were used," Ms. Richards mused. "He supplied everything and incorporated the extra cost into the class fee. He only wanted to work with particular products, and he didn't like for students to bring inferior ingredients in off the streets." She shook her head. "I apologize for interrupting, Pauline. Please go on."

"Well, I was the first student to get to class, and I noticed that my cake stand was a little tight. . . . It didn't spin as easily as some of the others." She raised and dropped her shoulders. "I knew that in order to properly perform the string work techniques, I'd need to be able to make the turntable spin well, so I swapped mine out with another one. Apparently, it became the one Daphne used."

"Okay. That explains the prints," Ms. Richards said. "It doesn't explain why no third set of prints was found . . . unless the killer was wearing gloves."

"I've seen a lot of people wearing gloves during their demonstrations," Myra said.

"It's not uncommon, especially when working with gel colors or kneading colored fondant," I said.

"Or gum paste," Pauline added.

"I suppose what I'm wondering is if any of you think this attack was planned as opposed to spontaneous," Ms. Richards said. "Did anyone see Jordan arguing with anyone the day before he was attacked?"

"I didn't see him arguing with anyone," I said. "But wouldn't Fiona be the best person to ask about that?"

Ms. Richards nodded. "She would be . . . if she and I could tolerate each other long enough to discuss Jordan."

"Why do you say that, Ms. Richards?" Mark

asked. "Wouldn't Fiona naturally want to get to the truth about who killed her boss?"

"I believe she would . . . but not if she had to do it through me." Ms. Richards sighed. "I have no idea what Jordan might've told her about me, but she thinks I lied about the reason I left him."

"The domestic abuse scandal?" I asked. "Sorry   I   I read about it online."

"Yes," she said. "That is why I left Jordan. He'd become too unpredictable. I loved him—I still love him—but I couldn't live with a man who couldn't control his drinking and who got so violent when he drank."

"I understand," I said. "But now that Chef Richards is . . . gone . . . wouldn't Fiona want to help you bring his killer to justice?"

"No. I do believe she'd help Jordan if she could. She'd work with the police. She wouldn't even talk with me," Ms. Richards said. "I saw her this morning, and she very definitively turned her head and walked in the opposite direction."

"Maybe she'd talk with me," said Mark. "I'm an investigator. Maybe I could get Fiona to open up . . . to tell me what she knows about the murder, what she knew of Chef Richards's life, who might've wanted to kill him . . . that sort of thing. I realize she's already told her story to the police, but retelling after some of the shock has worn off might help her to remember something she might've previously omitted."

"That would be wonderful," said Ms. Richards. "Thank you."

"Maybe the four of us could talk with her," I said, indicating Ben, Mark, Myra, and me.

"Five," Pauline said. "My future is at stake here too."

AFTER LUNCH, THE five of us went in search of Fiona. When we couldn't find her, we spoke to Kimmie Compton, who told us she thought she saw Fiona going upstairs. The front desk called Fiona's room for us and got her permission for us to visit her in the seating alcove near the second-floor elevators.

"What's this about?" Fiona asked when we essentially surrounded her.

In the elevator on the way up to Fiona's room, we'd elected Mark as our spokesperson. Now he said, "Fiona, I'm Mark Thompson. I'm a special investigator."

He didn't tell her he wasn't with the police. Of course, he didn't tell her that he *was*. He merely let her draw her own conclusions. Besides, Mark was special . . . particularly to Myra.

"I'd like to ask you a few questions about Thursday's class," Mark continued.

"I've already told the police everything I could remember," Fiona said.

"I know you have," he said gently. "But now that

the initial shock has worn off, I'm hoping that your going over everything one more time might help us to uncover some little clue we've missed. Would you mind doing that for me?"

"Of course not." Fiona visibly relaxed.

Man, Mark was good.

"Thank you so much," he said, taking a notepad and pen from his jacket pocket. "Fiona, did Chef Richards seem distracted in any way before class began Thursday morning?"

"No. He appeared fine," she said.

"Had he been troubled about anything in the days leading up to his visit to Brea Ridge . . . or couldn't you tell?" Mark asked.

"Oh, I could always tell when something was bothering Jordan," she said. "But he was fine. Everything was perfectly normal."

"So the two of you had a close working relationship," Mark said. "You talked with each other if there was something upsetting either of you."

"That's right," said Fiona. "He came across as abrasive—and he could be on occasion—but, overall, he was a good person."

"His former spouse has indicated that Chef Richards had a drinking problem and was abusive to her. Were you aware of that?"

Fiona pressed her mouth into a rigid line. "Lily Richards is a liar. Jordan did *not* have a drinking problem. He might've been a drinker when he was married to her, but who could blame him? She ran through money like there was no tomorrow, and she was a horrible flirt. Jordan was better to be rid of her."

Fiona's description didn't jibe with my initial impression of Lily Richards, but I remained silent. Better to let Mark do his job.

"Did you realize that Ms. Richards is here in Brea Ridge?" Mark asked. "She came here to the cake show to ask questions about what happened to her former husband. Since she identified the body, I'm assuming she was still his legal contact. Do you know whether or not she stands to profit financially from Chef Richards's death?"

Fiona's eyes widened. "I'll bet she does! That gold digger!" She got up and began to pace. "Do you think she might've murdered Jordan herself . . . to get his money?"

"Right now, I'm only fact gathering," said Mark. "I don't have enough evidence to go making accusations."

"What're *they* doing here?" she asked, nodding toward Pauline and me.

"Our fingerprints were on the cake stand that was used to hit Chef Richards," I said. "Pauline and I are trying to help point the police in the right direction, now that we've determined *why* both our fingerprints were on the stand."

"Yeah, I didn't think my cake stand spun well enough, and I traded it for Daphne's," said Pauline.

"But I certainly didn't hang around and clobber Chef Richards with it."

"Neither did I." I frowned slightly. "Isn't there a security camera in the kitchen?"

"No," said Ben. "I've spoken with the police about that. There are cameras in the ballrooms, in the restaurant, and in the hallways, but not in the kitchen."

"The killer must have worn gloves," Mark said to Fiona. "Did you notice any of the students wearing gloves?"

She shook her head. "Some of us prefer gloves all the time, and some of us don't. I wear gloves, even when I'm not working with something particularly messy, because I feel it's more hygienic. But I don't typically notice who is and who isn't wearing them." She sat back down. "Just wearing gloves doesn't make the killer one of the Australian string work students, though. . . . It doesn't even make him—or *her*—a cake decorator. Anyone could've put on a pair of latex gloves from the box in the kitchen before killing Jordan." Her eyes narrowed. "Are you positive Lily Richards didn't arrive in Brea Ridge until last night?"

"No," said Mark. "I'm simply going on what I was told. But you can bet I'll look into it."

AFTER TALKING with Fiona, Ben and Mark decided to follow up on Lily Richards's story that she'd arrived in town the night before. Myra, Pauline, and I returned to the cake show.

"What do you think?" Pauline asked Myra and me. "Do you think Lily Richards killed her husband?"

I shook my head. "I don't think she did. I'm inclined to agree with her that it's more logical that a man did it. Chef Richards was no spring chicken, but he was fairly stout."

"Still, if the woman knocked him out first with the blow to the head, drowning him would've been a piece of cake." Myra grinned. "Get it? Piece of cake?"

"We get it," I said. "Fiona sure doesn't like Ms. Richards. I wonder what Chef Richards said about his former wife to make Fiona despise her so much."

"Chef Richards was Fiona's mentor. Sometimes that alone encourages blind devotion." Pauline shrugged. "Oh, well, I'm off to check on my cake. I'll catch up with you later."

I was watching the door. It was nearing time for Alex to give his demonstration, and I hadn't seen Violet and her family at the inn yet. Myra told me that she was going to snoop around a little and that she'd see me at Alex's demonstration.

I took a seat on a riser where I could get a better view of the ballroom entrance, and at last I spotted Jason's red hair threading through the sea of heads. I stood and waved both arms.

"Jason! Over here!"

He looked up at the sound of his name, but he didn't see me. Before I could try again, China York climbed the steps to greet me.

"Hi, China," I said. "Could you help me get Jason's attention? Lucas and Leslie are supposed to help Alex with his cake decorating demonstration, and it's almost time for him to begin."

"Sure," she said. "I just want to tell you something

first. Antoine de Saint-Exupéry said: *Life has taught us that love does not consist in gazing at each other but in looking outward together in the same direction.*"

"Um . . . okay." China often philosophized in such a way that I had no idea what she was talking about.

"And there's a Latin proverb that says: *A man is not where he lives, but where he loves.* Think about it, dear. Are you and Ben looking in the same direction? If so, the only thing that matters is where your hearts are at." Before giving me a chance to respond, China said, "I'll go tell Jason and Violet where you are and that you're waiting for them."

"Thanks," I said to her retreating back, watching her pigtails bob like a young girl's as she tromped down the stairs.

By the time Violet, Jason, Leslie, and Lucas got to the risers, I'd already climbed down so I could go with them to meet with Alex. After hugging me, Leslie and the two guys hurried on ahead of Violet and me.

"Did China pass along any philosophical words of wisdom to you today?" I asked.

"No . . . but then I don't know her as well as you do," said Vi. "What wisdom is she imparting unto you?" She waved her hands around in a gesture that was meant, I'm sure, to look mystical.

"I guess I'd better start at the beginning, or else you'd be totally in the dark. Ben is considering taking a job in Kentucky," I said.

"What? You've got to be kidding!"

"I'm not." I took a deep breath. "And the worst part is that it's with his old college girlfriend."

Her eyes widened. "Nickie?"

"You know about Nickie?" I asked.

She shrugged. "Brea Ridge is a small town."

"China seems to think—if I understood her message—that if Ben loves me, it doesn't matter where he's at," I said.

"True . . . but if I were you, I'd keep him as far away from Nickie as possible."

Great. Vi seemed to think that if Ben went to Kentucky, I was as good as dumped. Did she see something I didn't? Could she tell that Ben wasn't that crazy about me? Or did she know how much in love he had been—and maybe still was—with Nickie Zane?

I was now eager to change the subject. "Chef Richards's ex-wife Lily is here. She apparently came in to identify his body last night and then came to the cake show this morning looking for answers."

"I hope she gets some," Vi said.

"So do I. Even if Ben doesn't go off to Kentucky, I might be going to the slammer if a more viable suspect doesn't turn up."

"Have you told Mom and Dad about this mess with Chef Richards?" she asked.

"No . . . and don't you," I said. "I'm innocent, so I'm sure to be exonerated . . . right?"

She inclined her head. "On the off chance

you've never seen an episode of *Dateline*, I'll say yes."

"Thanks," I said. "Big help, sis."

"I'm sorry. I'm just worried about you, and I think Mom and Dad should know," she said. "What if you end up getting arrested, and they see it on the news before you can break it to them gently? What if Mom has another heart attack?"

I rolled my eyes. "One, if Mom *ever* has another heart attack, it will most assuredly be my fault somehow. Two, if I *do* get arrested, it's unlikely it would make the news two hours away from here right off the bat. But in case it might, you can call and break it to them gently."

I wasn't as close to Mom as Violet was. I was close to Dad, but my relationship with Mom had never been great and it had soured even more after Todd tried to kill me. Mom had defended him—said it was an accident, that Todd hadn't meant to do it, that I *know* how I can be. . . . It still made me angry just to think about it. She hadn't wanted me to divorce Todd. She'd wanted me to give him another chance. I preferred not to give him or his gun a second chance.

Before Violet and I could talk anymore about Mom or Todd or Ben, Leslie came running back to see what was keeping us.

"Gosh, guys, hurry up!" she said.

"Sorry," I told her. "We're old."

"I know," she said. "But still, you don't have to go *that* slow."

"I *know*?" I repeated incredulously. "I *know*?"

"I'm kidding. You're not that old." Leslie giggled. "So, Aunt Daph, are you nervous about the awards ceremony? I am."

"So am I," I said. "Did your mom tell you about Alex's demo?"

"She did. She said he wants Lucas and me to be there with him, right?"

I nodded. "That's right."

"Are you up to that, Les?" Violet asked.

"Of course. I might be a little bit nervous standing up there in front of everybody, but I'll do it for Alex," she said.

By that time, we'd caught up to Jason and Lucas, who were waiting for Alex in the demonstration area.

Lucas, who'd overheard Leslie's last comment, said, "I'm not nervous at all. I'm a natural born showman. All my teachers say so."

"Yeah, and I'm worried you're going to find yourself in natural born detention because of it one of these days," Violet said.

"Aw, he'll be fine," said Jason. "I was a rowdy youth, and I turned out all right." He winked at Lucas.

"'A rowdy youth'?" Lucas scoffed. "Who are you, Dad, Ward Cleaver?"

At my surprised expression, Violet told me that the kids had been watching *Leave It to Beaver* and some of the other "oldies" on TV Land.

"Thank goodness," I said. "I thought we'd entered a time warp."

"Or a parallel universe," Lucas said. "That'd be fun."

"Yeah," I said. "I've heard those are a blast."

"Oh, good," said Violet. "Here they come."

I turned to see Molly, Chris, and Alex making their way quickly toward us. Leslie and Lucas raced to meet them.

"Are you excited?" Leslie asked.

"Thanks for asking us to help," Lucas said. "We won't let you down."

Alex merely smiled and led the way behind the table, where he began to take his icing, tips, pastry bags, and other decorating tools from a plastic bag. When he was finished unloading the first bag, Molly handed him the one she carried. Chris was holding a cake box.

"Did the restaurant allow Alex to bake a cake last night?" Violet asked.

"No," said Molly. "This is the cake that was made to be used in this demonstration. I believe a Mr. Conroy was scheduled to do the demo, but he backed out for some reason at the last minute."

"That's odd," I said.

"It was my understanding that he was sick or something, but then Ms. Compton said he was here today but that he still refused to do the demo." She turned to watch Alex, Lucas, and Leslie excitedly preparing for the demonstration. "I'm glad he did. I think this will be good for Alex."

"I think it will be too," Chris said. "At least, I hope it will." He placed the cake box on the table.

Kimmie Compton joined us and gave Molly a hearty handshake. "Thank you again—and thank Alex for me—for his agreeing to do this demonstration. I think it's marvelous to get young people interested in the art, and who better to do that than one of their own?"

"You're sure Mr. Conroy won't change his mind at the last minute and ask to do the demo himself?" Molly asked.

"Hardly. He's on his high horse about Chef Richards's death," said Ms. Compton. "Of course, it's a horrible tragedy that the man was murdered, but it was unforeseeable. Mr. Conroy thinks we should've planned a memorial into the festivities, but we simply did not have the time or the resources to do so."

"A memorial?" Chris spat out his words as if they left a bad taste in his mouth. "A celebration would have been more apt. That man was a menace. He's the reason Alex stopped decorating and had to go on antidepressants."

"Is that true?" a vaguely familiar female voice asked.

None of us had noticed that Lily Richards had joined us until she'd spoken.

"Yes, it's true," Chris said. "Several months ago, Alex entered a cake competition with a wonderful haunted house that he'd worked on for days. The house even had working lights and moving objects. Jordan Richards said there was no way a mere child could've made the house on his own, and he disqualified Alex from the competition. He broke that boy's heart."

"I'm sorry," Ms. Richards said. "I had no idea."

"This is Lily Richards," I said softly. "She's Chef Richards's former wife."

"Well, I pity you, then," said Chris. "Not because that monster is dead but because you were married to him in the first place. Because of him, Alex shut down for weeks. He has Asperger's syndrome, Ms. Richards, so he was delicate to begin with. But I don't care who the child is, or what condition he might or might not be in, you don't treat a child the way your husband did."

"I'm sorry." This time Ms. Richards's voice was a whisper, and tears welled in her eyes. "May I apologize to the boy?"

"That's not necessary," Molly said. "Chris, you're being mean. Ms. Richards didn't do anything wrong."

"I know. But *he* did. I came here to make him apologize to Alex for what he'd done." He clenched his fists. "I need to get some air. I'll be back in time to watch Alex do the demo."

"I'm sorry," Molly told Ms. Richards as Chris

walked away. "You certainly didn't deserve to bear the brunt of Chris's anger."

Ms. Richards took a tissue from her purse and dabbed at her eyes. "Still, I'm sorry that Jordan treated your son so badly. I know better than anyone that Jordan could be harsh and abrasive. Deep down, though, he had a good heart. He just didn't always show it. And he was a stickler for the rules. I can well imagine that he'd have behaved badly had he thought Alex had received help from an experienced baker."

We all fell silent momentarily as we watched the children setting up for the demonstration. Alex took Lucas and Leslie—each in turn—by the shoulders to position them exactly where he wanted them to stand.

"May I speak with Alex?" Ms. Richards asked.

"Of course," said Molly.

The two of them walked closer to the table.

"Hi, Alex," Ms. Richards said. "I'm Lily Richards. I was Chef Jordan Richards's wife. He wanted me to apologize to you for the way he treated you the last time you saw him. He knows what a good baker you are."

"Thank you," Alex said in his quiet voice.

"You're welcome. May I stay and watch your exhibition?" she asked.

He nodded.

"Thank you. I'm looking forward to it." Before she could rejoin our group, Gavin Conroy intercepted her.

"Lily . . . dear Lily . . . I'm so sorry for your loss," he said. "I'm sorry for the baking world's loss."

"Thank you, Gavin," she said.

"It's good that you're here," he said. "I plan to say a few words about Jordan later today . . . have a sort of makeshift memorial for those in the baking world who are here but who won't be able to attend his actual services."

"That's very thoughtful of you," said Ms. Richards.

"Would you like to say a few words about Jordan?" he asked.

"I might," she said. "Right now, I'm going to watch Alex do a demonstration for the children. Apparently, he has remarkable talent, but Jordan almost ruined his love of cake decorating."

"I doubt that Jordan's behavior toward the child was intentional," said Gavin.

"I wouldn't be too sure about that," Ms. Richards told him. "As I told the boy's mother, Jordan could be mean when he thought someone was breaking the rules . . . and he didn't always clarify whether or not they had before he formed his own conclusions."

"Still, it was one competition . . ." Gavin spread his hands.

"It was a *child*," Ms. Richards said. "Excuse me." She looked at me. "May I sit with you?"

"Of course," I said.

Poor Ms. Richards. She had to be going through

so much. It seemed as if she'd loved Jordan Richards, but she'd understood his temper and his shortcomings better than anyone. I wondered how such a classy, sensitive woman had wound up with Chef Richards in the first place. He had to have had some redeeming qualities buried under all that crabbiness . . . hadn't he?

And Gavin had called Chef Richards's former wife "Lily" . . . not "Ms. Richards." Was he being presumptuous, or were the two of them friends?

18

ONCE EVERYONE in the audience was seated, Alex whispered to Leslie. She nodded. Kimmie Compton introduced Alex and said he would be demonstrating a simple design that kids would find fun and impressive.

Alex looked at Leslie, and she wiped her palms down the sides of her jeans and said, "Hi, I'm Leslie Armstrong. My brother, Lucas, and I are helping Alex today. Alex doesn't like to talk very much while he works, so I'll be explaining what he's doing and that kind of stuff. Thanks."

Alex removed a teddy-bear-shaped cake from the cake box.

"As you can see," Leslie said, "Alex is making a teddy bear cake."

"Yeah," said Lucas, pointing toward the back left side of the ballroom. "Those people over there donated the pan. Whoever was supposed to do this demonstration before Alex took over made the cake, but Alex knows what he's doing. He'll do a bang-up job on the decorating."

"Earlier today, Alex colored his icing," said Leslie. "He's got light brown, dark brown, white, red, and black. He also has a variety of cake decorating tips."

"Look at her," Myra said. "She's practically a little Vanna White. She might be on one of those game shows one of these days. You never know."

Alex began icing the insides of the bear's ears light brown. He spread the icing on with a spatula and smoothed it down with a finger dipped in cornstarch.

"When you do one of these cakes, you always start by doing the smooth stuff first," Leslie said. "I didn't know that when I started out decorating, and I almost messed up my first shaped cake. So be sure and do the smooth parts before you fill in the rest with the stars."

Alex nodded and then finished filling in the bear's ears, paws, eyes, and bow tie. He then filled a pastry bag with dark-brown icing and filled in the rest of the bear with stars. He tipped the finished bear up to show the audience and they applauded in approval.

He sat the cake back down and held up his hand. "There's one more thing." He took out a recorder and showed it to the audience.

"This is a recorded message," said Leslie.

"I recorded the message," Lucas said.

Alex pressed the button, and Lucas's voice could be heard saying "Happy birthday!" Alex showed how the tiny recorder could be placed in a plastic bag near the bear's head so that when the button was pushed, it would appear that the bear was delivering the birthday greeting.

"You kinda gotta be careful with that, though," Lucas said. "Kids might not want to eat a cute cake that just told them *Happy Birthday*. One time my aunt Daphne made me a guitar cake that was so cool that I threw a fit and cried when my mom started to cut into it. If it had actually played music, no way would I have let them cut it!"

The audience laughed at Lucas's anecdote, and I smiled fondly. I remembered that cake. Lucas had wanted everyone to eat Leslie's princess cake and leave his guitar cake alone.

Following the demonstration, people from the audience—most of them children—gathered around the table to see the teddy bear cake. A couple of well-dressed adults hung behind. I thought I recognized them from earlier today in Pauline's front row.

Once the children had cleared out, the man and woman who'd been waiting approached the table.

"Hello, Alex . . . Leslie . . . Lucas," the woman said, looking at each child in turn. "My name is Marissa Allen, and this is Steve Pendergrass. We work for the children's television network KidzTV. We might be interested in having the three of you appear on an episode of *John and Joni.*"

"*John and Joni*? I love that show!" Leslie said. She clutched her fists up under her chin, and I could see that it was a struggle for her to keep from jumping up and down.

"Are your parents around?" Steve asked.

Violet, Jason, Molly, Chris, Pauline, and I had been standing nearby. We moved forward en masse when we heard Steve's question. I supposed it didn't matter that Pauline and I were not parents. We each had our own reasons for drawing near.

"I'm not sure a television appearance would be good for Alex," Molly said. "He has Asperger's Syndrome, and—"

"He'd be fine," Chris interrupted. "You saw how well he did here today."

"I would imagine the atmosphere on set would be much less stressful than appearing before a live audience was today," said Marissa. "The studio is a closed set, and the only people there would be the camera crew, director, and the actors who play John and Joni. And, of course, Alex, Leslie, and Lucas would be there." Marissa turned an unnecessarily charming smile on the children—she'd already won them over with the words "John and Joni."

Lucas turned to Violet and Jason. "Can we? Please? It would be so awesome!"

"Yes, can we, *please?*" Leslie asked.

"I don't know," Violet said, searching Jason's blue eyes for his reaction. "That really depends on what Molly and Alex think."

"Where is the show filmed?" Jason asked.

"In Atlanta," said Steve.

"See?" Lucas asked. "It's not that far away . . . not as far as New York or Hollywood. And besides, that's where Alex's uncle Chris lives!"

Steve smiled. "We don't want to pressure anybody." He handed one of his business cards to each of us. "But we do think this would be a fantastic opportunity for your children. Please consider it and call us up with your answer."

"It was nice meeting you," Marissa said. Then she and Steve walked away. I imagined they were off to see the rest of the talent on hand at the show.

"Alex, what do you think?" Molly asked him once Marissa and Steve were out of earshot. "Would you like to be on that show *John and Joni*?"

He shrugged.

"I think Steve was right," Jason said. "We all need to think this over and discuss it privately before making a decision." He handed Chris and Molly his business card. "This has my business and home numbers as well as my e-mail address. When you've decided what to do, and if you'd like to have Lucas and Leslie accompany Alex if he wants to go on the show, then please let me know."

"All right," said Molly. "I will."

I felt a yank on my left arm. It was Pauline. I allowed her to tug me several feet away from the others.

"Are you kidding me?" she asked. "Are you *kidding* me? I send a special invitation to every television executive I could find who is registered at this event, *and* I provide them with special—expensive!—gifts, and I barely get a nibble. This awkward little kid is already being invited to be on *John and Joni*?"

"Well, those executives were seeking a particular demographic," I said. "They work for a children's television network."

"Still, *I* could do a children's show," she insisted. "I could be an amusing villainous type . . . or a bumbling baker . . . or . . . or *something*."

"Didn't *any* of the producers you invited to your demonstration talk with you afterward?" I asked.

"A few of them stopped by to thank me for the gifts and to say they were worried I'd hurt myself. One or two said they'd talk with me later," she said. "And, of course, one of them gave back my head shot and said he wouldn't be needing it."

"Maybe most of them were merely trying to give you time to take care of your hand and compose yourself," I said. "That was a pretty painful injury."

"It wasn't that big a deal," said Pauline. "I was just startled, and I stuck myself."

"What startled you?" I asked. "Was it Gavin Conroy?"

She shrugged. "I suppose. I caught something moving out of the corner of my eye, and that's who it was."

"Did you know Gavin prior to the string work class we took on Thursday?" I asked.

"We'd met," she said.

"I hadn't met any of the other decorators in class prior to then," I said. "I guess I don't get around the circuit as much as the rest of you do."

"You will. Or, at least, you will if you stay in this business long enough," Pauline said. "You'll get to know some of the regulars."

"And that's how you know Gavin? He's a regular?"

"Of course he's a regular—has been for years," she said. "So are Lou Gimmel and that mousy redhead. I can't remember her name, but I know her when I see her."

"Do you get along with them?" I asked.

"Sure. I mean, we're not best friends or anything, but we're sociable." She frowned. "Why all the questions?"

"I guess what I'm getting at is do you think one of those *regulars* could be responsible for Chef Richards's murder?" I asked.

"Oh, goodness, no." Her eyes widened. "Do you?"

"All I know is this." I lowered my voice. "My fingerprints are on the cake stand used to knock Jordan Richards over the head. I know I didn't kill him. But I also know the police think one of us students did. Never mind getting arrested, I don't want that suspicion cast over me for the rest of my life."

"Neither do I," Pauline said. "But if we're innocent, we won't be arrested . . . will we?"

"I don't know," I said. "But you don't live here, Pauline. I do. Even if I was arrested but there wasn't enough evidence to convict me of murder, the people of this town would run me out of business because no one wants to buy a cake from someone suspected of murder."

She nodded. "I see your point. I guess all we can do is hope the police find the right guy." She suddenly seemed distracted, and I followed her gaze. One of the television executives was talking with Gavin Conroy.

"How long have you known Gavin?" I asked.

"For nearly five years," she answered. "Excuse me."

I expected her to walk toward Gavin and the television producer, but she went in the opposite direction. The television producer handed Gavin a business card and then left, so I wandered over to Gavin.

"Hey, Gavin," I said. "How's the memorial coming along?"

"It's shaping up nicely. Thank you." He inclined his head. "Would you like to say something on Chef Richards's behalf?"

"No, thank you," I said. "I didn't really know the man at all. Pauline might, though. Have you spoken with her?"

"I haven't. What makes you think she'd be interested?" he asked.

"We were talking earlier. She mentioned that she knew many of the decorators and sugar artists here from her years on the cake decorating circuit." I looked directly into his eyes. "She said the two of you have known each other for five years."

"Yes . . . we have." He glanced around nervously.

I took a chance. "I take it the two of you have been pretty close? Or that, at least, you *were*."

He cleared his throat. "Pauline shouldn't be talking about our private lives. That's none of your concern, and it isn't anyone else's business either."

"You're absolutely right," I said. "That's your and Pauline's affair." I quickly tried to change tactics before he walked away. "I saw the television guy talking with you. Good luck with that."

"I'm not interested in appearing on TV," he said.

"Is there always so much drama and excitement over the producers and executives who come to the cake shows?" I asked. "Or is this a special circumstance because they're now looking for someone to fill Chef Richards's shoes?"

"First off, there's no one who can adequately fill Jordan Richards's shoes," said Gavin. "In the second place, some decorators always go gaga over the producers in the hope that they'll be offered a spot on a show . . . even a guest segment on a morning talk show. Some of my compatriots act like complete idiots, fawning over the TV people like they were gods."

"Including Pauline?" I asked.

He scoffed. "You saw that reserved front row. What do you think? Now, if you'll excuse me, I need to get back to working on the memorial."

"Of course," I said. "You and Chef Richards must have been very close."

"I've already told you we were not," he said. "However, I feel a duty to show the man the proper respect in death."

"Right. I'm sorry."

"You *will* be at the memorial?" he asked.

"Of course I will," I said. "I wouldn't miss it. And I'm sure it'll mean a lot to Lily Richards."

"Maybe. I can only hope it will." Having said that, he strode off in the direction of the kitchen.

I wondered if he'd been given permission to use the kitchen to make refreshments to serve at the memorial service.

I was still staring after Gavin when Violet, Jason, Molly, Chris, Alex, Leslie, and Lucas surrounded me.

"We're going to do it, Aunt Daphne!" Leslie

said. "Mom, Dad, Molly, and Chris have been talking, and they're going to call the producers about us going on *John and Joni!*"

"That's fantastic!" I hugged her.

"I know, right?" she asked.

"Everybody at school will be so jealous," Lucas said.

"Now, keep in mind that they're only in the talking stages," Jason said. "There might not be anything come of this at all."

"Oh, yeah, sure," Lucas said. "That's why the guy was giving all of us his business cards. Those things aren't cheap, Dad."

"I hope it works out that you all get to go on the show," Violet said. "But your dad is right—sometimes they pitch ideas that don't work out. We just don't want you to get your hopes up only to have the whole thing fall through."

"You understand that too, don't you, Alex?" Molly asked.

Alex nodded.

"I've got a good feeling about this," said Chris. "I think it's all gonna work out and that you guys are gonna be stars."

Lucas gave him a high five.

Ben and Mark came up to us. I could see that Ben was nearly bursting with excitement.

"Great news, babe," he told me, hugging me to him with one arm. "There's surveillance footage of the night Chef Richards was killed after all."

"But I didn't think there were security cameras in the kitchen," I said.

"There aren't," he said. "But there are in the hallways *outside* the kitchen. We'll be able to prove that you're innocent."

I turned into his arms and hugged him fiercely. "Thank goodness!"

"Mark and I are going back to the police station to take a look at the footage ourselves," said Ben.

"Spread the word around among the other students, Daphne," Mark said. "I'll have Myra mention it around the ballroom so the spectators will know. Maybe this new evidence will loosen some tongues so we can get some eyewitnesses who saw something they didn't want to report previously."

"All right," I said. "I'll talk with Fiona and the other string work students."

"I'll call Myra and get her on the case," said Mark.

I laughed. "That shouldn't be hard to do."

Ben looked at his watch. "Let's meet back in the snack area in about an hour to compare notes."

"Sounds good." I was so relieved that this case was about to be solved.

19

AFTER MARK and Ben left, I was standing with Violet, Jason, Molly, Chris, Leslie, Lucas, and Alex when I spotted Fiona entering the ballroom.

"Excuse me," I said. "I'm going over to tell Fiona the news about the surveillance footage. Maybe it'll jog her memory about seeing someone talking with Chef Richards before he was killed."

I hurried across the room before Fiona could get entangled with someone else.

"Fiona!" I called.

She turned, smiled, and waved.

"I have wonderful news," I said. "I just learned that there is surveillance footage showing someone going to and from the kitchen around the time the coroner thinks Chef Richards was murdered."

The smile faded. "That's wonderful news?"

"Of course it is. It means we'll be able to find out who killed him," I said.

"That might be what it means to you. But for me, it means another trip to the police station, and I'm not looking forward to that." She sighed. "They'll have me look at the surveillance tape over and over. And then what if I'm not able to identify the person on the tape? The police will think I'm in cahoots with the killer or something."

I patted her arm. "It'll be okay, Fiona. They know you'll do your best. That's all you can do."

"I'm not so sure," she said. "I'm a stranger here. These people don't trust me."

"But they have their suspect on film," I said.

"But they don't know who it is. If they did, they'd have made an arrest already." She blew out another breath. "I don't want to find myself in the middle of something. I want to go home, put this mess behind me, and get on with my life."

"I believe you'll be able to do that whether you can identify the person on the surveillance film or not," I said. "Hopefully, that film means all this will be over sometime later today."

"In our dreams," she said. "Look, I need to go talk with Ms. Compton. See you later."

"See ya," I said.

Well, that hadn't gone a thing like I'd expected it would. I'd have thought Fiona would be thrilled to be able to identify the person who'd killed her boss and cost her the job as his assistant. Instead, she was reluctant to even view the surveillance footage. How weird was that?

I decided to seek out Gavin Conroy next. After all, he was trying to memorialize Jordan Richards. Surely, he'd be glad to know the murderer would be caught soon.

I found Gavin in the kitchen. Apparently, the inn's restaurant had given him permission to make some crudités and finger sandwiches for the memorial.

"Is there anything I can do to help?" I asked.

Gavin turned and smiled. "No, thanks. I appreciate the offer, though."

"I have good news," I said. "I just found out there's surveillance footage of someone going into and out of the kitchen around the time Chef Richards was murdered."

He nodded slowly. "That is good news, I suppose. It won't bring him back, though, will it?"

"No . . . but at least it will bring some comfort to Brea Ridge. We won't be afraid there's a murderer in our midst anymore," I said. "And it will hopefully give Ms. Richards some closure."

"Yeah . . . there is that," he said. "You know, I realize they had either already divorced or were in the process of doing so, but I believe she still loved him."

"I think so too. It's obvious in the way she came here to get answers about his death." I frowned. "Did either of them become involved with someone else after their separation?"

"I don't know. As I've already told you, I didn't know them all that well." He smiled sadly. "I just admired her . . . I mean, them, from afar, I guess."

"Are you sure there's nothing I can do to help you?" I asked.

"Not a thing," he said. "Go on back out to the ballroom and enjoy the show."

"All right," I said. "I'll see you at the memorial."

I next went in search of Lou Gimmel. He was the hardest to find, but I finally spotted him in the snack area.

"Hey there," I said, taking a seat across from him. "You're the talk of the show."

He chuckled. "Really?"

"Yes. I hear you might be America's next celebrity chef."

"Well, I hope so," he said. "There's nothing definite in the works yet, but I'm going to have an audition . . . talk with some people . . ."

"I wish you the best of luck," I said. "It would be so cool to be able to say that back in the day, you were my table mate!"

We both laughed. I then told him about the discovery of the surveillance tape that would make it likely that Chef Richard's murderer would be arrested soon.

"That's a relief," Lou said. "I was afraid that having a killer on the loose would taint the first annual Brea Ridge Taste Bud Temptation Cake and Confectionary Arts Exhibit and Competition."

"You know, I really hope they'll shorten the name next year," I said.

"So do I, but I wouldn't count on it." He laughed again. "It's selfish of me to say so, but another reason I'm glad this video has shown up is because until they find the killer, we're all suspects. Having a cloud of suspicion over his head wouldn't bode well for America's next celebrity chef, would it?"

"Indeed it would not," I said. "And I don't think that's selfish at all. I don't want any suspicion hanging over my head either. I've had enough trouble getting established in this town without being suspected of whacking Jordan Richards with a cake stand."

"I know what you mean. I'm completely ready for my life to take a turn for the better." He shook his head. "I recently suffered a breakup, and I'm trying desperately to find something to fill up my time instead."

"I'm sorry," I said.

"Thanks." He was silent for a second, and then he said, "You know what completely confounds me? She left me for a man who was every bit the snide, caustic, mean-spirited jerk that Jordan Richards was. Why do women fall for men like that? Why don't they want a man who'll treat them well?" He ran his hand over his forehead. "Take Lily Richards—she's an attractive, intelligent, kind woman. And yet she wound up with that jerk Jordan Richards."

"I don't know, Lou. I've done it myself. I had a wonderful guy that I'd dated all through high school. But then when I went to college, I met someone else. His name was Todd Martin, and he was the star football player and all-around big man on campus."

"He's the one Chef Richards was talking about that day in class, isn't he?" Lou asked. "The one who tried to kill you?"

"That's the one," I said. "I saw all the warning signs, but I ignored them. I thought that, sure, Todd was a bad boy, but that I was the one who could tame him. Little did I know, no one could tame Todd Martin. I broke the heart of the guy who adored me—and whom I still love to this day— because Todd seemed more exciting to me."

"Well, from what Richards said, you *did* find excitement," Lou said.

I grinned wryly. "Oh, I found excitement in spades. But now I have another chance with my high school sweetheart . . . I hope."

"I hope you do too, Daphne. But I don't think I'll ever have another chance with the woman I love . . . loved."

"Don't be so sure," I said. "You never know what might happen."

"It would take a miracle," he said. "But maybe I'll find someone new . . . someone who'll love and appreciate me for who I am and for what I have to offer her . . . which could be considerably more if I get a TV gig."

I laughed. "By now, that woman you loved is probably realizing what a huge mistake she's made. I knew almost immediately, but I felt I couldn't go back." I shook my head as if to clear away the memory. "But, whatever you do, I wish you the very best."

"You too," he said.

AFTER TALKING WITH Lou, I sought out Pauline. She was hovering near the demonstration area, and I figured she hoped to see some of the television executives. I talked her into joining me on the risers so we could chat for a second.

"Our worries are over," I said.

"They are? Have you heard something? Are the producers interested in me?"

"I'm talking about our worries about our fingerprints being on the cake stand used to knock Jordan Richards in the head," I said.

"Oh. What about it?" she asked uninterestedly.

"There is surveillance footage showing someone going to the kitchen around the time Chef Richards was killed," I said. "It'll put us in the clear."

"Oh . . . well, that *is* good, then," she said.

"Are you all right?" I asked. "You seem . . . distant."

"I'm okay, I guess," she said. "I'm just not feeling that well. That tetanus shot really hurt. Plus, I've had a headache ever since the medic gave it to me."

"I imagine your hand hurts too."

"It does . . . but not as bad as my arm where I got the injection," she said. "If you'll excuse me, I think I'll go upstairs and lie down for a little while."

"All right. I hope you feel better," I said.

She took a card from her purse. "My cell number is on here. Please call me at that number before the awards ceremony, would you?"

"Of course."

"I don't want to miss anything," she said.

As Pauline left the ballroom, I checked my watch. It was time for me to meet Ben, Mark, and Myra in the snack area. The other three were sitting at a table in the corner waiting for me when I got there.

"Any luck?" Myra said as soon as I sat down.

"Well, I told Lou, Gavin, Fiona, and Pauline," I said. "The only one who seemed even remotely thrilled that the surveillance footage was found was Lou Gimmel. He doesn't want the suspicion of murder to hinder his budding TV career. Fiona was worried she wouldn't be able to identify the person on the film, Gavin said catching the killer wouldn't bring Jordan Richards back, and Pauline felt ill and said she needed to lie down."

"Mark and I expect the killer to go looking for the hotel's copy of the surveillance video," Ben said. "Whoever it is—if he or she knows about the footage—"

"Which, by now, they should," Myra interrupted.

"Our killer should be trying to see the video to determine whether or not he or she can be identified from the tape," Ben continued.

"And you think that's why Pauline excused herself to go lie down?" I asked.

"She *did* shoplift that time in college," Myra said.

"I don't know," I said. "I really find it hard to believe that she's our killer. To go from shoplifting in college to bashing a man over the head with a cake stand and then drowning him in cake batter is a pretty significant leap. Myra, what did you discover about the spectators?"

"I don't know," she said. "I threw the information around to anyone who'd listen. Most of them were either like, *Well, that's good,* or they were like, *Yeah, yeah, move and let me see that cake.* I don't think the killer was out schmoozing on the ballroom floor. I think Pauline is the one. As soon as you told her, she took off, right?"

"Right . . . but I've had a tetanus shot before, and those things *do* hurt like the dickens," I said. "And they can make you sick."

"Wait," said Mark. "She had a tetanus shot this morning?"

I nodded.

"Then if she's sick enough to need to go to her room to lie down, we should check on her," he said. "She might need medical attention."

"I have her cell phone number. I'll call her." I took my phone and Pauline's card from my purse and tapped in the number. I shook my head. "It went straight to voice mail."

"Do you know her room number?" Ben asked.

"No," I said.

"Let's get someone from the inn's security staff to go see about her," Mark said.

"Yeah," Myra said. "We'll either find her sick in her room, or not sick in the place where they keep the surveillance tapes."

The three of us raced to the front desk. Mark explained the situation and said that someone with the inn's security team needed to immediately go to Pauline Wilson's room to make sure she was all right.

"She had a tetanus shot this morning and was ill when she left the ballroom," he said. "It might be an overreaction on our part, but we just tried to call her and got no answer. We want to make sure she's okay."

"We'll send security and the medic to check her out," said the desk clerk.

"Thank you so much," Mark said. "Do you mind if we wait here until you learn about her condition?"

"Not at all," she said. "Have a seat in the lobby, and I'll let you know as soon as I hear something."

We waited about ten minutes before we heard an ambulance drive up outside. Two paramedics sprinted through the double front doors with a stretcher.

"This way," said the clerk. She showed them to the elevator. "Room 143. Please hurry."

"Is that about Pauline Wilson?" I asked.

The clerk nodded. "Yes. It seems she's suffered a heart attack."

"Will she be okay?" Ben asked.

"I've told you all I know," she said. "I'm sorry."

Ben, Mark, Myra, and I got up and started walking slowly back toward the ballroom.

"What do you think this means?" asked Myra. "Do you think she's guilty and knows she's going to get caught, so that caused her to have a heart attack? Or do you think somebody poisoned her?"

"It could simply be that she had a reaction to the tetanus shot," said Mark. "The tetanus vaccine can cause an increased heart rate."

"And if she had a preexisting heart condition,

then it could've caused her to suffer a heart attack," Ben said.

We heard the elevator doors open. The paramedics strode by us with Pauline on the stretcher. I wanted to go over to them to ask if she'd be all right, but I could tell by the grim set of their faces that this wasn't the time to disturb them.

20

I'M GOING to the hospital," I said. "Someone should be there for Pauline."

"I'll drive you," said Ben.

"But what about the awards ceremony?" Myra asked. "Let me go to the hospital, and you stay here."

"No, it's okay. I'll try to be back in time for the awards ceremony." I placed my hand lightly on Myra's shoulder. "If I don't make it back and should happen to win something, would you accept it for me?"

She grinned. "Of course."

"Thanks," I said.

Ben and I rushed out the door to his Jeep.

"Do you think she'll be all right?" I asked him. "Wonder if she has any relatives nearby."

"The hospital personnel will determine all that," he said. "I'm mainly interested in finding out if the tetanus vaccination did indeed cause her to get sick or if it was something else."

"What? You think she was poisoned or something too? Has Myra beckoned you over to the dark side?" I barked out a short laugh before looking at Ben. He was serious. "Really? You think someone might've done this to her on purpose?"

"Someone killed Jordan Richards," he said. "Maybe they're afraid Pauline knows something. Maybe she *does* know something."

We got to the emergency room just minutes behind the paramedics.

"We're here for Pauline Wilson," I said to the nurse at the admissions desk.

"You'll have to wait until they get her into an exam room and stabilized," she said. "Then you can go back. You're family?"

I mumbled something about cake decorating and family that I hoped was unintelligible enough to pass muster and pressed my fist to my mouth.

Ben hugged me. "She'll be fine, sweetheart."

I clung to him and hoped that the nurse wouldn't ask us any more questions. I also clung to him because it was a wonderfully comforting thing to do.

"Don't let me go," I whispered.

"It's okay now. She's moved away from the desk," he said.

I didn't tell him that I was no longer putting on a show for the nurse. I meant it. I didn't ever want Ben Jacobs to let me go. Ever. I hugged him for an extra few seconds before reluctantly stepping out of his arms.

We were about to sit down when the nurse announced that we could see Pauline. We walked quietly into the exam room. There were three beds in the long room divided by curtained partitions. Only one of the other beds was in use. There was a young man with his arm in a sling sitting on the end of the bed. A woman I guessed was his mother held his uninjured hand.

Pauline was hooked up to a heart monitor and an IV.

"Hi," I said softly.

Her eyes fluttered open. "Daphne . . . what happened?"

"I was hoping you could tell us," I said. "You said you were ill and went up to your room to lie down. I mentioned to Mark Thompson that you'd had a tetanus shot this morning, and he became concerned that you'd had some sort of anaphylactic reaction to the vaccine."

"Nope," said a female doctor stepping around

the side of the curtain with a clipboard tucked into the crook of her left arm. "Ms. Wilson has a congenital heart condition. When the vaccine elevated her heart rate, it caused her to have tachycardia. We caught the arrhythmia before it caused a heart attack, though, and we should have that heartbeat back under control in no time."

"That's such a relief," I said.

The doctor checked Pauline's vital signs and the heart monitor and said she'd be back to check on her within just a few minutes but to ring for the nurse should Pauline need anything before then.

"I'm so glad you're going to be okay," I said after the doctor left. "Myra was afraid the same person who killed Chef Richards was trying to do you in." I chuckled to lessen the seriousness of my statement. "She thought maybe you . . ." I made exaggerated air quotes. *Knew too much.*"

Pauline gulped. "I do know something."

Ben stepped closer to the bed. "You know something about Chef Richards's murder?"

"Maybe." She furrowed her brow. "Or it could be nothing . . . only a coincidence. That's why I didn't say anything before now. But up in that hotel room, I thought I was going to die. And I decided that if I lived through that horrible episode, I would tell someone what I heard on Thursday after class."

Ben and I shared a look.

"What did you hear?" My voice was squeaky,

and I realized I both wanted to know and dreaded hearing what Pauline had to say.

"It was Gavin. That's why I was so jumpy when I saw him today," she said. "I was one of the last ones to leave the classroom Thursday evening. But Gavin lingered on purpose."

"Why were you one of the last to leave?" I asked her. "I know that you and Gavin had been an item at one time or another. Were you hoping to talk with him?"

"No. I can't believe he told you we'd had an affair," Pauline said angrily. "It was two years ago, and things have been awkward between us ever since. I was actually hanging around because I wanted to talk with Chef Richards. Gavin was waiting to talk with Chef Richards alone too. I finally gave up and decided I could talk with Chef Richards either before or after class on Friday."

"Why did you want to talk with Chef Richards alone?" Ben asked.

"I hoped he could use his connections to get me an interview or an audition at one of the cooking shows," she said. "They're as common now as houseflies. I knew there had to be at least one of them that could use my talent. That's why I'd arrived early on Thursday morning—to talk with him about his contacts . . . see who he knew . . . what he might be willing to do. But by the time Chef Richards got there, the class had started filling up."

"What about Gavin?" I asked. "Did he give any

indication of what he'd wanted to talk with Chef Richards about on Thursday?"

Pauline shook her head. "Not to me. But I could see how determined Gavin was. And I knew how stubborn he could be. He'd have outlasted me no matter what."

"Did Gavin seem angry?" asked Ben.

"Not at first," she said. "But when I stepped out into the hallway, I spilled my purse. I bent down to pick up the contents, and that's when I heard Gavin and Chef Richards arguing. I know I shouldn't have eavesdropped, but I couldn't help it."

"Did Gavin threaten Chef Richards?" I asked.

"I don't know," said Pauline. "He was telling Chef Richards that he was the best person for the assistant job and that Chef Richards knew it. He said he'd watched Fiona carefully during class and that she wasn't anywhere near as good a decorator as Gavin was. He accused Chef Richards of only hiring Fiona because she was a woman and because he was attracted to her. Then I heard the name "Lily" being thrown around, but they had lowered their voices and I couldn't understand what they were saying. Now that I've met her, of course, I know they were talking about Chef Richards's wife . . . or ex-wife . . . or whatever she was."

"Were you still there in the hallway when Gavin left?" Ben asked.

Pauline shook her head. "Once I'd picked up all my belongings off the floor and put them back into my purse, I got out of there. I didn't want either or both of them to come out of the ballroom and think I was spying on them."

"This argument took place in the ballroom," I pointed out. "Chef Richards was murdered in the kitchen. Wasn't he?"

"He was," Ben said, "but that doesn't mean that Gavin didn't continue to argue with Chef Richards and follow him into the kitchen . . . or that he didn't come back to continue the argument later."

"That's true," I said. "We need to get back to the inn and talk with Gavin." I gave Pauline my cell phone number and asked her to call me should she need anything. Then I promised I'd check on her later, and Ben and I headed to the inn.

In the car, I called Myra.

"Hey, Myra, has Gavin Conroy's memorial service for Chef Richards started yet?" I asked.

"Not yet, but it's getting ready to. Mark and I are in the demonstration area, where it's taking place. We thought the killer might show up at the memorial."

"You might be right on the money there," I said. "Ben and I are on our way."

The demonstration area was a somber place when Ben and I arrived. I tiptoed so the high heels of my boots wouldn't clack on the floor; and rather than sit down, Ben and I stood to the left of the risers and watched the memorial which was already in progress.

Gavin was finishing up a litany of Chef Richards's virtues that I, personally, was finding hard to swallow. First of all, from what I'd seen of the dearly departed, his virtues were few and far between. And given what I now knew about Gavin's argument with Chef Richards, Gavin's devotion to the man seemed just a little bit too contrived.

When Gavin finished speaking, he asked Lily Richards if she'd like to say a few words. Lily got up and took Gavin's place in front of the demonstration table. Gavin sat down in a metal folding chair to her right.

"'I come to bury Caesar, not to praise him.'" She smiled wryly. "Those of you who know—*knew*—Jordan personally will realize how funny he'd find that quote. He was an avid fan of Shakespeare, particularly the tragedies." She looked down at her hands. "Those of you who did *not* know Jordan personally—who only knew him as the snarky celebrity chef—would not realize that, although abrupt and often harsh, Jordan was a good man. He was honest—yes, sometimes brutally so—and opinionated, but he was passionate . . . especially about his craft. He demanded perfection of himself and of everyone around him. Many of the chefs and sugar artists I've spoken with over the years have said that Jordan was a tough mentor but that he brought out the best in them. He challenged them to become better than they were . . . and, in the end, they were more successful because of it. I know I will—and I hope you'll try to—remember the good things about Jordan and celebrate his life, his work, and his memory. Thank you."

The audience applauded Lily Richards. I imagined that most of them were sharing in my feeling of guilt over thinking that the man was a total jerk. When you saw him through his wife's . . . ex-wife's . . . estranged wife's . . . When you saw him through the filter of Lily's eyes and her misty, watercolor memories, he seemed a lot better than he'd appeared in real life.

No one else volunteered to speak. Gavin stood, placed an arm around Ms. Richards's shoulders, and thanked everyone for coming.

"If you'd like to remain in the demonstration area, the awards ceremony will be starting in fifteen minutes," said Gavin.

Most of the audience remained in their seats. Ben and I shared a look of exasperation, and then I shrugged.

"We have to do this," I said. "It can't wait." I strode over to Gavin and Ms. Richards. "Your eulogy was lovely, Ms. Richards."

"Thank you," she said.

Ben joined me. "Gavin, may we speak with you alone for just a moment?" He gave Ms. Richards an apologetic smile. "I'm terribly sorry, but this is urgent."

Gavin's mouth formed a thin, angry line. "Are you absolutely certain this can't wait?"

By this time, Mark and Myra were on either side of Ben and me.

"If Ben says it's urgent, Mr. Conroy, it's urgent," Mark said. "I suggest you come with us unless you'd prefer to air your dirty laundry in public."

He wasn't happy about it, but Gavin walked away between Mark and Ben. I turned to Myra as we followed behind them.

"How did Mark know Gavin had dirty laundry?" I asked.

"Oh, honey. *Everybody* has dirty laundry. One of them Eagles even wrote a song about it," Myra said.

Great. Now that song was stuck in my head.

Ben and Mark led Gavin—and, consequently, Myra and me—to a small conference room just outside the ballroom.

"What is this?" Gavin asked. "I need to be back in that ballroom. I *need* to be comforting a grieving widow. What's going on here?"

"You tell us," Ben said. "An eyewitness reports that you and Jordan Richards were arguing the evening before he was found murdered."

"So what if we were?" he asked. "Jordan was argumentative. Anyone who'd ever met the guy would vouch for that." His eyes narrowed. "Who are you, anyway? You're not a cop."

"No, I'm not," said Ben. "But I've already called them, and they're on their way here."

That was a bluff. Ben hadn't called anyone. In hindsight, it was a really good idea, and we *should* have called them before confronting a potential killer. I wondered if I could unobtrusively dial nine-one-one. I doubted it. I took out my phone.

"Sorry," I said. "Need to take care of something." I texted Myra: *Ben did NOT call the police. Would you please step outside the room and call them now?*

Myra nodded and then said, "I need to take care of something too." She did her oh-so-subtle wink-nod combo at me and then stepped into the hallway.

"I did not kill Jordan Richards," Gavin said. "Sure, I argued with the guy. I asked him why I didn't get the assistant job when I was clearly more qualified than that pink-haired piece of fluff Fiona. Jordan stuck up for her and said she had potential. I said he only wanted to get in her pants. That's pretty much the extent of our argument."

"He didn't insult your appearance like he did in class?" I asked.

"No. That was merely part of his shtick," Gavin said. "I knew he wasn't serious."

"Yet you gave it right back to him in the class-room," I said. "I admired you for that."

"Again, that was all part of the routine." Gavin spread his hands. "Haven't you watched him on TV? The chefs he works with best are those who stand up to him . . . those who don't cower around like . . . like that simpering Pauline Wilson."

"I'll agree that she simpered in class, but once she got out among the other competitors, she seemed to lose her timidity," I said.

"Yes, she did," Gavin agreed. "Maybe you guys should be talking with her."

"She's in the hospital right now," Ben said. "She had a reaction to the tetanus shot she was given this morning."

"Wow. Tough break." Gavin rubbed his forehead. "I don't know what you people want from me. I'll talk with the cops when they get here, but even if you're hotel security or whatever, you don't have any cause to hold me here. I've already told you I didn't do anything wrong."

"The witness also said you were talking about Lily," I said. "Would you care to tell us what that was about?"

"It's none of your business, but I will say that I thought Jordan was nuts to mistreat a beautiful woman like Lily. I'd come to know them over the years, and she's a wonderful woman. He was lucky to have her. Any man would be." Gavin opened the door. "I'm going back to the ballroom." He leveled his gaze at me. "When I win the wedding cake competition, I want to be there to collect my prize."

Myra stuck out her tongue at Gavin's retreating back. "What a creep. I bet he did so kill Chef Richards. Those two are birds of a feather."

Ben and I filled her and Mark in on our conversation with Pauline.

"Do you think Gavin killed the chef?" Mark asked.

"I have no idea," Ben said. "You're a lot better at this than we are. What's your gut instinct?"

"My gut's telling me that the argument Gavin Conroy had with Jordan Richards was more heated and more personal than he's letting on," said Mark. "I want to know why Conroy is so concerned about Lily Richards. Did the deceased leave her a big pile of money that Conroy would like to get his hands on? Or did he have a crush on the woman to begin with?"

"Or is Gavin feeling guilty because he murdered the woman's husband?" I asked.

Myra shook her head. "I'm not getting the guilt vibe from that guy. I think it's something else. Maybe Mark's right. Maybe Mr. Conroy has set his cap for the widow."

21

MARK, MYRA, Ben, and I went back to the demonstration area where the awards cere-mony would soon take place. I'd just started looking around for Violet when I heard her call my name.

"Over here!" She, Jason, Leslie, and Lucas were sitting on the risers midway up with Molly, Chris, and Alex.

The four of us climbed up to sit in front of them. I was directly in front of Leslie, and she bent forward and put her arms around my neck.

"I'm nervous," she said. "If I win, I think I'll

cry. . . . If I don't win, I *know* I'll cry. Competitions are hard."

"I know, sweetheart," I said. "But no matter what happens, we'll use this competition as a learning experience and grow from it."

"And if you don't win, you can always say that the judges were idiots or that the other competitors bought them off," said Myra.

I closed my eyes. *Way to come in there with a lesson on good sportsmanship, Myra.*

"At least, that's what I've always told myself over the years when I entered and lost contests," she continued. "It makes me feel better and keeps me from beating myself up over it."

I patted Leslie's arm and subtly shook my head, hoping that Leslie would catch on that I was telling her not to take Myra's advice. I needn't have worried. Supermom Violet stepped in.

"Whether you win or lose, darling, you created a beautiful cake," she said. "We're all very proud of the work you've done, and I hope you are too. If we were the judges, you'd most certainly win. But all forms of art are subjective, and the judges might look at things differently."

"Plus, they're not biased," said Lucas. "Or, at least, they're not supposed to be. Part of the reason we think you and Aunt Daphne have the best cakes here is because you're family. Right, Dad?"

"Thanks for pulling me right into the middle of

this, Sport," said Jason. "I think both Aunt Daphne and Leslie deserve to win. I'll leave it at that."

Fortunately, Fiona and Lou Gimmel waved to us at that moment as they made their way up the risers toward us, thus ending the awkward conversation about winning and losing.

"May we join you?" Lou asked.

"Of course," I said.

Leslie straightened back up, and Ben and I moved over to make room for the two newcomers.

"We heard about Pauline," said Fiona. "Someone said you went to the hospital to check on her. Is she okay?"

"Is she the one we saw the paramedics leaving with?" Molly asked.

"Yes," I answered Molly. "She accidentally stuck herself with a piece of floral wire this morning and had to have a tetanus shot. She apparently has a congenital heart defect that made her heart race once the vaccine was administered, and she almost had a heart attack." I looked back at Fiona. "She appears to be fine now. The hospital is just keeping her until her heart rate returns to normal."

"I'm glad she's okay," said Molly.

"So am I," said Fiona. "That's scary. Do you suppose she'd never had a tetanus shot before? You'd think a woman her age would've had at least one before now."

I shrugged.

"I'm not so sure it was the vaccine that caused her to be so sick," Myra said. "She told Daphne and Ben at the hospital that she heard a certain someone arguing with Chef Richards on Thursday. I think that person poisoned her to keep her quiet." She turned to me with the full mantle of authority and expertise that she most certainly did not have. "Did you check with the hospital to see if they ran a tox screen?"

"I . . . I didn't ask," I said. "Ben, did you?"

He simply looked at me with amusement, refusing to justify my question with a response.

Kimmie Compton stepped out into the center of the demonstration area. Gavin Conroy's makeshift memorial had been moved aside to make room for the trophies, plaques, and certificates to be awarded the winners.

"Thank you all for being a part of our first annual Brea Ridge Taste Bud Temptation Cake and Confectionary Arts Exhibit and Competition," said Ms. Compton. "We appreciate all our sponsors, our competitors, and our spectators for making this event such a resounding success. We'd especially like to express our thanks to those spectators who voted for cakes with their pennies. Those pennies will be donated to the local food bank and, given the number of filled cups, we think they will amount to a significant contribution."

Ms. Compton paused to allow the audience's applause to die down before continuing.

"And now let's get on to what you've all been waiting for—the winners!" She moved over behind the demonstration table where a stack of cards were waiting. She picked up the top card. "We'll start things off—naturally—with our beginners category. Third place goes to Kelly Anderson."

We all applauded as Kelly Anderson came forward to accept her plaque and prize basket.

"Our second-place winner is Brandon Campbell," said Ms. Compton.

Again, we applauded while Brandon went forward to claim his prizes. Our hands were going to be sore before all the winners had been announced.

"And, our first place winner in the beginners' category is Pam Barnett."

Myra gasped. "Pam Barnett is most definitely *not* a beginner! She's been decorating cakes for years! What a liar and a cheat! I should yell 'fraud.'"

"Please don't," I said.

Still, Myra fussed, and Mark and I tried to shush her. Mark finally persuaded her to lower her voice by saying that karma would come back to bite Pam in the derriere. That seemed to satisfy Myra for the moment.

"Another round of applause, please, for all our entrants and winners in the beginners category before we move on to the junior category," Ms. Compton said.

As I applauded, I felt Leslie's bony fingers dig into my shoulders.

"It's all right," I said softly. "You did a fantastic job on your cake."

Her little chin—also bony—joined her fingers on my right shoulder. It stayed there until the winners of third and second place in the junior category were announced. The fingers tightened as Ms. Compton started to announce the first-place winner:

"Leslie Armstrong."

She'd won! She and I emitted simultaneous squeals of delight. The rest of our group cheered.

"Go, go, go!" I said. "But be careful going down these steps." I felt tears prick my eyes. "I'm so proud of you."

As Leslie navigated the risers to make her way to the demonstration table, where her trophy and prize basket awaited, Ben put an arm around me, pulled me close, and kissed my cheek.

"You know, even if I don't win, her winning has made this competition a wonderful experience for me," I said. "All things considered."

"I do know," Ben said. "That's one of the things I love about you."

My heart nearly skipped a beat. One of the things he *loved* about me. Was he saying he loved me . . . or only that he loved certain things *about* me?

Leslie returned with her treasures, and we all oohed and aahed over them until we missed the first winner announced in the advanced category. We applauded and tried to look contrite.

Except Myra, of course. She exclaimed, "I'm so

happy for you, baby! This thing might not be rigged after all."

I rolled my eyes, and Molly giggled.

The other two winners in the advanced category were announced. These decorators were those who were skilled in decorating but who weren't professionals. I'd never heard of any of the winners in the category, and I thought they were probably from out of town.

I hadn't entered a cake in the professional category—only the novelty cake category and the wedding cake category. I was pleased, however, that Lou Gimmel took the top prize in the professional category and that another student from our Australian string work class took second place. It was the redhead whose name Pauline couldn't recall. I couldn't recall her name either and hadn't been paying attention when it had been announced.

In the floral sugar craft category, Pauline Wilson won first place. Ms. Compton said she'd see to it that Pauline received her prizes and asked us all to keep Pauline in our thoughts and prayers as she recovered from a bad reaction to the tetanus vaccine injection she'd had that morning.

Myra harrumphed her skepticism at the reported cause of Pauline's illness, but everyone pretended not to notice.

"Let's move on to the novelty cake category," said Ms. Compton. "Our third-place winner is Dana Mills."

We applauded as Dana went to collect her prizes. I continued to hold my breath. I didn't win third place. Would I win second? I'd been pleased with the way my superhero cake had turned out, but now I wasn't so sure. Had there been some flaw in it that I'd overlooked?

The second place winner was announced. It was Gavin Conroy. He accepted the prize, and I began to accept defeat. For some reason, I didn't think I could outdo Gavin. Was I that impressed with his decorating skills, or was I intimidated by his forceful personality and his inflated opinion of himself? Thinking of his forceful personality made me wonder if it was possible that Gavin had killed Jordan Richards. When the two of them argued, their tempers had to have escalated quickly. I could well imagine either one of them taking the argument too far.

I was still pondering that possibility when Kimmie Compton called my name as the first-place winner in the novelty cake category. It didn't really register that she'd said my name until Leslie squealed and threw her arms around my neck.

"Way to go, Aunt Daphne!" Lucas said.

I turned to look at them, and they were all smiling.

"Good," said Alex simply.

"Thank you," I said.

Ben squeezed my hand before I went down to accept my trophy and prize basket.

I'd beaten out Gavin Conroy! I hoped he

wouldn't kill *me* now. I met his eyes as I was returning to my seat. He gave me a supercilious smirk. I tried to smile, then dropped my eyes and hurried back to rejoin my group.

I'd barely sat back down before my name was announced again. I'd won third place in the wedding cake category.

"Our local girl is racking up the wins," said Ms. Compton. "Congratulations, Daphne!"

I was thrilled. Of course, there was a part of me that wished I'd won first place, but third place was a huge honor. The wedding cakes in this ballroom were gorgeous and represented hundreds of hours of painstaking work.

Once again, Gavin Conroy won second place. Lou Gimmel won first place in the wedding cake category. I was so happy for Lou. He seemed to be such a nice guy.

Ms. Compton gave her closing remarks and announced that the winning cakes would be photographed before they would be released.

"After the cakes have been photographed for our website and brochures, the decorators may pick them up," she said. "Again, I appreciate everyone coming out to lend your support of the culinary arts. Please join us again next year."

The audience had one last round of applause in them, and then everyone began milling toward the ballroom exits. Jason and Ben helped Leslie and me carry our prizes down the risers.

"If you'll give me your keys," Ben said, "I'll put these in your car."

"Thank you." I fished in my purse and brought out my keys. I took one final look at my goodies before Ben turned to leave with them.

"I'll be right back," he said.

Jason volunteered to go out with Ben, since he needed to put Leslie's prizes in their van. Lucas decided to go along and help carry the prizes because he figured Ben and Jason could use "another guy on the job."

I noticed that Leslie was busy talking with Alex, and—though it's as clichéd as it gets—I commented, "They grow up so quickly."

"Yes, they do," Molly said. "It seems like only yesterday that Alex was taking his first steps."

I wondered if his motor development had been delayed any by his Asperger's syndrome, but I didn't ask. I didn't want to appear rude, and it was none of my business anyhow. Besides, the child certainly didn't seem to have any difficulties now.

"I know exactly what you mean," said Violet. "We went from an Easy-Bake oven to the real thing overnight."

"I just hope this trip . . . this show . . . sets Alex back on the right track," Chris said softly. "Think about how much time he lost after that moron Richards set him back so far."

"I prefer *not* to think about that," Molly said.

"It's in the past. This competition *has* been wonderful for Alex. Hopefully, he'll get back into cake decorating and have a creative outlet again."

"I hope so too," I said.

Chris looked at his watch. "Shouldn't we be starting back soon?"

"I guess so," said Molly. "I just hate to leave. We've had so much fun."

Violet gave her a hug. "We'll definitely keep in touch. If nothing else, we'll get the kids together sometime this summer."

"If nothing else?" Chris scoffed. "They're going to be on that TV show. What was it called?"

"*John and Joni*," Leslie answered. "I hope we do get on that show. It would be the coolest thing *ever!*"

Alex grinned and nodded.

I too hugged Molly and said my good-byes to Chris and Alex. I believed some true friendships had been forged through this cake competition, and I was looking forward to seeing the three of them again. I knew Violet and her family were too.

I excused myself for a moment and went to congratulate Lou.

"You're the man of the hour," I said. "Congratulations!"

He swept me into a hug. "Thank you so much. I can hardly believe I did so well. The competition was fierce."

"I just hope you'll still remember tiny little Brea Ridge when you're a big star," I said.

"Well, *if* . . . and that's a big *if* . . . I ever do become a big star, you'd better believe I'll remember Brea Ridge." He laughed. "This competition has been a fantastic experience all the way around."

Fiona sidled up to his left. "Yeah, it has been a lot of fun . . . except for . . . well . . . you know."

Lou's smile faded. "Of course. Oh, man, Fiona, I didn't intend to be crass."

She dismissed his concern with a shake of her head. "You weren't. I'm sorry. I didn't mean to bring everyone down. I only wish I'd been able to participate in the competition. Chef Richards kept me on such a tight chain that there was no way I could find time to work on anything . . . you know . . . outside of work."

"Still, I'm very sorry for your loss," Lou said.

"Any chance you're looking for an assistant?" Fiona asked him.

"Um . . . not at the moment, but if that changes, I'll keep you in mind," he said.

She began digging in her purse for a business card. "I know I've got a stack of cards in here somewhere. . . ."

"Hold that thought," Lou said. He looked relieved as he left us to walk over to the television producer who'd motioned him over. It was one of the men I'd seen talking with him the day before.

Good for Lou.

I noticed that Fiona was still frantically search-ing for a card. Poor Fiona. I excused myself from her when I saw Ben coming back into the ball-room.

22

THANK YOU for putting those in the car," I told Ben. "I might take them by the house on my way to see Pauline. I thought I'd volunteer to take her prizes to her."

"You're planning on coming back here, aren't you?" Ben asked. "I thought we'd have dinner in our room."

I smiled. "That sounds wonderful. I'll feed Sparrow when I go by the house, then."

"Great." He looked down at the floor.

"What about Sally?" I asked. "Would you like for me to go by and feed her too?"

"No," he said, looking back up at my face. "I took care of her earlier today." He took a deep breath. "There's something I need to tell you."

"All right." I gazed at him expectantly, but he didn't immediately elaborate. "Ben?"

"Yeah . . . Let's step over here and sit at one of these empty tables for a minute." He waved to someone.

I turned to see that it was Mark to whom Ben had gestured. Mark was now headed our way.

"Is there some new development in the case?" I asked. "Did you guys find out something else?"

"Not . . . not quite," Ben said.

"Did you tell her?" Mark asked.

"I was getting ready to." Ben placed his hand at the small of my back. "Let's sit down, and I'll explain everything."

I didn't like where this was going. Had there been *good* news in the case, we wouldn't have needed to sit down to talk about it.

Ben pulled out a chair for me. I sat down and looked up at him warily. Ben sat to my left, and Mark sat directly across from him. I didn't know how Mark had managed to get out of Myra's sight for an instant—especially when he was getting ready to talk about an ongoing investigation—but he had.

"We—I—have a confession to make," said Ben. "You know the surveillance footage that showed someone going to and from the kitchen at around the same time Chef Richards was murdered?"

I nodded.

"It doesn't exist," he said.

My jaw dropped. "It got erased?"

"There never was any surveillance footage," Mark said. "We told you and Myra and everyone else that in order to plant fear in the killer's mind. We hoped that would make him tip his hand."

"You *lied* to me?" I asked Ben. "You made me think I was in the clear when I was not? I'm still a suspect in Jordan Richards's murder?"

"We took a risk," Ben said.

"You gave me false hope!" I said.

"Daphne, you're not going to be arrested for killing Jordan Richards," said Mark. "Even if you *were* guilty, the police don't have enough evidence to charge you. They don't have enough evidence to charge *anyone*."

"That comes as little comfort to me now." I pushed back my chair. "I'm going to talk with Kimmie Compton and see if she would like me to take Pauline's prizes to her."

Ben came after me as I walked away. "Daph, please, Mark and I thought it would work."

"I get it," I said. "I only wish you'd have let me in on the plan."

"I wish we had too," he said. "Please forgive me

and come back here and have dinner with me this evening."

"All right." I did forgive him, but I needed to be alone for a few minutes. In just a short time, I'd gone from being a suspect to being exonerated to being a suspect again. That realization hit me like a punch in the stomach. I so desperately wanted this ordeal to be over. Now I didn't know if it ever would be.

As I was making my way back toward Kimmie Compton, I was intercepted by China and Juanita, my favorite cashier from Save-A-Buck.

"Congratulations on your wins!" Juanita grasped both my hands. "I am happy for you."

"Thank you," I said.

"Where are your trophies?" China asked. "I wanted to see them up close."

"Ben has already put them in the car for me, but please come by the house anytime and take a look. I'm going to put them both on my mantel in the living room."

Juanita let go of my hands and spun around to look at a cake someone was carrying out. "Ooh, isn't it beautiful?"

"It is," I said, smiling at Juanita's excitement.

"Myra told us that the girl who made the flowers—Pauline, was it?—got poisoned," China said.

I rolled my eyes. "She did not get poisoned. She had a reaction to the tetanus shot she was given after she accidentally stabbed herself with a piece of floral wire this morning during her demonstration."

"I wouldn't be too quick to dismiss Myra's theory," said China. "A lot of times killers use conveniences like that to cover their tracks."

"But why would someone want to harm Pauline?" I asked.

"Maybe she knows who killed Jordan Richards," China said. "She didn't stab herself until that big guy showed up."

"You mean Gavin Conroy," I said.

China nodded. "Maybe she thinks he did it."

"Maybe he did," I said.

"No matter what, the person who did do the murdering now believes Pauline knows the truth, right?" Juanita looked at China. "Is that not what Myra told us?"

"That is what she told us," China said. "Either way, there's still a killer on the loose, so you be careful out there, Daphne."

I promised her I would. "I'm going to run over and see Pauline for a minute. I'm hoping to deliver her trophy to her. I think that would cheer her up. While I'm at the hospital, I'll try to find out exactly what she knows . . . or thinks she knows." To make Myra happy—because I knew word would get back to her—I said, "And I'll ask her if the doctor ordered anyone to run a tox screen."

China nodded. "Good idea. Let us know if we can help."

"Thanks, China," I said. "I will."

I approached Ms. Compton. "Hi."

She turned and smiled at me. "Hi there. Congratulations on your successful competition."

"Thank you so much," I said. "I'm going over to the hospital to check on Pauline. Would you like for me to take her prizes over? They might cheer her up—especially the trophy."

"They very well might. That would be wonderful," said Ms. Compton. "Please tell her I'll be over to check on her later this evening if she hasn't been released when I finish up here. And please also let her know I'll box up her prize-winning flowers as soon as they're photographed, and I'll keep them safe for her."

"I'll do that." I started to go pick up the trophy and prize basket but stopped and turned back to Ms. Compton. "May I ask you a question?"

"Of course," she said.

"Do you have any theories on who murdered Chef Richards?" I asked.

She pursed her lips. "I honestly don't. I know people can get awfully upset and protective of their craft. And you can hurt someone's feelings in an instant about their work and not even realize you've done so. But I believe this was more personal. For a person to kill a man, I would think—hope—there would be something more valuable at stake than a cake, or a technique, or a criticism."

"So would I." I picked up the trophy and prize basket. "I'll be back soon."

"Take your time, dear," she said. "It will take at least two hours for all the cakes to be photographed."

BEFORE GOING TO the hospital, I went by my house to drop off my trophies and prize baskets and to feed Sparrow. The cat came running to greet me when I unlocked the door. For a stray that wouldn't come near me before I'd spent weeks coaxing her with prosciutto, she now looked forward—albeit cautiously—to my presence.

"Hey, Sparrow," I cooed. "How's my pretty girl, huh?" I set the prize baskets on the counter and went back out to get the trophies.

"Check these out," I told the cat when I returned. "First place in the novelty cake category and third place in the wedding cake category. Not too shabby, huh? No, it's not shabby at all."

Sparrow meowed her agreement . . . or her hunger. More than likely, it was her hunger.

I opened a can of cat food and poured it into her dish. Then I filled her water dish before going into the bathroom to freshen up. First things first— I washed my hands in case any of the smelly cat food juice got onto them. Next I touched up my makeup.

Ben hadn't been subtle about his hope that dinner in the room he'd rented would turn into an overnight stay, so I packed a bag just in case. I was still a tad miffed about his lying to me about the surveillance footage, but I knew his heart had been in the right place.

Considering the placement of Ben's heart led me to wonder if he was any closer to making his decision about leaving Brea Ridge for Kentucky . . . and Nickie Zane.

I dropped a rollerball dispenser of his favorite perfume into my overnight bag. Hey, Nickie wasn't getting him without a fight.

Not that I'd *kill* her over him. . . . If he didn't choose me on his own, I didn't want him. Really. *Really*.

Kimmie Compton had made a good argument earlier. People seldom kill over mere hurt feelings like criticism of their string work or their icing techniques. People kill when something they truly care about is threatened—a career, a loved one, a lifestyle. Who had something that Chef Richards had threatened? Or what did Chef Richards have that someone else wanted?

As I brushed my hair, I decided to start with what Chef Richards had that someone else might want. He had a lucrative career as a celebrity chef. Lots of the decorators who came to the first annual Brea Ridge Taste Bud Temptation Cake and Confectionary Arts Exhibit and Competition wanted that.

I thought it was something Fiona wanted, but I wasn't sure. Either she wanted to be the celebrity, or else she wanted to work for the celebrity . . . doing much of the work but getting none of the glory. That was confusing to me. Fiona was confusing to me. It had appeared that she'd wanted to enter the cake contest—and goodness knows her work was above par—but Chef Richards had kept her too busy to give her time to prepare a cake for the competition. Had he kept her too busy on purpose, not wanting her to get a taste of success? Had he truly kept her that busy? Or had Fiona used Chef Richards as an excuse *not* to enter the contest because she'd been afraid she might fail? Also, Gavin had accused Chef Richards of hiring Fiona just to "get in her pants." Had Fiona and the chef been having an affair?

Pauline Wilson definitely would have loved to have unseated Jordan Richards as the reigning celebrity chef. But seeing that she was in the hospital recovering from a near heart attack caused, in part, by a congenital defect, would she have had the strength to hit Chef Richards hard enough to knock him out or to drown him in cake batter? I kind of doubted it.

Gavin Conroy was certainly strong enough to knock out Chef Richards and then suffocate him in the cake batter, but did he want to be a celebrity chef? He didn't seem as eager to please the television executives as Pauline had. Of course, Pauline had taken things to the extreme, but still, Gavin simply hadn't appeared to be impressed by them at all. Were Mark and Myra right? Was Gavin interested in Lily Richards? And if so, why would he feel the need to knock her former husband over the head in order to pursue a relationship with her?

Still, even though the couple were either separated or divorced, Ms. Richards seemed dedicated to Jordan. But Fiona had called her a horrible flirt and claimed that Ms. Richards had lied about Jordan's drinking problem. Fiona had told me that she didn't have a current partner. Was she holding out hope for a serious relationship with Chef Richards? Maybe she thought they'd make the perfect celebrity chef couple. But if that were the case, she wouldn't have killed the man . . . not unless he'd told her in no uncertain terms that they would never be a couple—celebrity or otherwise.

Fiona hadn't wasted any time asking Lou if he needed an assistant. On the other hand, she hadn't wasted any time asking me if *I* needed one. Maybe Fiona was desperate for money. Had Chef Richards not paid her? Had he cheated her somehow?

I let out a growl of frustration as I turned off the bathroom light and carried my overnight bag into the kitchen. How did one narrow down a field of suspects from the list of people who despised Jordan Richards? He could have possibly constituted a threat to at least two students with regard to their careers and/or their personal lives. I thought a moment. And Chef Richards had been a threat to Alex. In fact, he'd been more than a threat to Alex. He'd caused the child to have a setback in his emotional development. But wasn't Chef Richards already dead when Alex, his mother, and his uncle had arrived in Brea Ridge?

In addition to all the people I knew of who might've wanted to kill Chef Richards, there were hundreds of other visitors to the first annual Brea Ridge Taste Bud Temptation Cake and Confectionary Arts Exhibit and Competition who might've come here just to do the old boy in. The police might never catch Chef Richards's killer.

23

I DROVE TO the hospital, planning to ask Pauline about the argument she overheard between Chef Richards and Gavin Conroy. If she knew something that could possibly implicate Gavin in Chef Richards's murder, she needed to come forward with it before it was too late . . . before Gavin left Brea Ridge.

When I arrived, I asked the nurse in the emergency room how Pauline was doing.

"She's doing just fine," said the nurse. "In fact, I'll be bringing her paperwork in soon. She needs to look it over and sign a couple of things, and then she'll be free to go."

"Great. She's staying at the Brea Ridge Inn, and I'll be going back there," I said. "I'll be happy to give her a ride."

"Excellent." The nurse smiled. "I was planning on calling her a cab, but you know how slow those things are around here. The only ones we have are those driven by Winnie Amos and Jack Griffin, and getting either one of those to roll off the couch on a Sunday afternoon is like pulling teeth."

I laughed. "Thanks for taking such good care of Pauline."

"That's what we're here for." She nodded toward the trophy. "What did she win?"

"First place in the floral sugar craft competition," I said.

"Well. Good for her."

I went into Pauline's room. I wanted to be discreet in case she was getting changed, so before stepping around the curtain into her area, I called, "Congratulations!"

Based on the nurse's report, I expected to see Pauline dressed in the clothes she had arrived in this morning rather than in the hospital gown. Instead, she was not only still wearing the gown, but she was clutching the blanket up around her chin so tightly that her knuckles were white.

"Pauline, what's wrong?" I asked, placing her

trophy and prize basket on the table. "I thought you'd be getting ready to go. The nurse told me it was only a matter of getting the paperwork filled out before you can leave. Are you feeling sick again? Should I go get the nurse?"

She rapidly shook her head as her eyes darted to the right.

I followed her gaze but didn't see anything. "Why don't I get the nurse?"

"No! Please . . . don't. I'll be fine." Again, her eyes darted to the right.

I noticed the toe of one sneaker behind the curtain. I gasped.

Despite Pauline shaking her head like crazy, I asked, "Who's there?" When I didn't get an immediate response, I pulled back the curtain. "Chris? What're you doing here?"

"I . . . came by to . . . talk with . . . her," he said.

"Why were you hiding?" I asked.

He shrugged.

It seemed unlikely that he had been about to pop out and yell *Surprise*. What could he possibly be up to that would make him feel that he should try to hide in a hospital room?

Before I could ask him, the nurse brought in Pauline's paperwork.

"I'll step outside while you're taking care of that," Chris said.

"I'll go with you," I told him. I didn't want him

to leave, and I was determined that he was going to tell me what he was doing hiding in Pauline Wilson's hospital room.

After he and I stepped into the hall, I asked him again, "What are you doing here, Chris?"

"I was afraid Pauline was going to implicate me in the murder of Jordan Richards," he said.

"Why would you think that?"

"At the awards ceremony, Myra said that Pauline overheard *a certain someone* arguing with Chef Richards," he said. "She looked right at me."

"Myra was just bragging," I said.

"You mean Pauline *didn't* hear anyone arguing with Chef Richards?"

"She did. She heard Gavin Conroy and Chef Richards arguing but that was right after class on Thursday." I frowned. "So you're saying you argued with Chef Richards too?"

"Uh . . . yeah . . . I did." He shrugged. "Molly, Alex, and I got into Brea Ridge on Thursday evening. We were staying at another hotel, but I went to the inn looking for Jordan Richards. I wanted to make him apologize to Alex for the way he'd treated him. I wanted Richards to make things right with Alex . . . to tell Alex that he was a good cake decorator." He ran his hand over his face. "Alex has struggled so much since that incident at the cake show a few months ago. The kid hasn't been the same. I just wanted my nephew back."

"What did Chef Richards say when you confronted him?" I asked.

"He told me I was an idiot and he asked if I really expected him to believe that he'd done irreparable harm to a child simply by telling the child that his work was too good to have been done without help," said Chris. "He said most kids would've been flattered by that. I told him Alex wasn't *most kids* and that I didn't care whether Chef Richards believed it or not. I explained that Alex had Asperger's Syndrome and that he hadn't decorated since Chef Richards had been so rude to him."

"Wait," I said. "You're not telling me Chef Richards refused to apologize to Alex, are you?"

"That's exactly what I'm telling you. And I told him he *was* going to apologize to Alex first thing Friday morning—that I'd be bringing my nephew to his class. I told Chef Richards that if he didn't want to be embarrassed in front of his students, he'd better step out into the hallway when he saw us at the door. So, uh, yeah . . . he and I had a pretty heated argument." Chris put his hands in his pockets. "I thought that Pauline had overheard us and that her testimony, combined with that surveillance footage, would put me in the kitchen close to the time Chef Richards died and that I'd take the blame for hitting him on the head with that cake stand and then shoving his face into the vanilla cake batter."

"Well, I'm not sure anyone would blame you if

you had, given the circumstances," I said. "After getting to know Alex these past couple of days, I'd want to at least dump the cake batter over Chef Richards's head for the way he treated that boy. I can imagine how you and Molly must have felt."

Chris smiled. "Well, thanks for understanding. I'm going to take off. Molly and Alex are waiting for me back at our hotel. I'm going to follow them as far as their house in North Carolina tonight and then go on home to Georgia tomorrow. Please apologize to Pauline for me. I didn't mean to scare her. I just wanted to explain what she might've overheard."

"I'll tell her," I said. "You guys have a safe trip home."

"Thanks, Daphne."

As Chris strode down the hall, the nurse came out of Pauline's cubicle.

"Ms. Wilson is dressing and will be ready to go in just a couple of minutes," said the nurse. "I wish I'd have been off this weekend. I'd have sure loved to see all those pretty cakes."

"I wish you had been able to come too," I said. "There were some really beautiful ones on display."

"That's what Ms. Wilson was telling me earlier today," she said. "Oh, well . . . maybe next year." She returned to the nurses' station.

I stepped up to the closed curtain. "Pauline, it's Daphne. Do you need any help with anything?"

"Is that man with you?" she asked.

"No, he left," I said.

"Good. He was creeping me out." She pulled back the curtain. "Let's get out of here."

"You've had a horrible day," I said. Call me Captain Obvious.

She smiled and picked up her trophy. "It wasn't all bad."

"I know Ms. Compton will be happy to see you."

"You said that guy left," she said. "He wasn't going back to the inn, was he?"

"I don't think so. Pauline, what did he do to make you so afraid of him? He seemed all right to me."

"It wasn't what he did or said. It was his attitude. He just . . ." She blew out a breath in frustration. "He just came across as menacing. He wanted to know who I'd heard arguing with Chef Richards and what I'd heard."

"What did you tell him?" I asked.

"I didn't tell him anything. I asked him to please get out of my room," she said. "And then he heard you talking to the nurse, and he hid behind the curtain. Now do you see why I was freaked out?"

"I certainly do," I said. "I can't figure out why he'd feel the need to hide, though, if he was only here to talk with you."

"Because he was a nut," said Pauline. "He was so nervous about what I might've overheard."

"From what I've seen, he is a little high-strung," I said. "He was afraid you'd heard him arguing with Chef Richards and would implicate him in the murder."

"What was he arguing with Chef Richards about?" she asked.

I explained the situation between Chef Richards and Alex.

"Poor kid. Still, I don't know why the uncle would've thought my hearing him arguing with Chef Richards would be such a big deal," she said. "Everyone argued with Chef Richards."

"And yet you stabbed yourself with floral wire when you saw Gavin Conroy during your demonstration," I said. "Do you think Gavin killed Chef Richards?"

"Do I think he did it? Yes. Like Chef Richards, Gavin has a violent temper. Do I have any evidence that Gavin killed the chef? No." She shook her head. "I wish I did. Then you and I would be off the hook."

"Maybe we can put our heads together with Mark—the private investigator—and with Ben and come up with some sort of trap where we could trick Gavin into confessing," I said. "What do you think?"

"I guess it's worth a shot. But could we do it tomorrow over breakfast?" she asked. "I'm really exhausted, and I just want to go back to the inn and crash tonight."

"That sounds like a plan," I said. "I'll talk with Mark and Ben and see if both of them can meet us for breakfast."

I drove Pauline back to the Brea Ridge Inn. She took her trophy and prize basket and went to find Kimmie Compton, and I stopped by the front desk.

"Hi," I said to the clerk. "Has Gavin Conroy checked out yet?"

The clerk tapped a few computer keys, looked up, and said, "No. Would you like for me to ring his room for you?"

"No, thanks," I said. "I'll catch up with him later."

I walked over to the seating area and called Ben. "Where are you?" I asked when he answered.

"I'm still with Mark and Myra in the snack area," he said. "Where are you?"

"I'm in the lobby," I said.

"Great." He lowered his voice. "I'll head on up to our room and be there when you get there."

"Wait," I said. "Why don't we have dinner with Mark and Myra? We can eat in the inn's dining room and go over this case one last time."

He sighed. "But I was really looking forward to some alone time with you."

"We'll still have it, I promise," I said. "I just feel that we all need to put our heads together on this investigation one last time before we completely give up. Pauline is fairly sure that Gavin Conroy killed Jordan Richards, but she doesn't have any proof and doesn't know how to get it. Maybe Mark can help us figure that out."

"All right," Ben said. "The three of us will meet you in the dining room."

"I'm on my way." He sounded really disappointed that he and I weren't having dinner alone in our room. I wondered if that was a good sign or a bad one. Maybe he was going to tell me his decision about Kentucky. If he was staying, I'd like to know that right this minute. If he was going, I'd prefer to delay his announcement for as long as possible.

I was walking in the direction of the dining room when I met Gavin Conroy in the hallway. I thought, *Speak of the devil . . .*

"Hi, Gavin," I said. "Are you going to dinner?"

"Just finished up," he said. "I'm ready to go up to my room and rest awhile. It's been a trying day."

"Well, if I don't see you before you check out, have a safe trip home."

He smiled. "You take care, Daphne."

I continued on to the dining room, wondering why Gavin Conroy had suddenly seemed nicer than he ever had. Was it because he knew he was *this close* to getting away with murder? Or was he simply glad to have the competition behind him?

I stood to the right of the maître d's podium and waited for Ben, Myra, and Mark to join me.

Kimmie Compton and Pauline Wilson entered the dining room.

"Hello, Daphne," said Ms. Compton. "I'm treating Pauline to dinner this evening. She's had such an awful ordeal. Would you care to join us?"

"I'd like to, but I'm waiting for friends," I said. "I appreciate the offer, though."

"Maybe next time, then. By the way, Pauline told me about that man skulking about the hospital," Ms. Compton said. "If he shows up here again, I think we should have security throw him out."

"I don't believe he meant her any harm," I said. "As I explained to Pauline, he told me that he wanted to make sure she understood why he'd been arguing with Chef Richards."

"And I told Daphne that *everybody* argued with Chef Richards," said Pauline.

Ms. Compton smiled as she lifted and dropped one shoulder in a semishrug. "Maybe his death was our own little version of *Murder on the Orient Express*."

The hostess arrived and took Ms. Compton and Pauline to their table. I didn't express my wish to the maître d', of course, but I hoped Ben, Myra, Mark, and I got a table far enough away from Pauline Wilson and Kimmie Compton that we wouldn't have to worry about them overhearing our conversation.

When Ben, Myra, and Mark did arrive, the maître d' informed us that the only table for four that he currently had was in the back but that if we'd like to wait at the bar until another table became available, we shouldn't have long to wait. I quickly told him that the table in the back would suit us fine.

"I hope you guys don't mind," I said once we'd been seated. "But Kimmie Compton and Pauline Wilson are here too, and I don't want them overhearing what we have to say."

"I don't think anyone will overhear us here," said Myra. "We might need a bullhorn to get the attention of our waiter." She noticed my disapproving glare. "Which is completely all right with me."

"It's fine with me too," Ben said. "I'm ready to put this entire episode behind us." He had an edge to his voice that told me he was still put out over the fact that we weren't having dinner alone in our room.

"I'm more ready than you are," I told him. "I'm one of the suspects in the murder. Remember?"

"Of course I remember," he said. "It's just that we've been over and over and over this, and we can't come up with anything new."

"Then let's take it from the top and review what we know one last time," I said.

24

AFTER THE waiter brought us drinks and took our orders, I removed a small notebook and pen from my purse.

"Mark, do you or Ben want to do the honors of laying out what we already know?" I asked.

"Ben, you go ahead," said Mark.

"Fine. I'll set out what I know, and you guys jump in when you have something to add," Ben said. "Will that work?"

We all agreed that it would.

"Chef Jordan Richards arrived in Brea Ridge on Wednesday afternoon," said Ben. "He gave a workshop here in the Brea Ridge Inn ballroom early Thursday morning. Sometime Thursday night, he was found suffocated in a large bowl of cake batter with a head injury."

"Vanilla cake batter," I said, mostly to myself as I wrote.

"How do you know it was vanilla?" Mark asked.

I raised my eyes to his. How *did* I know? I'd heard it somewhere . . . very recently. "Oh, I remember. It was Chris . . . Alex's uncle . . . he mentioned it. Why? Is that important?"

"It's important that he knew the flavor," said Mark.

"That's not common knowledge?" I asked.

Mark shook his head. "The police never mentioned what flavor of cake batter Chef Richards was found drowned in. It wasn't in any of the records. They omitted it on purpose. Chris knows the flavor because he was there."

"Yes, he admitted that," I said. "He was afraid it was he that Pauline overheard arguing with Chef Richards in the kitchen."

"But Pauline didn't hear anyone arguing in the *kitchen* with Chef Richards," said Ben. "She heard them arguing in the ballroom following Thursday's class."

I frowned. "That's right."

"Chris either *did* something or he *knows*

something," Myra said. "We need to find out which."

"I don't have his number, but Molly gave me hers," I said, as I took my phone from my purse. "Should I call her?"

"Yeah," Mark said. "Call and ask for Chris's number."

"Okay." I took out my phone.

Before I could call, the waiter brought our food. I thanked him and then, to be courteous, I went into the hallway to call Molly.

She answered on the first ring. "Hey, this is Molly."

"Hi, Molly. This is Daphne Martin."

"Oh, hi, Daphne. I'm using my hands-free device since I'm driving, so I couldn't see who was calling," she said. "I didn't forget anything, did I? I'm the world's worst for doing that."

"No," I said with a little laugh. "I was just wondering if Chris is with you. I think he might know something that could help the police solve Jordan Richards's murder."

"I told him not to go to the inn Thursday night," she said. "I've been heartsick ever since I heard what happened to Chef Richards. I told Chris that two wrongs don't make a right."

"What do you mean?" I asked. "You don't think Chris had anything to do with Chef Richards's death, do you?"

"I don't know," she said. "I hope and pray that

he didn't. I told him that bullying that man wouldn't solve a thing, and now here he is a suspect in the man's murder."

"He isn't a suspect," I assured her. "We just think he might've seen someone or something that would help the police figure this whole mess out."

"Okay. He's not with us, though. We brought separate vehicles because he and I didn't get off work at the same time on Thursday. He's following us in his truck." She gave me Chris's cell number. "I should've never let him come with us. I knew that temper of his would get him in trouble."

"It'll be fine," I said. "You don't know that Chris did anything wrong. Besides, it's obvious Chris is crazy about Alex . . . and I don't think Alex would have done the demonstration if Chris hadn't encouraged him to do it. He's a good influence on Alex, and I don't think he'd do anything that would ultimately damage his relationship with his nephew."

"You're probably right," she said. "Alex is napping in the backseat, so I can tell you Chris has been the only father figure in Alex's life for the past ten years. Alex's dad just couldn't take Alex being— as he put it—different."

"I'm sorry."

"Me too," she said. "I hope you find the answers you're searching for . . . but I pray that they don't involve my brother."

"So do I, Molly." We said our good-byes, and I

returned to the table instead of calling Chris. I didn't want everyone to wonder where I'd gone, and I didn't quite know how to approach Chris. I preferred to get the others' input before doing so.

I returned to the table. I felt a little guilty when I saw that they'd waited for me before beginning to eat.

"Thank you for waiting," I said. "It wasn't necessary, though."

"Now she tells us," said Myra, digging into her chicken breast. "I'm starved."

"Did you talk with Chris?" Ben asked.

"No." I explained to them what Molly had told me. "Based on what she said, I'm really scared that Chris could be the one who killed Jordan Richards. I told Molly that I didn't think Chris would do anything that would jeopardize his relationship with Alex. And I honestly don't think he would . . . on purpose. But we all saw this weekend how quickly he can fly off the handle."

"You definitely need to call him, Daph," said Mark. "You just have to be careful in how you go about it."

"Maybe I could ask if he saw anyone else in or around the kitchen when he was there . . . or if there might've been someone heading in that direction after he left," I said.

"That would work," Ben said. "You'd be asking him to give you the information without actually coming out and accusing Chris of anything."

"That sounds good," I said. "Let's finish our dinner, and then we can go up to our room, put the phone on speaker, and talk with Chris."

Mark and Ben shared a look I couldn't decipher, and then Ben said, "Okay."

What did Mark know that I didn't?

WHEN WE ALL got to the hallway outside our room, Ben looked at us with resignation. Mark shrugged. Myra grinned. I tilted my head like a confused puppy dog.

Myra knew too? Even Myra? And she hadn't told me whatever it was that she knew and I didn't?

Then Ben opened the door.

Red rose petals had been strewn from the doorway to the table for two by the window.

"Oh, Ben," I said, my mouth gaping open.

"It's all right," he said.

"It's not all right," I whispered. "You planned a lovely, romantic dinner for us, and I spoiled it."

"You didn't spoil anything," said Ben. "You were right. We need to get the issue of Chef Richards's murder resolved so we can move on past it."

"When this is over, I promise you the best dinner in the world," I said. "Or, at least, in Brea Ridge . . . and the most passionate—"

He smiled and placed his index finger over my lips before I could share any more intimate details in front of Mark and Myra. "Deal. Let's call Chris."

I dialed Chris's cell phone number and put my phone on speaker.

"Hi, Chris. This is Daphne Martin," I said when he answered. "I have Ben, Mark, and Myra here with me, so I have you on speaker."

"Okay. I'm driving, and I think I'd better pull over for this conversation. Hold on a second."

We waited for Chris to find a good place to stop. Then he came back on the line.

"I've kinda been expecting this call," he said. "I figured I'd messed up somehow. What did I do?"

Ben, Myra, Mark, and I exchanged glances. I shrugged, figuring it was better to simply tell him the truth. We wanted him to be honest with us. We should offer Chris the same courtesy.

"You told us about the vanilla cake batter," I said. "The police didn't reveal what kind of batter Chef Richards was found lying in."

"I swear to you, I didn't kill that man," said Chris. "I'll turn around tonight and come back to Brea Ridge and make a statement to the police. It's what I should've done in the first place, but I didn't think anybody would believe me."

"Tell us what happened," Ben said.

"Well, it's like I told Daphne. Molly and Alex got to Brea Ridge before me on Thursday. They went to the hotel and checked in and then went to Bristol and did some shopping and stuff. When I got into town, the three of us met up at that steakhouse there in Brea Ridge. We had dinner, and the more I thought about how Jordan Richards had done Alex, the madder I got. I blew up and said I was going over to that inn and hunt him down." He expelled a breath. "Molly warned me not to go. I should've listened to her."

"You found Chef Richards in the kitchen?" I prodded.

"Yeah," he said. "I asked them at the front desk. They told me he was in the kitchen and that he had asked not to be disturbed. I told them I'd talk with him later, then. I pretended I was going to one of the guest rooms, but I found the kitchen, and there he was."

When Chris fell silent again, Mark urged him to continue.

"I started out trying to be calm and reasonable," said Chris. "But it didn't take but a minute for my temper to get out of control. I mean, I tried to explain to Chef Richards how much he'd hurt Alex, and he didn't even care! I told him about Alex's condition and how he'd had to go on antidepressants after the episode at the cake show, and he said if Alex was that far gone, he'd have had to go on medication anyway. That's when I lost it."

"What did you do?" My voice emerged just above a whisper.

"I picked up that cake stand, and I hit him with it." He quickly added, "But I didn't kill him. I swear, I didn't. Chef Richards was not dead when I left that kitchen. I felt his neck, and he had a pulse."

"Why didn't you call nine-one-one?" asked Mark.

"I've been arrested for assault and battery once before," said Chris. "I was afraid that if I got charged again, I'd do jail time. Plus, the old man wasn't hurt that badly. Yeah, the blow knocked him out, and he probably got a concussion; I knew he'd wake up with a bump on his head but otherwise be okay."

"How could you possibly know that?" Myra asked.

"I've been a brawler all my life," he said. "I know when somebody's seriously hurt and when they're not. He wasn't."

"So you're saying that when you left, Chef Richards's face was *not* planted in that bowl of cake batter," Mark said.

"No, sir, it was not. That's exactly what I'm telling you," he said. "I knocked him out, but I didn't drown him. Somebody else came along and took advantage of that situation." He expelled a breath. "Let me talk with Molly at her house, and then I'll turn around and come back to Brea Ridge and give a statement to the police. I didn't tell Molly and Alex what I did. In fact, I'd planned to slip off from them on Friday and apologize to Chef Richards and beg him not to press charges. I didn't figure that would do me any good, but I didn't want Molly and Alex to suffer for what I'd done either."

"Chris, did you wipe your fingerprints off the cake stand before you left?" I asked.

"No," he answered.

"Someone must have," I said. "The police didn't mention there being any unidentified prints on the stand. Were you wearing gloves?"

"In this weather?" Chris asked. "No, I didn't have on any gloves."

"Did you see anyone else near the kitchen . . . either when you were going into or coming out of there?" Ben asked.

"No." Chris paused for several seconds. "Hey, wait, there was one thing. I saw a purse on the counter. After Myra said that Pauline Wilson had heard someone arguing with Chef Richards, I thought she was the one who had been there. I thought she knew what I'd done and would think I'd killed the guy."

"Wait. You saw a purse on the counter?" I asked. "The woman wouldn't have left without it. She must've still been there."

"What did the purse look like?" Myra asked.

Myra was an expert on purses and shoes. She always noticed them.

"It was pink," said Chris. "And it had a clasp at the top."

"Was it a structured bag with small handles? Or was it a hobo with long straps?" Myra asked.

"Uh . . . I don't know," he said. "The bag was fairly small. It had handles rather than shoulder straps. Oh, and the clasp was undone. The purse was open part of the way, and there was a white glove sticking out of it."

Myra and I said simultaneously: "Fiona."

"Are you sure there was no one else in the kitchen while you were there?" I asked Chris. "You didn't see anyone? In particular, you didn't see anyone with cotton-candy-pink hair?"

"I'm positive," he said. "I'd have remembered cotton-candy hair. But I'm positive about that pocketbook too. That's why I thought Pauline could send me up the river."

"Fiona must've stepped out for a minute before you went into the kitchen," Ben said. "Maybe she heard the two of you arguing and decided not to go back into the kitchen until you were through."

"And when she came back and found Jordan Richards unconscious, she might've seen an opportunity she simply couldn't pass up," I said.

OUR NEXT ORDER of business was to find Fiona. Well, *I* thought that should be our next order of business. Mark and Ben thought we should call the police. So we did that first. Like me, Myra was ready for action.

Besides, we'd already called the police once and had them come when we thought Gavin Conroy was going to give us trouble. They'd rushed right over, and it hadn't amounted to anything, and they weren't terribly thrilled with us over that. I wasn't anxious to get them involved again until we were absolutely positive something big was going down.

"We need to find Fiona before she checks out of this hotel and makes it across the border, never to be heard from again!" Myra said.

Myra could be a little dramatic when excited. Unless the woman had a supersonic jet waiting for her in the parking lot, there was no way Fiona could make it to any border—other than a state border—tonight. And I'm fairly certain all of these United States extradite criminals to other states in the union in which they are wanted for questioning in a murder investigation.

Mark calmed Myra sufficiently for Ben to make the call to the Brea Ridge Police Department. Once the phone call had been made and Ben had reported that there were deputies on their way over, Mark told Myra that she could now go from room to room kicking in doors and overturning mattresses.

Her eyes brightened. "Really?"

"No, not really," he said. "That would take too long. We need to know which room Fiona is staying in and go from there."

"Of course," said Myra. "Why kick in *all* the doors when only one is necessary?"

"The only trouble is that the people at the front desk aren't going to be forthcoming with that information until the police get here," I said.

"There might be a way around that." Mark took out his phone and called someone. Within five minutes, there was a Brea Ridge Inn security guard at our door.

"Hey, Jim," Mark said. "Thanks for getting here so quickly."

"No problem, man," said Jim. "What do you need?"

Mark quickly explained that we were looking for Fiona and that we suspected her of murdering Chef Richards. Jim called the front desk and told them he needed Fiona's room number. When he ended the call, he said, "Let's go."

With Jim in the lead, Mark, Myra, Ben, and I strode down the hall to Fiona's room.

Jim knocked on the door. "Hello. I'm with Brea Ridge Inn security. Is anybody in there? If so, would you open the door, please? I need to speak with you."

When he got no response, he knocked again and repeated the introduction. He gave anyone inside a third warning and then said he'd be using his passkey to enter the room. There was still no response, so Jim opened the door to the room.

The room was empty. There were no clothes hanging in the closet. There was no suitcase on the floor. There were no toiletries on the sink.

"She's gone," I said.

"We've got to find her," Myra said.

"I'll call the front desk and see if she's checked out," Jim said.

"Ben and I will check the parking lot," said Mark. "Ladies, you should return to the room until we find out what's going on."

"Return to the room?" Myra squawked. "We're not some helpless females who need to be molly-coddled here. I'll have you to know we've stopped killers in their tracks before."

"Killer," I said. "It was one killer. And, as I recall, you and I did *not* stop anything. If the police hadn't shown up—"

She whirled to face me. "Whose side are you on?"

"You know I'm on your side, Myra, but maybe they're right. Maybe we should wait in the room."

She narrowed her eyes and studied me for a full thirty seconds. I know. I counted.

"All right, then." She turned back to Mark. "Let us know when you find out something."

We left the room, and the men and the women went in separate directions. The men headed for the elevator.

"You've got a plan, don't you?" she whispered when she thought the men were out of earshot. "I can tell. You've got a plan."

"It's not exactly a plan," I said. "It's more of a hunch."

"Well, clue me in on it, sister," she said.

"I figure that if Chris was so sure that Pauline knew something, Fiona might be under the same impression," I said. "I think we need to get to Pauline and warn her."

Myra nodded. "Good idea. Of course, it might be too late. We might find Pauline dead."

I seriously doubted it, but I didn't say so. In fact, I was all for letting the men do the rest of the legwork and the heavy lifting. I would just as soon have gone back to the room Ben had rented for the two of us, dumped those rose petals in a bubble bath, and waited for him to join me. But by buying time by checking on Pauline and telling her about Fiona, I was getting Myra out of the men's way while letting her believe she was still a crucial part of the plan.

That is truly what I thought I was doing . . . right up until the instant that Myra and I saw Fiona slipping furtively into Pauline's room.

25

MYRA STARTED slapping my forearm and pointing. I nodded to let Myra know that I too had seen Fiona sneaking into Pauline's room.

"What do you think she's doing?" Myra hissed.

"I don't know," I answered. "We should call the guys."

"By the time we call the guys and get them up there, Pauline Wilson will be as dead as four o'clock yesterday," she said.

"A.m. or p.m.?"

"Both. Now, stop stalling. If you're not going

in after her, Daphne Martin, then I most certainly am."

"All right, all right. Just don't go marching up to the door half-cocked," I said. "We need to have a plan."

"I have one," said Myra. "I'm going to knock on that door and when Pauline lets me in, I'm going to tackle Fiona."

"Myra, that'll never work!"

My words fell on deaf ears. By the time they'd left my mouth, Myra had already begun pounding on Pauline's door.

"Open up!" she called. "This is the police!"

Okay. That was the part of the plan she'd neglected to mention.

"If you don't open this door within ten seconds, we'll be forced to use our battering ram to knock it down," Myra threatened.

I groaned. She was going to get us both killed . . . and probably Pauline too. I texted Ben: *Get to Pauline's room. Now!*

I got to Myra's side at the precise moment that Fiona flung open the door. Naturally, she was brandishing a small pistol.

"I knew you weren't the police." She spat the words right into Myra's face. "Since when does the police department hire old women?"

Myra came around with a left hook that neither Fiona nor I saw coming. When Myra's fist connected with Fiona's face, the younger, less stable woman staggered and dropped her gun. I quickly scooped it up and trained it on Fiona, who I was now positive took advantage of another brawler's quick temper to seize the chance to kill Jordan Richards.

"Nobody calls me 'old,'" Myra growled.

It was very Sam Elliott of her. I was proud. I felt like the Sundance Kid to her Butch Cassidy. I was thrilled out of my mind when Mark and Ben arrived in moments, and Mark pried my fingers off the handle of that gun.

"ALONE AT LAST," Ben said as he unlocked the door to our room.

"I'm sorry I spoiled your original plan," I said.

"I'm glad we can put the entire Jordan Richards's murder behind us and move on with our lives."

We stepped into the room.

"The rose petals are a wonderful touch," I said. "Earlier, before Myra and I saw Fiona sneaking into Pauline's room, I was thinking of how nice it would be to fill the tub with bubble bath and some of those rose petals . . . and me . . . and you. . . ."

He began kissing my neck. "That would be nice."

I smiled. "I'll start the water."

I stepped into the bathroom and started filling the tub. As I started back into the bedroom to get my overnight bag, Ben met me in the doorway.

"I meant to do this in a special, romantic way, but . . ." He got down on one knee and took a small blue velvet box from his pocket. "All of a sudden, I'm just desperate to do it."

I gasped and immediately felt tears prick the backs of my eyes. "Ben—"

"You're everything to me, Daphne. Will you marry me?"

By then I was crying so hard, I could only nod. I finally managed to squeak out a "yes."

Some time later, after we'd mopped up all the water that had overflown from the tub and had called down to the front desk and requested more towels, I lay in Ben's arms and traced his jawline with the back of my hand.

"I thank God every day that I was given another chance with you," I told him. "I'll make you the best wife ever."

"I know you will," he said. He kissed me softly. "I love you, Daphne. I think I've loved you all my life."

"And I've loved you all of mine," I said. "I just made a stupid mistake."

"We all make mistakes, babe."

"What about Kentucky?" I asked. "Did you make your decision?"

"Yep." He smiled. "I think I'm much better suited to life here in Brea Ridge."

"Oh, Ben, thank you!"

"That's why I was working last night and couldn't

be here with you," he said. "I'd made a promise to Nickie to help her get her magazine off the ground. And last night, I completed three articles for the first issue. She's paying me for my time, and I told her that I was hoping the payment for those three articles would go toward paying for our honeymoon."

I drew in a breath. "You told her that?"

"I did. And she wished us well," he said. "About that honeymoon . . . where would you like to go?"

"As long as I'm with you, I don't care where we go," I said. But the longer I lay there considering it, the more I got to thinking about how nice it would be to go to some tropical island. "How much do you think we'll have to work with?"

"I don't know. Tell me where you want to go, and we'll see what we can do," said Ben. Then he chuckled.

"What?"

"If we don't have enough, maybe we can persuade the reigning welterweight champion Myra Tyson to go a few rounds in a charity event," he said.

Epilogue

THERE'S A lot of excitement around Brea Ridge these days. Ben and I are planning a late summer wedding. Violet and Leslie are thrilled and are helping me look at gowns, wedding invitations, and decorations. I, of course, will be making the wedding cake.

Lucas, Leslie, and Alex are television stars! Okay, not really, but they did make an appearance on *John and Joni*. It was a very small role, but all three of the kids were thrilled. And they all got autographed photos of John and Joni. It turns out

John and Joni are cute teenagers pretending to be younger than they are, and Leslie is now head over heels for John and certain that she'll marry him someday. Hey, you never know.

Both Lucas and Leslie have kept in constant contact with Alex since the first annual Brea Ridge Taste Bud Temptation Cake and Confectionary Arts Exhibit and Competition. Alex has returned to cake decorating and is doing really well. Molly says he's happier than he was even before that fateful competition and the horrible episode with Chef Richards.

Chris had to spend three months in jail but was allowed to serve the time in a Georgia facility on a work release program that wouldn't interfere with his job. He also had to attend an anger management class and pay a fine.

Myra and Mark are still dating and doing well, although Mark now has a competitor for Myra's affections. When Myra went home that Sunday night after decking Fiona, the "demon" Chihuahua was waiting on her porch once again. I guess Myra had decided she'd had enough of everybody's guff that evening, so when the dog ran barking at her, she barked right back at him. He ran and hid under a bush. Then Myra went into the house and got the dog some roast beef. She named him Bruno, and now he adores her. The feeling is mutual. Although Bruno is fed "that dog food recommended by the vet," he still gets his roast beef on a regular basis.

Fiona is in jail awaiting trial. After hours of questioning, she finally confessed to the Brea Ridge Police Department—my money is on Officer McAfee as the interrogator—that she took advantage of Chef Richards's unconscious state to finish him off in the cake batter. She says she didn't really intend to kill him . . . that it just sort of happened.

"I began to think about how he'd always treated me . . . how he had more money than the Queen of England . . . how he took credit for my hard work . . . how he acted like I was so inferior to him . . . how he wouldn't help me get ahead in the pastry world . . . how he'd used me and cast me aside. I looked down at him lying on that kitchen floor, and I despised him," Fiona had told the police. "I wanted him dead. And I took the bowl of cake batter, and I shoved his face in it. Then I wiped off the bowl and the cake stand, and I ran all the way to my room. I wasn't even sure he was dead until I went to check on him about an hour later. Then I called the police."

Residents of Brea Ridge waffle back and forth between wanting the formerly pink-haired waif (whose hair has now faded to a dull, lifeless brownish gray) to plead insanity and walk away scot-free to wanting her to get life imprisonment. The ones who want her to plead insanity and be released from jail are the ones who are familiar with Chef Jordan Richards.

Still, as Lily Richards would point out, none of

us truly knew the man. Not even she knew him as well as she'd thought. She has set up a scholarship in Chef Richards's name benefiting students who want to study the culinary arts.

I'm sitting in the living room looking at a bridal magazine when Ben comes in and sits down beside me.

"So, have you given any more thought to our honeymoon destination?" he asks, nibbling my neck in a way that makes it hard to think about anything.

"I have," I tell him. "Do you think we could go to Hawaii . . . and then swing back by Tulsa for the Oklahoma State Sugar Art Show?"

ACKNOWLEDGMENTS

Fɪʀsᴛ ᴏғғ, I'm thankful to God for His many blessings. I'm also thankful to my family: Tim, Lianna, and Nicholas. Your love and support and patience (around deadline time!) is terrific. Thank you, Robert Gottlieb, agent extraordinaire. Thank you, Kerry Vincent, for your unwavering support and encouragement. Thank you, Rosemary Galpin, for contributing the recipes found in *Battered to Death*'s "Daphne's Kitchen Recipes" section. And, thank you, Dean Koontz, for your kindness and generosity.

Daphne's Kitchen Recipes

Rosemary Galpin's Royal Icing

(For those of you who might be unfamiliar with royal icing, it sets up to a hard, smooth finish.)

INGREDIENTS

3 pasteurized egg whites (at room temperature)

½ teaspoon vanilla extract

½ teaspoon cream of tartar

1 teaspoon piping gel or light corn syrup

4 cups confectioners' sugar

Yields approximately 2 ½ cups

DIRECTIONS

In large bowl, combine the egg whites, vanilla, cream of tartar, and piping gel and hand mix until well blended.

Add confectioners' sugar gradually and continue to hand mix until sugar is incorporated and mixture is shiny, approximately seven to ten minutes. You can use a hand mixer on low, but do not overmix as this will incorporate air and cause bubbles and breakage when applied with bag.

Add food coloring if desired.

Strain mixture through a white knee-high stocking to remove any lumps before use.

Store unused icing in the refrigerator for up to three days, in an airtight container with a damp paper towel covering the top.

Rosemary's Carrot Pumpkin Pecan Cake

INGREDIENTS

1 package white cake mix

1 package butterscotch instant pudding mix

1 teaspoon cinnamon

¼ teaspoon nutmeg

¾ cup canned pumpkin

½ cup milk

3 large eggs

½ cup canola oil

2 cups peeled, finely grated carrots (pat between paper towels to remove excess moisture)

1 cup raisins

½ cup chopped pecans

DIRECTIONS

Preheat oven to 350°.

Lightly grease and flour two 8-inch round cake pans.

Combine cake mix, pudding mix, spices, pumpkin, milk, eggs, and oil in a large bowl and mix on medium speed until smooth (approximately two to three minutes).

Add carrots, raisins, and pecans and mix until well blended.

Split the batter evenly between the two pans. Tap the pans on a hard surface to level the batter.

Bake forty minutes or until a toothpick inserted in the center comes out clean.

Cool ten minutes on wire racks then remove from pans to cool completely.

Hint: For even cooking and to prevent doming of centers, invert a stainless steel flower nail in the center of each pan before adding the batter. Remove the flower nail when the cakes are turned out of the pans.

Ice with cream cheese frosting.

RECIPES SUBMITTED BY ROSEMARY GALPIN

Rosemary Galpin is the owner of Memory Makers Specialty Cakes of Luling, Texas. Rosemary is the 2012 OSSAS Grand Wedding Cake Competition silver winner. Visit Rosemary on Facebook at *www .facebook.com/gayle.trent.Memory-Makers-Specialty -Cakes*.

AUTHOR'S NOTE

TO PROVIDE the Australian string work instruction in *Battered to Death,* I used the tutorials provided by Pauline Bakes the Cake (www.paulines cakes.com/2010/04/australian-string-work-rolls -royce-of.html) and Cake Walk (www.melcakewalk .blogspot.com/2010/06/oriental-stringwork-part-4 .html).

I very loosely used the structure of the Oklahoma State Sugar Art Show to serve as a template for the First Annual Brea Ridge Taste Bud Temptation Cake and Confectionary Arts Exhibit and Competition. The Oklahoma State Sugar Art Show (www.oklahomasugarartists.com) is held each year in Tulsa in conjunction with the Tulsa State Fair. The Oklahoma State Sugar Art Show will celebrate its twentieth year in 2013. The event is hosted by Kerry Vincent, *Food Network Challenge* judge and master sugar artist. In 2004, Ms. Vincent was inducted into the International Cake Exploration Societé Hall of Fame, and she was inducted into the Dessert Professional Hall of Fame in 2010. In addition, Ms. Vincent has also created her own unique sugar craft techniques, including Vincent Marquetry.

For readers interested in pursuing a career in cake decorating, you might be interested in visiting the International Cake Exploration Societé (www.ices.org). The International Cake Exploration Societé (ICES) is an organization made up of both beginning and experienced cake and sugar artists from around the world. The organization provides support, encouragement, and continuing education for cake and sugar artists.

Another valuable resource for those readers interested in cake and sugar artistry is Wilton (www.wilton.com). Wilton has long been the most recognized name in cake decorating. Their website offers a discussion forum, publications, step-by-step instructions, and products for sale.

ABOUT THE AUTHOR

Gayle Trent is a full-time mystery writer. In addition to the cake decorating series written under her own name, she writes an embroidery mystery series under the pseudonym Amanda Lee. She lives in southwest Virginia with her husband, two children, two dogs (who are both currently snoring at her feet), and four cats (who are most likely off somewhere plotting to take over the world).

If you've read the first book in the cake decorating series, *Murder Takes the Cake*, then you know that Sparrow is based on a real-life cat that came to visit Gayle and had kittens in her backyard. Two of the Trents' four cats are Sparrow's remaining kittens.

Please visit Gayle online at www.gayletrent. com, on Facebook (www.facebook.com/GayleTrent andAmandaLee?ref=hl), on Twitter (twitter.com /GayleTrent) or on Goodreads (www.goodreads .com/author/show/426208.Gayle_Trent).

Printed in the United States
By Bookmasters